"Remember when you left my class?" Cathy made her way into the apartment uninvited. "What do I say to the students every year?"

"I… I don't know," Britty snuffed out her cigarette in a dirty ashtray.

"Sure you do. What do I say just before my students leave for the Sr. High class?"

"I guess – to say hello when they see you."

"Yes." Cathy looked up at her and waited.

"Hello?"

Cathy smiled. "Hello again. And?"

"For the boys to hold the door open for you."

"Very good. You're not a boy."

Britty gave a throaty laugh. Cathy slightly lifted a finger, a signal to Andi to mute what she knew was the verbal slap her cousin was tempted to give.

"And?"

"That you'll be watching? I thought you were kidding!"

# Mrs. Covington's
# Sunday
# School
## Dropouts

# ALSO BY CONNIE MILLER PEASE

**BOOKS**
Trouble at the Bagel Café

**MUSICALS**
*Children's Musicals:*
A Light At Christmas
Come, Messiah!

*Full Length Musicals:*
Whither
Found
Just One

**SHEET MUSIC**

Here Comes April Rain
I Hope To Love You
I was Always There
In My Dreams
Just One
Softly Now He Comes
The Gift God Gave You

Find the author at www.myfiresidechat.com

# Mrs. Covington's
# Sunday
# School
## Dropouts

## Connie Miller Pease

*To a minister who loved words and a piano teacher who loves music,*
*Calvin and Jean. How fortunate I am to call myself your daughter.*
*The paper-thin veil between us will be lifted some wonderful day.*

*To my cousin, Cathy Jean. The sun still breaks into*
*a million diamonds when it hits the lake.*

# Prologue

*Peter said, 'Lord, you know that I love you.' and then Jesus said, 'Take care of my sheep.' Peter knew sheep were stupid and stubborn and could smell up the sheep pen, so he knew Jesus wasn't saying this just because it had a pretty ring to it. No, Brandon, no one ever, ever adequately anticipates the cleanup.*

Mrs. Covington couldn't quite put her finger on what had started it, but thirty minutes into the Sunday service, her mind had wandered far enough to conclude: 1. A trip to the bakery shouldn't send you to hell, and she was honor-bound to remove her rock-hard resentment over the refreshment committee dumping the whole donut Sunday inaugural effort in her lap. 2. The question of how long it would take for the bakery clerk's comments about the number of whiskey shots she had downed the night before and an astounding amount of information about an amorous fellow by the name of Frank to leave her memory might be unanswerable. Heaven forbid, but perhaps Alzheimers was good for something. Cathy pinched the bridge of her nose between two fingers, closed her eyes, and took a deep breath.

A surreptitious glance at the stained glass windows revealed they were sparkling this morning with unusual clarity. One bright beam ran down the polished wall, onto the wine colored carpet, touched a cushioned pew and the coloring page of three-year-old Chloe Simpson, and landed squarely in Cathy's lap. Cathy sighed. That was nice: sunshine in your lap. Much better than the donut Sunday inaugeral effort.

Of all the things that could fall in your lap – trouble or trials or treasure – the simple touch of sunshine was best. It was almost as if God took cheerfulness and made it into something you could see and feel. It was like a stained glass cleanser for the soul.

Cathy ran her hand over her wrinkled brow and tried to concentrate. Nope, her mind was a mess.

She was meeting Andi for lunch at the new tearoom, Entitea, down several blocks and across the street. At least there was leftover meat loaf in the refrigerator at home.

However, Andi's interest was piqued by anything that stirred her aesthetic sensibilities, and indulging her cousin was, in and of itself, gratifying, if for no other reason than to watch what happened when Andi walked into a room. Beauty might be fleeting, but the Lord had seen to it that Andi Clemens was exempt from that rule: completely and utterly exempt. Her presence made grown, sophisticated men gape. She had brought more than one board meeting to a standstill by merely crossing her legs. She could lay any woman flat with her stunning looks even if she was their senior by some forty years and had six kids now grown and on their own, though she'd buried two others plus a husband. Andi might find it a somewhat intricately carved cross to bear, but Cathy found it a dependable source of amusement.

Cathy listened intently for a minute. The minister was on verse five of the ten-verse passage. Pulling a peppermint from her purse and popping it into her mouth, Cathy reviewed the lesson she had taught that day to the ten students in her Sunday school class. Rappelling out the window of her second story classroom had seemed like a good idea at the time. Dan and Kenny, two of her former students who had some climbing experience, had loaned their equipment and expertise for the hour. Cathy's eyebrows knit in a vee. Would the class even recall it was the Apostle Paul who was lowered over the city wall in a basket or would they simply remember Mr. Kipton yelling at them? That man had no imagination, which could explain why his wife always seemed to hover on the threshold of a smile without ever crossing over.

Cathy's classroom was plastered with posters and wild paint colors. A full-size sarcophagus stood in the corner, a leftover prop from a colorful VBS years ago. A small hot cocoa bar in the corner sometimes held a pan of homemade caramel rolls, and a sign on the door said *It is only when you fear as you ought to fear, that you need not fear at all.* She had, at one time, considered having those words as a kind of password to enter the class, but had settled, instead, for a ceiling that boasted a multitude of glow-in-the-dark stars. A few times a year, Cathy would flick off the lights, shut the blinds, and encourage her class to lean back and think about the vast cosmos; about a Creator so magnificent that wonder mixed with fear was the only natural reaction to have. Middle School students, after all, needed to think about something other than what was said during lunch at school the week before or whose voice was changing.

A fleeting frown crossed her face. Many of those same students had one day walked out the church door without a backward glance; those one-time students – some interesting, some obnoxious, some boring, some with real promise – who what? Who thought those lessons didn't apply to them? She mentally ticked off each face and name, where she had last known them to live and the inferences she had drawn when asking around about them. Cathy's face grew hot and she set her mouth determinedly as she added up the hours she had put into preparing a lesson each week, twelve months of every year, for easily forty years.

What were students accountable for? Cathy bit her lip and played with the corner of a page in her Bible. She might give it one last effort before they found out too late.

By the time verse ten had been expounded and everyone was adequately inspired, or pretended to be, Cathy was stuffing a small notebook into her purse. In the notebook, the names of forty-seven former Sunday school students had been written in increasingly harried script. Thank heavens God could transform anger over donuts and their accompanying complications into something at least worthy of consideration.

Maybe the donut incident of June 28th wouldn't send her to hell after all.

# Chapter 1

*Ha ha, no, Jesse. Sin is rarely just an action. Unless you're an animal, behavior begins with your thoughts... and thoughts are as hard to control as the tongue. It can be done, but requires some effort from us. We must always own our own actions. The blame game is as old as Eden and as unwinnable, unless you're in politics.*

Green and black tilework covered the restaurant's exterior, and 'Entitea' was written in fancy black script on a black sign above the entrance. As she opened the door, Cathy inhaled the faint scent of oolong tea that hung in the air. Contemporary décor had always left her feeling slightly cold, and she shivered imperceptibly as her footsteps echoed across the checkerboard linoleum.

The hostess led her to a table by the far wall. There it was; the courteous and indulgent nod that hid the disinterest just beneath it. She'd seen it a hundred times. She was retired, widowed, and growing soft in the middle. What else could be expected?

Blending in or, in this case, drawing no interest, admittedly had its advantages. You could observe others without being seen: like that fellow at the table over by the opposite wall she caught ogling the date of the man two tables away and the phone number being passed from her to him via the waiter. You could make faux pas left and right and few would notice. It was like wearing camo without the mindless pattern. She, Cathy Covington, was the cover girl for the uninteresting part of the crowd.

Of course, she could be excused for a few extra pounds, having had six kids of her own and, on her own, seen them through puberty and beyond. She had the same auburn hair color she'd had as a teenager, but at 60, who really cared besides a hair stylist named Nate? Her husband had disappeared years ago when the children were still running around just for the sake of it and the two of them were full of more dreams than cash. She'd always suspected foul play, but a body had never turned up and she'd had to wake up each morning with an unanswered question instead of a husband.

Theirs was a humble house on Maple Lane, a short block in Pine Point. A small town within flirting distance of the Twin Cities, Pine Point's sidewalks meandered along neighborhood streets and past downtown businesses, some of which had been established no later than the 1940s. Church doors were rarely locked. Teachers taught the children of their first students.

Part of the town's appeal was also part of its peril. It held fast to an antipathy for what others considered regular politics. Folks didn't shy away from writing in a candidate if those on the ballot failed to excite their interest. In fact, on more than one occasion, election results had turned into something of a surprise party for the newly elected. In fifty years, only one resident had turned down his newly elected post. People still knew his name. It wasn't uttered in polite circles. City ordinances gave residents a wide berth. The town council believed that as long as you behaved yourself, you could do as you chose. The Metropolitan Council was the equivalent of a four-letter word.

The town's population might do business in the city, but their lives were anchored in Pine Point. Pine Point, in the minds of a very determined City Council and a constituency with a small town heart, remained an island unto itself. It's motto: *Independence: Not just for 1776.*

Cathy settled into an unyielding chair at her chrome and glass table and looked around. She was the only person over thirty-five in this room filled with groups and couples wearing casual chic. Simultaneously, someone knocked over a glass, a few men murmured, silverware clattered to the floor, and a cook's expletive resounded from the kitchen. The manager grabbed a waitress and told her to get some burn ointment from the kit on the back wall.

Shutting off her cell phone, then glancing toward a corner of the ceiling, Andi walked over to join her. "Scale of one to ten?"

"I give this place a negative two," Cathy replied.

"Knowing how you love form and function…"

"Knowing how I prefer a comfortable chair and a table that…"

"Could withstand a bar brawl."

Cathy looked down at the glass tabletop in front of her. Her eyes met Andi's with a look that said "and they call this a table?"

"What is that, anyway?" Cathy nodded to the speakers mounted near the ceiling.

Andi cocked her head for a moment. "I believe some sort of stringed instrument. Could be a sitar, but that would be hazarding a guess, and I just came through road work on I-35, so I need to sip on something before I'm in the mood for another hazard."

"Ever the comedian. I mean the song."

"No idea."

3

The waitress came and took their orders, though her eyes never left Andi.

As the server walked away, Andi commented, "Interesting name, Muffy."

Cathy unsuccessfully fought the smile that had tugged at her lips since the girl had introduced herself. "I can't imagine what it's short for." Cathy cleared her throat. "How goes retirement?"

"Just a different set of men hit on me now. Volunteer work has its own entertainment. I hadn't known volunteering at a non-profit could be so sexy." Andi sipped the Godzilla Vanilla Tea that had just been placed in front of her. "I've no regrets. The firm is in good hands, but I miss the work. What is that, anyway?"

"Mai Tai Chai."

"What about you? Are you still satisfied with your decision to close up the studio?"

"Ha, ha! Studio? If you can call a cove in the living room a studio…" Cathy shook her head. "I was getting impatient with my students."

"You? Impatient?" Andi teased.

"I know, I know. Anyway, it's best for now; a brief, but necessary 'retirement.' I needed a sabbatical though I couldn't, correction, can't, afford one. At any rate," Cathy sipped her tea, "I can start up again when I'm ready. The fall, I suppose, in order to pay the winter's heating bill." Cathy wrinkled her nose. "I won't go back to the second job even if I have to eat dandelions."

Andi nodded. "I can't blame you, Nebuchadnezzar."

"For now, as far as everyone is concerned, I'm retired with a silently understood 'and.' *And* apparently I spend my days yearning to do everyone 'a little favor.' Retirement, as anyone would tell you if they had the nerve to be truthful, makes everything you do without merit. Evidently, it is more important to stifle a yawn in a meeting than to make a meal for someone who's sick and, as we all know, unpaid work doesn't take time like other work." Cathy reached down and pulled the notebook from her purse. "However, I've been toying with a bit of inspiration I pulled from church today."

"Oh yes. What's his name – Gingham? Bingley?"

"It's Bingham, and he's a fine young man. A bit young, but dedicated, and smart enough to know he doesn't know it all. Actually, I was thinking of some of the students I've taught in that church over the years."

"Those darling little Middle Schoolers."

"Yes. Darling," Cathy replied wryly.

"Well, what do you expect when you insist they eat grasshoppers during the lesson about John the Baptist?"

"They were crickets and they were chocolate-covered. I think it was a lovely option for the ones who didn't want to roast grasshoppers they caught and brought to class." Cathy paused, then qualified, "Well, at least until the very, very minor fire. I still think Francie's mother over-reacted." She paused again, then added, "The property committee will get over it and the elders needed to pray for less histrionics in that family anyway."

"Or when you bring a machete when talking about the wars for the Promised Land?"

"And a club," Cathy interjected as though it was unthinkable to leave it out. "Too bad I couldn't find an ox goad. Even a javelin would've helped." She looked up at Andi, whose mouth quirked to one side.

Her cousin had not changed since they were girls scrambling over fallen branches on their way to their fort hidden in the middle of a woods; property for which Andi had, in adulthood, paid a pretty penny and now owned. Cathy was the same girl who was with her on the lake in the fishing boat in the quiet just before dawn when the sun's rays hit the water and exploded in shiny brilliance. She was the same girl who told ghost stories in the middle of the day because, to her reasoning, it was the only way she could indulge in the forbidden thrill and still sleep at night. She was the same girl who had written deep, intimate, love songs about boys who, because she didn't have the nerve to look them square in the face, much less talk to them, she ignored whenever she saw them. She had loved life messily then and couldn't have compartmentalized hers if she'd wanted to. Her cousin had, after the thing with her husband, developed a determination that ignored propriety from time to time, perhaps, but underneath she was the same avid spirit.

"I think, perhaps, a variety of weaponry makes it a bit more realistic. Plus, Middle School boys love blood and guts. It's one of their favorite units."

"You haven't nailed anyone to a cross yet, have you?"

"Not yet."

Andi rested her chin in her hand and raised her eyebrows.

Cathy sat back in her chair, bouncing her fingers off each other. "It seems to me that if I go to the trouble of teaching them, they ought to go to the trouble of integrating what they're taught."

"Oh yes," Andi cajoled, "we're all so very adept at that. Fortunately for us, God doesn't follow us around with that ox goad you wish you had."

"Maybe not an ox goad, but He does search us out. You know it as surely as you have a son named Jonathan now in the ministry. But He's been known to give up, and when that happens it's called hell," Cathy calmly replied.

"And some of these students are on their way?"

"Either going straight to or taking a detour."

"Ooh. This is getting interesting," Andi squinted one eye.

Cathy took a bite of the alfalfa sprout-stuffed sandwich that had just been placed in front of her. "Thank heavens for Dijon or this would have exactly no taste."

She looked up as Andi rhythmically tapped her index finger on the table.

Cathy had always loved baiting the hook. It did not bother Andi as long as she was not the one being baited. When, however, she was, it was one of her pet peeves.

"What?" Cathy mumbled through her cup as she took another sip of tea. "The least they could do is have a decent cup. What is this, green or blue? It can't seem to decide for itself."

"It's having an identity crisis," Andi replied impatiently. "Don't give me the big brown eyes act, Cath. I've known you since we drooled on each other's toys."

"They're hazel. My eyes have their own identity crisis."

"They were brown when you were short enough to walk under a mailbox. Out with it."

"I was wondering what harm there would be in doing just a – I don't know – a follow-up of sorts. You know, kind of check in on things with one or two..."

"One or two...," Andi repeated.

"Or seven or twenty."

Andi reached for the list resting on the table in front of her cousin. She scanned down to the bottom of one page, looked up at Cathy, and flipped to the next page. "It appears there are more than one or two or seven or twenty here."

"And seeing whether a little nudge could push them back on the straight and narrow. Besides, it's not even a complete list."

Muffy came by and asked whether they needed anything. Cathy wiped her mouth and looked forlornly at her plate. Her effort went unnoticed.

"No, thank you," Andi smiled.

Muffy bumped into the next table as she walked away.

"Some people need more than a nudge, cuz; they need more like a bulldozer."

"You know, Andi, I've always tried to steer clear of anything having to do with bull," Cathy replied with an innocence that she had used to her advantage for half a century at least, "although in recent years doze is definitely in my vocabulary. I do think some of these," she pointed to the list, "need a reminder in the form of a visit, heavy-handed or otherwise."

"Ditching the kamikaze prayer route, for now, in favor of hand-to-hand combat," Andi murmured. She perused the list, popping a grape into her mouth.

The door opened, and the sound of the new guests bumping into each other and squawking like geese in late autumn just covered over the tearoom's background music. Andi sipped her tea and continued to examine the list until the women recovered from first sight of her.

"That fruit plate is the size of a saucer. Aren't you hungry?"

"Checked this place out yesterday. Ate before I came. Hmmm. I seem to recall this James Mehan giving you fits."

"Oh, I'll get to him; but I believe I'll start small. The state pen is a little farther than I want to drive this week."

"You know how when you start one project, ten others suddenly materialize?"

"Yea, what is that about anyway? It must be an invisible law of the universe," Cathy shrugged, "and, if so, there's no fighting it. But, really, Andi, I can't think of much that would come up."

"You *will* let me in on this, won't you?"

"You've been with me on every adventure that made me laugh or cry."

"Or hiccup," Andi interjected.

Andi motioned for the check. A man at a nearby table gave a loud gasp as the lid of his laptop fell shut, smashing his fingers, two waiters ran into each other, and the cook uttered another expletive from the kitchen.

# Chapter 2

*Sometimes, class, if the front door is locked, you must go around back or, as they say, climb through the window. In a way, that's what Ehud did. He did what the others had not thought to do. Plus, he was mega brave. No, Britty, I don't believe that holds true for your boyfriend, who, by the way, you're too young to date.*

Cathy struck a match, igniting a small flame in her kitchen fireplace. She'd had a morning fire for the better part of the thirty-five years she'd lived there. Even warm days deserved a crackling start. Somehow, a fire provided comfort in good circumstances and bad and everything in between, including a house with inadequate insulation and life in the Midwest where a warm dawn was as rare as a green lawn in November.

The kindling glowed from a Ben Franklin stove in a corner of the room, a personal indulgence made in a kitchen befitting an abode the size of a postage stamp. The fireplace had not been Cathy's idea, but it had been her salvation. One morning shortly after her husband had disappeared without a trace, workmen hauling it in the back of their truck had knocked at her door. They had carried it in and installed it, all in less than a day. They had left behind a cord of wood with a note from Andi. The note was still in Cathy's dresser drawer underneath her long johns where she had saved it. She wondered, again, what she had missed in tracing the path to his business or in the boxes of things from his office that had sat in the middle of her bedroom for fourteen months afterward.

Cathy leaned against the counter and gazed out the window, thinking of summer days when the neighborhood kids would have a homemade parade up and down the street with everything from trombones to guitars to kazoos struggling through numerous renditions of *When the Saints Go Marching In.* The Serling girls had twirled batons and thrown them high in the air to the trepidation of the nearest onlookers. A few of the neighbors had attempted cartwheels and handsprings, but that had ended when Johnny Blakely cracked his wrist trying to impress her daughter, Christy, by walking on his hands. It had been a good place to raise kids, but three of the homes were busy only on holidays now, their owners' children spread all over the country. A few still resounded with the din of adolescent drama. Johnny Blakely was an orthopedic surgeon at Inova Fairfax.

She frowned. A red squirrel was stealing seeds from the bird feeder. She pulled her sons' old BB gun from the broom closet, kicked the screen door open and took a shot. The squirrel scrambled up a tree and hid in its branches, unharmed. She returned to the kitchen. This week it was red squirrels: 3, Cathy: 0.

Cathy's little residence, though it had been filled to bursting with six kids, two dogs and a working mother, had only a single renovation, a deck, despite time's demands. The conglomeration of wallboard, paneling, and bookshelves her sons had rescued from the curbside due to neighborhood home repairs did not count. The boys had created two necessary and distinctly effective basement rooms with the detritus. Besides, that was less a renovation and more a great outlet for creativity, testosterone, and hammering loud enough to compete with her daughter, Christy's, occasional outbursts of temper. It was during those days that she had learned to treasure the discovery of aspirin, and had even written the Bayer company a fan letter.

Hostas the size of Galapagos Tortoises lined the flagstone walkway to the front door. A large potted geranium stood near the entrance, which was flanked by snowball hydrangeas. The small deck held two rockers, a small table, an old towel, and a broom, and it jutted out from the back. A brimming vegetable garden took up half of the backyard.

The coffee maker stuttered on, sending the deep aroma of Bahama Sunrise flavored coffee, ground fresh at Grammie Mae's Confectionery, through the room. Moving about the kitchen, she opened the old refrigerator and grabbed a Styrofoam box from the center shelf. Considering it for only the briefest of moments, Cathy whistled once between her teeth, and an English springer spaniel came barreling around the corner of the kitchen, neatly leaping over Cathy's feet and landing directly in front of its dish. She bent down and patted his head. "Good boy, Harry. I hope you like the sandwich left over from yesterday."

The dog nuzzled the sandwich apart, swallowed the prosciutto whole without tasting it, and flopped down while it held the bread between its paws, tearing it apart, eating only a few pieces. Alfalfa sprouts littered the floor untouched.

"My sentiments exactly." Cathy scooped up the debris. She turned her head in the direction Harry looked as he perked his ears.

"You'd really do that?" Andi breezed through the back screen door. "Poor Harry. First you name him after the prince that tends toward trouble and then you give him prosciutto from Entitea? By the

12

way," she poured coffee into one of Cathy's pink gingham patterned cups and sat in a wooden chair at the sturdy farm table, "you can hear that whistle of yours from a block away."

"The neighbors get to have teenagers, I get to whistle for my dog," Cathy replied flatly.

Andi reached into a white paper bag she'd tossed on the table. "Here, Harry. Have a glazed donut."

The dog trotted over, grabbed it from her hand, and guiltily crawled under the table with his loot.

"You're welcome." Familiar with her cousin's propensity for unusual breakfast menus, she looked around the kitchen. "What? No salad? No ham sandwich this morning?" She pulled a donut out of the bag and held it up.

"Have I ever turned one down?" Cathy settled her plump form into the chair opposite her cousin, taking the pastry and her first bite in one motion. "How is your assignment coming?"

Andi gave a loud sigh.

"Now come on, cuz. Assessing the lay of the land diminishes mistakes by half."

"As I recall, doing so scared Israel out of their wits and preceded them wandering around in the desert for forty years."

Cathy took another bite of her glazed donut. She wiped a corner of her mouth with her finger and licked it thoughtfully.

"I made phone calls and drove around the city – not something that would even remotely make it onto a list of happy outings for me – scouting addresses like a taxi driver for the better part of a day; actually, into the wee hours, and not all lovely locations, eith..." A memory stopped her mid-word. "I didn't realize how many dry cleaners there are."

"Imagine that."

The kitchen light flickered, then went out.

"I suppose there's no use in offering – again – to pay for some rewiring," Andi called after her cousin who was already half-way down the stairs and headed unerringly toward the fuse box.

The light came on again, and Cathy, appearing at the top of the stairs, slightly out of breath, replied, "In a word, no. Besides, it blows only when I use the coffee maker and the washer and dryer at the same time. I asked just one little thing of you."

Andi looked at her and loudly slurped the remainder of the coffee from her cup.

"Oh my, aren't *we* getting testy?"

Andi held out her empty cup.

"Here. Let me give you a refill," Cathy said after the better part of a minute.

"I wish you had let me use a computer."

"They scare me. People find things out about you on those things. They get your tax records."

"They'll never get yours," Andi snorted, "since they're keeping company with your computer in a box in the closet."

"And take money out of your bank account," Cathy insisted, ignoring her cousin's comment.

Andi inclined her head in a manner that showed either disbelief or pity, but not agreement. "Do you know what it's like to talk your way into the back room of a post office?"

"I can't say that I've ever..."

"And then to hear boxes toppling from three corners of the room, not to mention sweet talking a man who is surely dear to a wife who sees him as though he still has hair to comb..."

"Now I'm sure it wasn't as bad as all..."

"And, after having your arm squeezed at least three times and your thigh patted..."

"I don't want to hear it..."

"To put information into your pocket which feels as though it's burning all the way through your skirt..."

"You wore a skirt?"

Andi nodded.

"Not the coral and black."

"The same. I changed before I came over. I didn't want to excite the dog."

Cathy closed her eyes and shook her head. "That poor man."

"How else could I be sure to get the information?" Andi defended herself.

"Results?"

"A mailroom that is taking them probably ten minutes..."

"You're underestimating... "

"To put back together," Andi shook her head, digging through her purse, "and this."

Andi pulled out a sheaf of misdirected letters and forwarding addresses.

Cathy jumped up, hurried over to a small roll-top desk in the living room, and retrieved her Excalibur replica letter opener.

"Thank heavens we live in Pine Point," Cathy muttered as she grabbed them and started sifting through the bunch; opening them and as quickly scanning their contents and discarding them.

Andi's finger tapped the edge of her cup.

"These would end up in the garbage anyway. We're just recycling them," Cathy responded. "Ah! I knew we'd get a lead or two..."

"A *lead* or *two*? I essentially ransack a post office for a *lead* or *two*?!"

Harry trotted over and sat in front of Andi, his signal that he expected her to pet him.

"Don't you take her side and try to calm me down," Andi muttered to Harry as she reached down and scratched him behind the ears.

"Ah, ah, ah; does the parable of the lost lamb mean anything to you?" Cathy raised her eyebrows and gave her cousin an innocent smile.

Cathy held up a change of address request. "See? Little Britty Kellihurt." She tilted her head to one side, remembering. "She was such a sweet thing until her eyelashes started entering the room three seconds before she did."

Harry snatched a discarded envelope from Cathy's lap and, holding it between his paws, chewed it into mulch.

"And her parents said they had no idea where she lives, when all they had to do was a little minor investigating. You'd think they'd figure out that well-intentioned phone calls that go unanswered will never get them anywhere. Parents these days," Cathy shook her head. "Anyway, this is just going to be a little remedial visit. She's only been out of my class for several years. Wanna come?"

"Wouldn't miss it."

# Chapter 3

*Jesus told us that he'd give us a more abundant life. That does not mean a life with more money or fewer problems, but it does mean a life of amazement, challenge, and adventure. In other words, class, when you turn your agenda over to God, hang on to your hats.*

"I thought it would be best just to drop in," Cathy shouted over the noise of the freeway. "Honestly, Andi, do we really have to have the top down?"

"Oh yeah." Andi nodded her head to the beat of a new CD as she swerved around a van filled with kids and beach toys. She called to the driver next to them, "Don't be jealous. This can be you in twenty years!"

Cathy wrinkled her nose at the faintly sweet sour scent of invisible car fumes. "I don't think she heard you. And you're underestimating again. Did you see the halter top she was wearing?"

"She certainly was a perky thing."

"I'm not going to touch that. Exit 54B." Cathy peered at a map as she frantically tried to keep her hair from blinding her completely.

They drove to a part of the city where the hazy gray of a changeable sky seemed to lose its depth of color, but still taunted the day's premature heat. The distressed brick buildings around them offered cheap rentals. A couple of old houses with faded sheets for curtains and porches sagging to the point of near detachment from the structure were interspersed between the other buildings. Two pawnshops and several no-nonsense bars crowded within a couple of blocks served familiar patrons. Beat up cars were parked at a few points along the curb. Nearby, broken glass was scattered in the gutter. A shiny black Lexus cruised slowly down the street.

"Very cosmopolitan," Andi said under her breath after she'd put up the roof of her Porsche Spyder. They'd gotten out of the car, and she'd double double-checked the locks. She felt around in her purse. "Oh great. I forgot my cell. Have you broken down and gotten a cell phone yet?"

Cathy looked her way and deliberately blinked once.

"Well you don't have to look daggers my way." Andi glanced around her. "No doubt there are plenty in this neighborhood already."

"I thought you carried," Cathy muttered between her teeth.

"I didn't want to bring it into the voting booth, which, as you'll recall, we stopped at prior to this lovely little outing." Andi scanned the windows of the buildings on the street.

"Poor Mr. Proctor." Cathy shielded her eyes against the bright sun relieved momentarily of its cloud cover.

"I hear widow-makers run in his family," Andi continued. "I wonder who will get the vote for this special election?"

"I always vote for the minister."

"What?"

Cathy defended herself to Andi's aghast look. "I figure his morals can help the town council and the council stories can make his sermons more interesting."

Andi's eyes darted back and forth between the building and her car. Clutching her bag, she glanced over her shoulder. "What was that with them sneaking the Logjam Days' parade committee chair onto the ballot?"

"Nobody wants to do it, so they decided to put it to a vote as long as there was a special election anyway. The committee should've started its planning a year ago, so it's sure to be a mess at this point with the parade only a few months away. Can you imagine pulling a ninety minute parade together for an audience of over ten thousand?" Cathy laughed. "Pity the sucker who gets it." She turned in a circle, squinting at the building numbers. "See there? I think that must be it."

They entered a brick apartment, climbed the worn, narrow stairs to the third floor, stopping only once for Cathy to catch her breath, and knocked.

The door opened a crack, then a bit wider. "Mrs. C.. C.. Covington?"

"Oh, hello, Britty. We were just in the neighborhood and I thought I'd stop by to say hello. Hello."

"But how..."

"Remember when you left my class?" Cathy made her way into the apartment uninvited. "What do I say to the students every year?"

"I... I don't know," Britty snuffed out her cigarette in a dirty ashtray.

Cathy sat down on a couch that was off-white, reminding her of the oil rag she kept in the trunk of her car.

The efficiency apartment looked as cheap as the rent, from the stained, threadbare rug underfoot to the dirty window that offered a view of the brick building next door.

Andi wrinkled her nose. Her clothes would need to be hung outside overnight, and if the stale smell of the apartment building penetrated them any further it would take at least a week. She shut the door, shoved her sunglasses up on her head, and tried to not breathe.

"Sure you do. What do I say just before my students leave for the Sr. High class?"

"I guess – to say hello when they see you."

"Yes." Cathy looked up at her and waited.

"Hello?"

Cathy smiled. "Hello again. And?"

"For the boys to hold the door open for you."

"Very good. You're not a boy."

Britty gave a throaty laugh. Cathy slightly lifted a finger, a signal to Andi to mute what she knew was the verbal slap her cousin was tempted to give.

"And?"

"That you'll be watching? I thought you were kidding!"

Cathy smiled benignly and glanced sideways at an open can of Spam on the counter. She gestured with her arms. "Sooo, this is the place, eh?"

Andi eyed the leggy blonde up and down, then smiled with her mouth only.

Britty pulled her cami down to meet her shorts.

"I'm sorry, Britty. I've always said manners preempt comfort, and here I am breaking my own rule! This is my cousin, Andi Clemens."

"Pleasure." Andi extended her hand.

While Britty shook it, Cathy said, as though the idea had just occurred to her, "Say! How about we all go out for coffee? It's on me. You must know of some good little cafes around here, Britty?"

"I... I can't. I have to meet somebody in about 5 minutes."

"Too bad," replied Andi.

"We'll wait," Cathy said cheerfully at the same time.

Britty looked panicked. "Wait. I think it wasn't until tomorrow. Yea. I got the days mixed up. I have to meet 'em tomorrow."

Cathy stood. "Lucky us! Do you need your purse?"

"Need a shirt?" Andi said under her breath as Britty shuffled to the far side of the room to retrieve her purse from beside the unmade bed.

The three settled into their chairs at Ed's Diner, five blocks away. A waitress hurried to look for a mop for Tables 3 and 7.

"I don't suppose you have any pink cups?" Cathy queried their server.

The waitress' eyes narrowed as she shook her head slightly.

"Ah well. We shall have to do with the ever-creative white," Cathy mumbled to herself after the waitress had taken their orders.

When they'd been served and Andi had polished her silverware with a Kleenex from her purse, Cathy said, "So you graduated from High School – last year?"

"Actually, I'm takin' some time off from school. I decided I wanted to get a feel for what's out there, ya know? Kinda takin' my time, ya know?"

"And what are you finding 'out there'?"

Britty rummaged in her purse for something and then put it down again. "Oh, ya know, just havin' good times. I have a job that pays great."

"Wonderful! Where is it?"

"A convenience store. They pay real good. The manager's a little uptight, but, hey, they can't all be kittens."

Andi nodded as though it was costing her a great deal to do so.

Britty studied Andi. "What kind of mascara do ya use?"

Andi looked at her in silence until Cathy kicked her under the table. "You couldn't afford it."

Britty began to speak, but Andi held up her hand. "And don't for a minute think you could shoplift it. That store has security that makes the Pentagon look like a Walmart," she continued in a voice that lent finality to the topic.

"And that apartment! Good rates?" Cathy continued.

"Oh yea. Great. You wouldn't believe what some of those places charge. My boyfriend gets a little off rent for mowing, shoveling snow in the winter, things like that. Only, they just let him go. They're so anal retentive about when to do things."

"Indeed." Cathy pressed her lips together as she smoothed the napkin in her lap. "You must be thrilled to have found an apartment in the same building as your boyfriend!"

Britty paused. "Yea."

"I noticed last Sunday that your mom got a shorter haircut."

Britty looked at the wall.

"She said they haven't seen you. She said you don't answer the phone."

"Too many rules. Always finding fault. Who'd want to talk to that?" Britty answered derisively.

Cathy motioned to the waitress for a coffee refill. The waitress did not notice.

After a minute, Andi raised her index finger, and the waitress started over to their table. A booth full of young men suddenly broke out in raucous laughter, which abruptly stopped with a sharp look from Andi. A man at the counter spilled his Pepsi.

Cathy leaned forward and winked at Britty. She whispered, "You're a high school dropout living with her boyfriend."

"He must be a real catch," Andi commented dryly.

"He's hot." Britty pulled a cigarette from the bottom of her purse. "Last one," she sighed.

"I haven't had a smoke all day. Mind if I share?" Andi asked longingly.

Andi might not be able to pull off the innocent act like her cousin, but she was not above, on rare occasions, doing a little play-acting of her own if she thought the situation warranted it. She was no slouch at it, either.

Giving her a stunned look, Britty lit it, inhaled, and passed it to Andi who dropped it in her water glass and stirred.

"What'd ya do that for?"

"Just doing what feels good," Andi replied. "I'm probably like your boyfriend that way."

Cathy sat back. "I was just saying, Britty, I'm wondering if you'd even get to be assistant manager of that convenience store if you went back and finished up. Got your GED or something."

"I think of that every now and then." Britty still glared at Andi. To Andi she said, "You don't know Mitch. He's not like that. We're gonna get married."

"Line number twenty-three in the player's handbook," Andi murmured with a hint of boredom.

Cathy looked long at the girl across the table. "You remember what I taught you about this?"

Britty stiffened with undisguised displeasure.

"You're a pretty girl. You're wasting your pretty years. When you're lying in bed tonight and everything is quiet, would you think about this visit? Ask some questions this week. Put Mitch on the ropes. Don't back down."

A few customers looked their way at the sound of Britty's throaty laugh.

As they dropped her off in front of her apartment, Cathy slipped a twenty-dollar bill in Britty's hand.

"One more thing. They miss you at Sunday school."

"Oh that was great." Andi rolled her eyes as they pulled onto the street.

Cathy caught sight of Britty in the rear-view mirror. It was possible she was saying something about never setting foot in church again, but Britty was disappearing fast (you had to love a Porsche), so she couldn't be sure. Cathy peered closely at the list. "I think we have time for one, maybe two, more visits today. I think there's one only a mile away. Looks like 24th and Martin. Turn left!"

Andi swerved left, drove a few blocks and parked. The few blocks' difference had improved the neighborhood to the point where Andi simply patted the dashboard of her car upon parking.

"Britty never was one for confessing sins, even when she was in my class." Cathy got out of the car and started walking. "Some people don't like the whole self-examination thing. But you never know. Maybe one of these days she'll try it on for size."

"Hope it fits her better than that cami," Andi jibed.

"Now Justin: he was real good at confessing. It just came out more like bragging, so the point got lost a bit. I believe he should be..."

A bell tinkled as Cathy pushed open the door of an engine repair shop and stepped onto the chipped linoleum floor. The office smelled of oil and stale coffee. There was a beat up pop machine in the corner and six metal folding chairs lining the walls. Shelves behind the counter held a variety of motor oils, plastic funnels, jugs of antifreeze, and cardboard air fresheners interspersed among other items.

A man in his mid-twenties came through the door from the back room. His slim build contrasted with the bulge of his well-defined muscles. He had shoulder length brown hair and wore a torn faded red T-shirt and oil stained jeans.

"Well if it ain't Mrs. Covington in the flesh!" He cracked a smile and strode over to hug her. As he came around the counter, he glanced at Andi and tripped. Cathy caught him by the shoulders and smiled.

"Give me a minute, Justin. I just want to soak in the sight of you. How've you been?"

"Still a sinner if ever there was one," he replied happily. "What're ya doin' in this part of town? Gotcherself motorcycle problems?" He laughed at his joke. "Hey, you'll never believe what I got 'n the back. A car smashed like a banana in a peanut butter sandwich. They had to pull the sucker out with the..."

The bell over the door rang. A middle-aged man wearing a brown suit entered and strode straight over to Justin, like a guided missile.

Cathy studied him. He was unremarkable looking in every way except one. He had a small scar under the left side of his jaw line. It appeared to be an old burn about the diameter of a cigarette. Most people wouldn't notice it because they were taller than her 5 feet, 2 inches and wouldn't see it from the perspective she did.

"Do you have the lease Mr. Dowling sent? It was due yesterday," he said without preamble.

Justin paled. "I have it, Mr. Masotic. I just – the rent increase seems awful steep."

"Take it or leave it. He's charging you that rate as of yesterday, signed or unsigned."

"He can't..."

"Take it or..."

Andi took a step toward the man and dropped a lipstick on the floor.

Mr. Masotic glanced over and did a double take. His words evaporated into thin air, and he involuntarily bent down to pick it up and hand it to her. She nodded a wordless thanks and turned to Justin.

"I hate waiting, sugar." She winked.

Looking a bit flustered, Mr. Masotic said, "I'll be back next week. You'll have it in your hand and signed or you'll be out on the street by closing time."

He turned and strode out the door, choking back a cry of pain as he slammed his finger in the door while sneaking a look back at Andi.

"Thanks, Ms..."

"Mrs. Clemens." Andi reached out to shake Justin's hand.

Cathy peered out the door and watched as the man walked down the street and stopped at a dry cleaners, pulling some papers from his suit coat pocket as he entered.

Justin let out a loud sigh of relief.

"Is that your landlord?"

Justin shook his head. "That's just his employee, I guess. I call him Dowling's henchman." Justin chuckled at his joke, but didn't sound very convincing. "Ya know," he unlocked the soda machine and grabbed a cola, "it doesn't seem that long ago that he raised the rent. Now he's doin' it again. Want one?"

"Diet," they replied in unison.

Justin laughed as he grabbed the cans and shut the door. "It feels good to laugh. Every time I see that guy's shadow, I 'bout feel like losin' my lunch."

"So move," said Andi.

"I wish." Justin motioned them to a couple of the chairs and pulled one over opposite them. "It was hard findin' a space in the first place," he explained. "This place was offered dirt cheap. I signed the lease before he could change his mind. I'll be the first to admit I'm not much for readin.' Now I'm thinkin' I shoulda read that thing more careful. I hadn't figured he'd be way ahead of me.

"I got in and got started, and he started nickel and dime-in' me for little things. Then he started raisin' the rent bit by bit. Now it's just crazy. The startup costs of the garage strapped me nigh until Jesus comes back," he raised his can to Cathy, "and I don't think I could afford to change locations at this point what with related costs and possible loss of regular customers."

Justin shook his head. "Honestly, Mrs. Covington, if you and your friend here hadn't shown up, I might be roundin' up a posse right about now." He pulled his hair into a ponytail, securing it with a rubber band he kept on his wrist.

"Now Justin," Cathy said hurriedly, "The minute you lose your temper is..." She raised her eyebrows and waited.

Justin squinted, then blurted out, "The minute you lose! I remembered! Good times in that class of yours, Mrs. Covington." The man laughed. "Aw, I'm just teasin.'"

"You don't look like you're teasing," remarked Andi.

"I'll admit this much: that's one guy I'd like to see smashed in that car back there."

Andi flinched, and Cathy stood suddenly. "You wouldn't have another diet soda, would you? I can't believe how thirsty I am."

"Sure thing." Justin moved to the vending machine as Andi glanced gratefully at Cathy.

"Hey!" Justin slapped his thigh, "Let me show you ladies around this place of business while I still have it."

"I thought you'd never ask!" Cathy said brightly.

An hour later, they thanked Justin as he held the door open for them. Having drunk soda from the vending machine, having learned a bit about small engine repair and Justin's new girlfriend, and having elicited a promise from Justin to stop in for Sunday school the next Sunday, the two women started back to the car.

"Sorry about Justin saying that about the car in the back."

"Painful memories come out of the blue whether someone says something or not," Andi replied. "It's always an eternity ago and always yesterday."

It's curious that no one talks about that particular quality of death, but no one does. Loss offers something akin to time travel for those left behind. Death's visitation seems like an eternity and like the blink of an eye. In those bleak and blessed moments spent with the dying, time is suspended altogether. The days and weeks following loss are perpetual twilight. Eventually, the ensuing years pick up where all was halted, as if someone had called a brief recess and now it was over. The days wander less blithely along, but wander nevertheless, and the death seems to have been a very long time ago. Then one day, no matter which day nor where, something – some scent, sight, or song, or some memory – melts time completely and brings one immediately back to the moment as if no time has passed at all.

Andi knew it and Cathy knew it. That knowledge was a well-known acquaintance about whom they weren't certain how they felt. Love and its memories were worth the price of sorrow, but no one said it wasn't a steep price.

"Memories," Cathy continued resolutely, "that is, good memories, are nice, but hope is better, and you have both."

"Irrevocably. Only the pitiful want to be pitied."

"Now that I know you're okay: I hate waiting, SUGAR?" Cathy asked incredulously.

"I said the first thing that popped into my head. Can I help it if I happened to watch an old movie last night?"

Cathy rubbed her temples. "I think the stale smoke from Britty's apartment is catching up with me. Want to get some take-out chicken and go back to my house to sprawl on the furniture like two old lizards?"

"Yes to the first two, speak for yourself to the third, except the sprawl part. I'll race you to the recliner."

# Chapter 4

*When Paul says to give thanks in all circumstances, he means we need to remember that there will be good times and there will be bad times, but God is always the source of good in the midst of good and bad alike. Yes, Patrice, even when your parents don't let you go to the mall every weekend. In fact, you should be especially grateful for that.*

Cathy wiped her fingers and swallowed the last bite of chicken. "Funny running into Carter like that."

"Nice of him to pick up supper for his new wife."

"Nice of you to pay for it. That's one match that will face more than its share of trouble, her having the baby three weeks after the wedding. I know they were trying to make things right."

"Not sure I disagree," Andi nodded.

Cathy looked out the window, considering the disagreements and agreements and agreeing with them all. "Mmm. Lots of things to consider. A terrible case of the 'what ifs' will crop up the rest of their lives, no doubt."

"Like cold and flu season; dependable and annoying."

"Anyway, I hope he knows they're welcome back. Just when they need the support most, they disappear." Cathy blinked. It would be funny if it wasn't so absurd. People always act as though the sin apparent to others, the sin known publicly, is worse than the sin that remains private. Over centuries of people, of cultures and expectations, this ridiculous belief remains when, in reality, whether sin is known or unknown, it remains a silent influence of life's consequences. Whether act or excuse or rationalization, this belief continues on its merry way without someone calling it out for what it is: an unoriginal lie. "Think I'll see them Sunday?"

Andi leaned her head against the back of the chair and closed her eyes. "They've got a baby that needs loving and no one does that better than a church, no matter how clumsy it is at going about it. It probably helped that you hugged him."

"He's a hugger, that boy. Even in Middle School, he was always hugging the girls. Hugging is probably what started the trouble in the first place, but I know what you mean." Cathy sighed as Harry licked her fingers. "Now Britty, she was more of a..."

"Let's not talk about Britty," Andi interrupted with irritation.

"I wonder what she'll think of that note I asked Justin to drop off at the convenience store," Cathy mused.

"It depends on how superstitious she is."

"What harm can a little Bible verse do?"

"*Faith is being sure of what we hope for and certain of what we do not see?* That girl isn't going to think of the book of Hebrews. She's going to think of a certain Sunday school teacher who said she was always going to be watching."

"Huh." Cathy gave a half shrug. "And that Mr. Masotic fellow," she continued, squinting, "too bad you had to sacrifice your lipstick. Did it break much?"

Andi shook her head. "It was nearly used up anyway." Andi popped the rest of her biscuit into her mouth while she went to

31

the kitchen to get the teakettle. "Let's not forget Mr. – oh what was it – Bowel, Dowley..."

"Dowling, I think," Cathy ventured.

"Green, Black, or Herbal?" Andi called from the kitchen.

"Oh, certainly not herbal. I'd rather lay awake half the night staring at the ceiling."

"Herbal it is." Andi came into the room with a tray holding a teapot, two mugs, and a can of Mountain Dew.

"*Really*, Andi."

"I'm telling you, it really perks up a cup of tea. You should try it sometime."

"When I turn 21 again I will."

"What Justin needs, beside a clean rubber band for his pony tail, is information. You know, you could read up on property ownership and rental law in Perry's old books." Andi poured the soda into her half-filled mug.

In addition to her Ben Franklin stove, the bookshelves spanning two of Cathy's walls were her harbor. They held theology and fantasy; classic literature from the Greeks to contemporary; essays and history; as well as how-to books, devotionals, and philosophy that required multiple perusals. They were, in essence, the world within reach; a musty, comforting ministry of print. Only one shelf had remained untouched over the years, the one holding books from her husband's office.

"The cash from the sale of the rental properties certainly helped put the kids through college." Cathy yawned.

"You could've used it earlier."

"And then they couldn't have used it later," Cathy calmly replied. They both sighed.

"Besides, I had you to bring me groceries every so often," said Cathy, recovering with a laugh.

"At least you allowed me to do that. You know, Cathy, it's hard to watch someone you love be poor."

"It's hard to be watched," Cathy murmured.

"The kids didn't care," inserted Andi.

"Kids define dignity differently, as well they should. They loved their Auntie Andi's generous spirit. You could not have found more grateful recipients."

"Anyway, for me to have not brought a few groceries every so often would've been immoral. My kids were over here eating you out of house and home half the time."

"And, the other half, mine were running around your yard, jumping in fountains and destroying them. And a few hedges."

"Only one fountain..."

"A very large one."

"And rose bushes. Don't forget my dear roses. I still miss that little one by the river near the back by the woods. Oh, you know the one."

"Never did learn my Latin, but, yes, it was the prettiest little thing. Sorry about that. You never replaced it," Cathy added contemplatively.

"It was vintage. Irreplaceable."

The cousins sipped their tea in a companionable silence. Harry yawned, stretched, and pawed at the door.

At length, Andi said, "I suppose the pirates did need a safe place to bury their treasure. They couldn't have guessed it wouldn't take well to being dug up and replanted."

"Twice." Cathy got up to let the dog out.

"I *was* impressed with Camden for managing a shovel a good foot and a half bigger than he was. How's his building business going, by the way?"

"Booming. Calls from his work sites every Friday. There are times I almost wish the pirate treasure would've been real." Cathy peered into the dark while Harry sniffed the bushes. "It would have been very gratifying to offer Justin an alternative and put Mr. Masotic in his place today."

The sweet scent of her neighbor's freshly mowed grass hung in the air. Cathy began to hum *White Christmas*. Suddenly two doors slammed nearly simultaneously and the shot of a BB gun from the direction of the back door punctuated the air.

"Get it?"

"It's a bit dark," Cathy excused herself. She returned from the kitchen with Harry trotting behind her and wandered over to her wall of bookshelves. "There's a whole shelf of books I suppose I could peruse," she mumbled, staring at the books. "After – well, 'after,' I lost heart for going through his things. Never did."

Harry nuzzled her leg with his muzzle, then plopped down a few feet away.

Andi came up behind her and grabbed a book from the shelf. An envelope fell to the floor. Picking it up and turning it over, Andi froze, then gave a low whistle. "It appears you mightn't have needed those groceries after all."

Cathy reached for the envelope and opened it, then stood for a minute, unmoving. She stumbled back into a stuffed chair as she read it once, twice, then three times. "I don't believe it."

Andi took the paper from her cousin and examined it. "Whether you believe it or not, it's genuine."

Andi handed the envelope back to her cousin. The two women stared at each other.

Finally, Cathy looked down again. "And me with the computer the kids gave me in the closet," Cathy whispered, squinting at the paper. She swallowed. "I can't imagine why I didn't know about this Micr... Microsoft stock."

"Perry probably thought he'd wait to tell you after what he thought was an initial bounce settled down. It was still a new company then. See?" Andi pointed to the date. "I wonder if he got in on it early the first day it was offered? It's got to be worth easily..."

"Don't say it. It will just make me nervous."

The two women stared at each other in silence.

"Want to sleep over tonight?" Cathy asked. "You can have the guest room."

"I'd say that's better than the tub. There's a time and a place for whirlpool jets, after all."

# Chapter 5

*It does seem coincidental, Ike, that the donkey was standing there and available for Jesus to ride for the Triumphal Entry. Oftentimes what we regard as a mistake or a coincidence was God's intention all along or, perhaps, in answer to someone's prayer. There are times when we never know what prayer it was in answer to or for what purpose it happens.*

Andi stayed long enough the next morning to make Cathy a breakfast of poached eggs, toast, and coffee. Cathy ate a half slice of toast and sipped her coffee twice, letting the remainder grow cold while she stared at the table. Andi gave her a quick tutorial on investing and taxes and gifts while Cathy nodded distractedly. She had let Cathy cry on her shoulder.

At one point, she said, "You know, Cathy, the usual response to found money is excitement, not whatever it is that you're having."

Andi lapsed into silence. Finally agreeing to take the envelope to her financial advisor and ask him to hold it for Cathy until she could meet with him, she left.

The first day brought a thunderstorm suitable enough for scary stories told around summer campfires. The second day, Cathy sat in her living room rocker and rocked back and forth until dusk. The only time she moved was to let Harry out to do his business and to go to bed at 7:00. The third day, Cathy talked with Harry as she switched the fuse that had blown the night of the storm. She mumbled to him while he followed her as she wandered from room to room, finally landing in her rocker once again. She made sporadic comments to him throughout the afternoon. As the sun sank low in the sky, she began talking to the Lord as she was prone to do when she was upset: without proper greeting and in sentences that only the Almighty Himself could decipher. She did not bother to turn on her lights when dusk turned everything to shadow. Harry jumped up on the bed and slept next to her until she rolled over on his paw, at which point he crawled under the covers and rested his head on the crook of her knee. Cathy spent the next few days in seclusion, her home a retreat and Harry her therapist.

She should be jumping-up-and-down grateful rather than digging-a-hole worried, and she apologized to God. The air seemed to have something extra in it just now; something she had sensed at varying points in life. God was abundantly patient with her and, as surely as the necessity of ant traps in May, she didn't deserve the extravagance of it. Was He amazed at her lack of faith or simply amused? Cathy was pretty sure she didn't want to know.

The morning was already sunny and promised the kind of heat that slows people's breathing, pulls sun worshippers to the beaches, and drives everyone else into air-conditioned buildings. Cathy was wrapped in a blanket, a chair pulled up next to the Ben Franklin stove, drinking coffee and staring into space when the phone rang for what seemed like the tenth time. By now, the incessant ringing had begun to remind her of an obnoxious repetitive note in some weird EDM recording. She picked it up, but didn't get it hung up again fast enough before she heard the voice on the other end.

"Cath?"

She should have known. Andi never was one for pulling the covers over her head and praying for daylight. "Hm?"

"You need to snap out of it."

"Mm hm."

"Either you snap out of this or the Lord will snap you out of it Himself and then where will you be? My prayers don't stop at the ceiling, you know."

Cathy nodded.

"I've already started a kamikaze prayer blitz the likes of which defies the imagination."

Cathy looked out the window. There was a red squirrel eating seed from the bird feeder. Cathy slowly scratched the corner of her twitching eye.

"I mean it, Cathy."

Harry laid his chin on Cathy's foot.

"I don't understand. You sail through Perry's disappearance, but finding out you're rolling in clover has you in shock."

Cathy leaned her head back on the chair and closed her eyes.

"Cathy? Cathy!"

Had her cousin stomped her foot?

Cathy sighed. Obviously, Andi wasn't going to stop ranting until she gave her some sort of response. "You had a front row seat, so you know I didn't sail through anything; the waters were plenty rough. I just didn't have time to be catatonic then. As you recall, *you* were the one who convinced me to stop my detective work and care for myself and my children. The wound I walk around with is still open, even if it *is* ignored by everyone, including me."

The doorbell rang. Cathy got up, peered around the corner of the kitchen and squinted. "Someone's at the door. I'll have to call you back."

Cathy hung up, dropped the blanket on the chair, and looked down at her slipper-clad feet. At least she had dressed today, though worn-out denim capris with a sagging elastic waistband and a stretched-out tee shirt with a bullhorn and the words *Don't Forget Dynamics* pushed the definition of 'attire'.

Harry politely waited for her to get a few feet from the door before he began barking maniacally. She snapped her fingers to quiet him. He continued to bark. She grabbed his collar, gave him the look, and pulled open the door. It was Mr. Proctor's widow, Clara. She was standing stick-straight and was wearing a flowered dress with sensible sandals. They were brown with wide straps and rubber soles.

A sudden wave of compassion washed over Cathy, and, despite her desire for solitude, she invited her in. Upon being ignored by their guest, Harry laid down and licked his paw.

"Clara. How are you doing? Keith's death was such a shock to all of us."

Clara stood in the middle of the living room. "I still can't believe it," she replied, dabbing one eye with the corner of her sleeve. "But I can't talk about that right now or I'll get to sobbing. Public sobbing."

Clara shook her head as though such a thing was beyond demeaning and walking around with a lump in one's throat instead was at least civilized.

"I understand. Learning about the loss... it isn't the end of it," Cathy said, groping for words.

A look of surprise crossed Clara's face, then an old memory.

"That's right. How long ago was it? You didn't seem like the sobbing type." Clara's eyes narrowed. "You didn't change your routine," she commented, suspiciously.

"Children preclude an abundance of time or privacy."

Clara nodded slowly, as though she was pulling scenes from her memory. She straightened, looking slightly like an army recruit. "They tried to reach you, but couldn't get through for some reason. They told me, since the special election was due to my dear Keith's passing, I could be the one to tell you."

"Who tried to reach me?" No. She would not feel guilty for ignoring the phone. Whoever 'they' were could just hunker down and deal with it. She had other things to think about just now.

"City Hall. You were elected Logjam Days' parade committee chair."

Clara stuck out her hand and Cathy shook it automatically, then sat down on the couch.

"But I didn't run," Cathy disputed her.

Clara raised her eyebrows as if to say 'Since when does that matter?' She then looked at her watch. "There are some people coming here for an impromptu victory party in precisely five minutes. Perhaps you'd like to..."

Clara gave Cathy a meaningful look up and down.

Cathy didn't move.

"But I wasn't on the ballot," she reiterated, shaking her head as though it would make Clara's announcement null and void.

"You'll recall it was a write-in. Nobody wanted it. Congratulations!" She looked again at her watch. "Three minutes."

Cathy scratched her head. She got up, looked out the window, into the kitchen, and up at the ceiling. Her mind felt like a clogged highway. She looked at her dog, who looked back with an expression of concern and a sympathetic whine. "I've got to see what I have to serve people. If you'll excuse me... "

"The secretaries are picking things up at Mortens," Clara said.

"Nice," Cathy said reflexively when she heard the name of the town's only caterer.

"But if I may be so bold, perhaps a dress or suit would be more in order right now?"

The doorbell rang.

Clara pushed Cathy out of the room, muttering, "She was right. The funeral was only the beginning," under her breath. "I'll get it," she called to Cathy's retreating form.

The party was in full swing by the time Cathy returned to the living room five minutes later. The mayor was making lousy jokes and the city manager was laughing at them. Two secretaries were standing by the coffee table, eating cream puffs and gossiping. Clara, the only one who seemed concerned with decorum, was walking around the room with Cathy's coffeepot, filling Styrofoam cups with Summer Solstice coffee from Grammie Mae's Confectionery and placing coasters on available table spaces.

The Director of Public Works was drinking a diet lime soda when he saw Cathy out of the corner of his eye. He immediately held his fingers to his teeth and whistled. The room became silent, then burst into applause as they spotted Cathy.

"Let me shake your hand, Parade Committee Chairwoman!" exclaimed the mayor, glancing down. "On behalf of Pine Point, we congratulate you on your election!"

The room began buzzing again as everyone returned to their conversations.

Cathy managed to get the mayor's attention again. "Shouldn't this be an appointed position?"

"No, no, no, no, no. The parade committee volunteers have always elected the chair from within. Unfortunately, those volunteers have dwindled, especially after last year's fiasco. We now have a total of one, and he doesn't want it. The clock is ticking, the parade being just a few months away. He called me and asked for help. Did I mention he's my sister's oldest boy? Hence, the city election. Don't you read the newspaper?"

A sandy-haired fellow approached Cathy and stuck out his hand. She was struck by the resemblance between him and the mayor.

"Why, Heck!" Cathy exclaimed meaningfully.

"I didn't know if you'd recognize me, Mrs. Covington."

"I never forget my Sunday school students."

Heck's face grew slightly pink.

"I'm busy with other stuff now," he replied, rather officiously.

The effort of a smile crossed Cathy's face, and she tilted her head. "You remarried, I heard."

"I was too young the first time. I didn't know what I was getting into," he said.

"That's what they all say," muttered Cathy.

"What?"

"What? I didn't realize I said anything. Two kids now?"

"They came with the package, yep." Heck appeared to study the floor by her feet.

"I'll be looking for you to bring them to church one of these days," Cathy persisted. "And look at us. Now we're colleagues. You never thought you'd see that day, I'm guessing."

"It's weird," Heck agreed. "Meetings are the second Monday of the month."

Heck seemed to want to set this thing back on track.

"We might need to have more than a monthly meeting at this point," Cathy said with a growing anxiety that began at her toes and traveled up to her midsection. "At City Hall?"

"No. Down at the Corn Hut."

"I'll see you then," Cathy said as Heck backed away to allow room for Hal Kingsley, who apparently felt an encouraging speech coming on.

The party had continued half an hour longer. Cathy suspected most of City Hall was glad for a break in routine, even though her living room kept them as crowded as chicks at a trough.

Harry had escaped to her bedroom as soon as he had sniffed everyone to make sure they were harmless. He had begun giving the mayor's secretary, Gloria, a look that indicated she was suspect, but Cathy had rushed over and grabbed him by the collar. She wished there was some way she could reassure Harry that half of Pine Point would have agreed with his assessment, but the phrase 'manipulative bitch' was something he would have understood differently than she intended and something Cathy would not have uttered aloud anyway.

Cathy had just closed the door after the parting guests and fallen prone on the couch, accidentally knocking over someone's half-drunk coffee, when the back door slammed.

"Would you grab a wet cloth from the kitchen?" she called.

Andi's face appeared in the kitchen doorway and she lobbed the washcloth, hitting Cathy squarely in the face. She stopped mid-stride and looked around the living room. "There has not been enough time for you to do this to your home."

Cathy sat up and examined the mess. "And yet, here it is."

Andi looked Cathy up and down and shook her head slightly. "When we were talking on the phone you sounded like you were in more of a bathrobe and slippers mood than a pink – and brown – what is that – paisley?"

Cathy looked down as if discovering her dress for the first time. "I grabbed the first thing I could lay my hands on. This, I'll have you know, is from Emma Peeble's garage sale."

Andi began slowly winding a strand of her hair around her index finger.

"Those garage sales are the talk of Pine Point!" Cathy said defensively. "She has some of the best things you'll find at any garage sale within twenty-three miles. I honestly don't know how she does it."

Andi furrowed her brow, closed her eyes, then opened them again. "Are you wearing your fuzzy pink slippers for the sake of the ensemble or for comfort?"

Cathy looked down at her feet. Well, that explained the apparent deference of those she had visited with at the party. And here she had thought manners from the far East were suddenly taking over the City Council.

"Maybe I'll get you a cup of coffee. Do you want a cup of coffee?" Andi said gently. Despite her fervent prayers, her cousin had finally and completely gone off the deep end.

Cathy began fanning herself. "Is it hot in here or is it just me?"

"I'm rather warm, myself." Andi went back into the kitchen and opened the refrigerator door. She came back with two Diet Cokes. She popped them both and took a long swig before handing the other to Cathy. Sitting down next to Cathy on the couch, she cleared the coffee table with one sweep of her arm, and put her feet up, leaning back. "Talk to me," she ordered.

Cathy didn't know whether to laugh or cry. Andi massaged the bridge of her nose between two fingers.

"I've officially snapped out of it."

"And I'm supposed to believe that why?" replied Andi, unconvinced.

"I had a visit from the folks down at City Hall."

"What?"

"You just missed them. They came, they saw, they conquered."

"That dark of a day, huh? Did they leave anything of value behind?"

"Just remnants from Mortens."

"Nice," Andi answered reflexively. She examined a mostly empty plastic tray, reached over and popped a miniature quiche in her mouth. Harry promptly began eating the rest, knocking the tray to the floor in his exuberance.

"I've been elected Logjam Days' parade committee chair."

Five minutes passed while Andi choked on her quiche, then laughed until tears ran down her face. Fifteen more minutes went by as the two women sat side by side on the couch, staring into space, silently contemplating the past few days.

"You must admit, God has a great sense of humor," Andi concluded, choking back her laughter.

"Hm," was Cathy's articulate and unamused comment.

# Chapter 6

*"Do not worry about your life, what you will eat or drink; or about your body, what you will wear." That, class, is a verse I hang on to for dear life. I encourage you to do the same. Life is more than food, and the body more than clothes.*

Cathy waved good-bye to Andi as they parted ways in front of the financial planners Andi had used for years. The suite was housed in a tall building, the exterior of which reflected its surroundings as a lake reflects the sky.

"Casey'll take good care of you, Cath. He's as dependable as an old shoe," Andi called softly over her shoulder.

"I believe he just might be able to afford a new pair now," Cathy replied in a low voice.

A few feet away, a fountain spewed water skyward. Cathy walked over, sat on the side of it and tried to clear her mind. The amount of time in which things had come at her hadn't allowed for clear thinking or assessment. It was like being in an Impressionist painting. Where did she go from here? Should she tell other people and, if so, who? Or maybe that would be the worst thing she could do. What in the world did someone do with extra money besides blowing it all? It was a cinch she'd never had to figure that one out. There had to be responsibilities of some kind to go along with this type of thing, didn't there? There should be some plan of action, obviously. It was too bad she had no idea what it should be. If she thought about this any longer, her mind might just become even more fuzzy than Monet's best work. It had been less than a week and already she needed a break.

Cathy spied a coffee shop across the street. There is something comforting in a hot drink. It soothes first your hands, warming them to the fingertips with more immediacy than a pair of gloves, and then streams through your body like a necessary blanket. However, there wasn't a soft snow falling, or an icy rain, or even a cool breeze. It was July.

Cathy crossed and stepped up to the counter. After all, the newly wealthy had just as much right as the middle class to overspend on something they could make for a nickel at home. "Hello. I'm in need of a little jump start, but it's rather warm out today for coffee, don't you think?"

The barista nodded.

Cathy squinted as she scanned the menu board. "Sorry. The print is a bit small. Can you suggest something?"

The barista suggested an iced coffee; an idea upon which Cathy gratefully jumped. "Ha! Brilliant!" She received a confused look in return. "Put a lot of something in it to sweeten it enough to drink, will you?"

The barista started listing Cathy's options for a sweet coffee drink, but gave up as Cathy walked away to look out the window. Who came up with this stuff? Cold coffee. The marketing whiz who thought of selling it was a genius.

She involuntarily cringed as she handed the girl a five and took the cleverly decorated cup. As she sipped the cold drink, Cathy puzzled over the last few days. Those days reviewed, uninvited scenes traipsed through her memory like so many garden gnomes.

After her husband, Perry, had gone, she had become hypersensitive to audible changes so that she could abruptly wipe her quiet tears away when anyone entered the room. Her youngest had been born not two months after Perry's disappearance and, with no time for self-pity or a decent maternity leave, she had plowed ahead with the determination of a mother bear. Those days of seemingly endless exhaustion – for what?

Cathy looked into her five-dollar coffee. Some days she had dug through the bottom of her purse and under couch cushions, looked in the corner of every cupboard, and laid every last penny and nickel in the center of the kitchen table, praying there was enough to pay the water bill. She'd had to pass by sidewalk sales, thinking how ironic it was that the only people who could save money were those who could afford to buy things when they were on sale.

The unmet wants of her children were never far from her mind, even now. So many regrets: the things they could not have, the trips they could not take, and the activities they could not afford. When they went to the zoo, it did not harm them to pass up the ice cream cart, but it would've been so much better to have been able to say 'no' out of regard for their character development rather than out of necessity.

All of those things and more were now known to be needless if she had known years ago what Andi had stumbled upon comparatively few hours ago. Whoever said they had no regrets was either in denial or lying outright.

She slid into a chair at one of the bistro tables on the walk outside the coffee shop and leaned back. People in business suits walked hastily in and out of the store. She had walked as hastily, but never to buy expensive coffee. There always seemed to be twenty things to do in half the time it would take to do them.

A couple of college students joked around with each other, procrastinating before they opened the textbooks in front of them. There had been late nights when she had stayed up with a teenager working on homework into the wee hours. She could still feel sand in her eyes as she had struggled to stay awake in the place just between sleep and consciousness which enveloped her as she sat upright until 2:00 am.

A couple walked through the door, hand in hand. Oh, Perry. Were there any other details her husband had thought unimportant to mention?

A familiar sense of loss washed over her again as it had in so many unguarded moments and unexpected places for twenty-five years. She had met Perry Covington while in college. He was the teaching assistant for a business law class she had squeezed into her junior year. Their friendship had developed into courtship and marriage as though it was the most natural thing in the world. When they were apart, they each felt slightly perforated. Perry might have disappeared, but the love – the irreplaceable, irrevocable, unquenchable love – never had. How many different ways she could have learned about the stock. Perhaps Perry would have surprised her with this over cocoa some quiet winter day or as they swayed in the hammock under dapples of summer sun. Instead, on an unremarkable day, years after the fact, she had discovered his happy secret and wasn't happy at all.

Wildflowers lined the highway in delightful chaos. The greens, the deepening purples and ambers of groundcover spread in careless design under sketches of cloud pictures dispersed over a wide sky. Sun diamonds sparkling on ponds and lakes beckoned, while heat waves quivered off the pavement into the air. All competed for Cathy's attention on her drive home, but she saw none of them. Unbidden memories had done what her other efforts had not.

By the time she pulled her car into the driveway, Cathy had decimated half a box of tissues, but she had also made some decisions about the house and about going through Perry's things regardless of the emotional whiplash. She would buy the cemetery plot she had not been able to afford and lay down a monument for her lost husband. It would have a small cross at the top by his name and it would be engraved with one word: "Loved." And she'd make a supper fit for the old days when everyone still lived under one roof. No, it would be *better* than the old days: she'd include meat.

The rich aroma of two cheesecakes wafted through the kitchen. Six dozen caramel rolls cooled on the counter. Dishes were piled in the sink and Harry licked the floor. Cathy, barefoot with her hair in a messy bun, cradled the phone between her ear and shoulder while she paged through a cookbook with one hand and jotted down needful ingredients with the other.

"Cam? You need to come over for dinner tomorrow night. No, just you. You'll have to leave your family for one night if that's okay. I don't want to set up extra tables in the living room and the deck. I'm having your brothers and sisters, too. No, I'm not sick. 'Fraid not, but that fuse is only a sporadic nuisance. Let's not get into it now, Cameron. Maybe we can talk about it when you come, hmm? No, no. I'll do all the cooking. Be here by 6:00. Give the deadlines to your foremen to worry about. It will take you too long to get here from

Chicago otherwise. Of course I'll make a cheesecake. You can sleep over and drive back in the morning. See you later. You're a wonderful man, don't you forget that."

"Tom? Dinner tomorrow at 6:00, here, you and your brothers and sisters. I'm sure Candy can manage without you for one evening. Give her my love. How's the book coming? Oh, what does your editor know? Find a way to convince him to leave it in if it means that much to you. You know you're the best."

"Christy? Come on over for dinner tomorrow night. Give yourself a break. Dan can take care of the twins. It'll be good for him. It'll remind him that there's life outside a courtroom. Oh crumb, hold on."

Cathy grabbed the BB gun from her broom closet and took a one-handed shot at a thieving squirrel.

"No, the shot went wild. I got a black walnut. Great! See you then, and remember, you're a blessing to everyone. Come on, now. Don't argue with your mother."

"Katie? Are you free tomorrow night for dinner? It would be good for you to take a night off from the restaurant. They'll be able to run it without you for one night. Of course I'll make a cheesecake. Can you bring some of those flavored syrups from your kitch... sure, I'll try anything once. You know you're on your way to being the best restaurateur this state has ever seen, don't you? Just remember they love you for more than the food, dear. See you soon."

"Alden? I'm having a dinner at the house tomorrow night. Hm, there's always room for your girlfriend, but I think I'd like just the seven of us this time. Oh, no reason. Just feel like reminiscing. No, I'm not sick. Can you make it all that way in time? Just plan to sleep here. You can beat the morning rush hour and make it back to the ER in plenty of time for the next appendectomy. See you then, and remember, when you heal a body you touch a soul." Cathy laughed. "You said it with me this time! Yes, yes. Cheesecake it is."

"Tab? How 'bout your mom's cooking tomorrow night? Knew you'd say that. Of course I'll make some caramel rolls for you to take back with you. Can you get out of classes soon enough to get to town by 6:00? Just because it's grad school doesn't mean you can skip. You're a wonderful man; I'm proud of you. Later, baby boy."

Phone calls made, Cathy mindlessly stared out the window. What was bothering her? Something seemed like a woodpecker tapping to get into her consciousness, but for the life of her, she couldn't figure out what it was

The kids were due to come in another half hour. Cathy plopped onto the couch and swung her ballet-slippered feet onto the cushions. She was no dancer, but she had discovered years ago, during one of her personally-mandated life explorations, that she loved the comfort and sense of joy they gave to her. She'd ditched the class after three months, bought some muscle pain relief cream, and kept the slippers. She arched her back and stretched. Harry jumped up to join her and licked her ankle while she hummed the last few bars of *Auld Lang Syne*. Cathy smiled and leaned her head back, closing her eyes.

Her little children with sticky hands, limitless energy, and innocent faces had soaked the energy right out of her while they were growing. It had been hard to watch them walk out the door one by one, but she had chided herself that she was raising them to be people, not pets. Once she had managed to let them go, to soar in their own directions, she had been rewarded. They were decent people, devoted Christians, and loyal friends who viewed life with a dependable sense of love and humor. The phone connections never grew cold. Their lives were better than perfect: they were contented.

The beginnings of a puzzled frown crossed Cathy's face, but it was interrupted by a quick knock. Someone threw open the door and a spontaneous combustion of shouts of greeting and kisses and hugs followed. Harry jumped from person to person, receiving scratches and petting enough to last a week. Tab headed for the kitchen to graze before they sat down for the meal and the others quickly followed, opening the refrigerator and cupboard doors and tearing off pieces of each other's caramel rolls to pop in their mouths. Though it was twenty minutes before the designated time, they were right on schedule. It was a family thing.

Cathy looked around the crowded table with a satisfied smile. She had so far managed to put off their questions about the impromptu family gathering, and, to their credit, they had all gamely put up with it. The talking and joking had been non-stop since their arrival. And while they had been enjoying each other and teasing each other, a growing uncertainty pestered her. She was about to drop a bombshell on them. She hesitated at the thought now that they were all together, and she remembered how happy they had all been despite certain deprivations and the troubles that had accompanied them. She got up to pour herself some more tea. Standing at the counter stirring in some honey, her thoughts swirled in her mind.

Cathy excused herself to let Harry outside and accompanied him into the yard. What did people do when they couldn't have a fresh air talk with God? Really. That population must be as close to exploding as corn in a hot popper.

It is said that times of meditation are good for the body and that quiet is good for the soul. It was good advice, though a bit thin. If there was something, someone with a broad range of vision that saw not only all the pieces of a moment, but how those pieces fit in all of history, why would a person not inquire of that source? And if that source understood all that a person could not, and if that invisible presence was willing to be accessed, why in the world would a person ignore it?

What should she say? Finding the stock was like some belated conversation with her husband. Perry's disappearance hung in the air like a specter. What would it do to the kids, even if they were all grown? Would it plunge them all into some untouchable depression, some desperate search for their father all over again? Maybe they had held on to things they had never expressed to her. That was what kids did sometimes even though they were grown. Whether adult or child, she would always feel a little bit responsible for them even when the responsibility was more theirs than hers. The link of responsibility forged in parenthood never grew weak. Maybe it wasn't in the form of making a meal now, but children, no matter their age, benefited from the wisdom of their elders; of their parents, or, in her case, parent. That's the way it was with families. The web of relationship was a perpetual influence whether or not it was consciously realized. Would this news help them or would it cause trouble?

She didn't want them gaining friends the likes of which were suddenly friendly simply due to a different number in their bank account. They already had friends who were real friends based on mutual affection. If she told them, every new friend after that could be suspect.

She wasn't even sure what *she* thought about it, despite days of wandering through the rooms of her house in her fuzzy slippers, talking to her dog like she was only half sane.

Cathy stood for a while in silence. The slight breeze touched her hair like a reassuring caress, and she let out a long sigh she had not known was waiting to be released.

Spending more time outside than she'd intended, she walked resolutely back to the backdoor. As she re-entered the kitchen, each face turned her way. Cathy cleared her throat and made her announcement.

# Chapter 7

*There will be things in life we're proud of – like Friday night's football game, right, Jake? But there's another Friday, Good Friday, that isn't about pride. It's about having someone take what we deserve and handing us what we don't deserve, instead. It's about getting heaven when we – even the best of us – deserve hell.*

"You didn't tell them?" Andi, still in a white silk robe and slippers, stood in the doorway of her house. Her jaw had dropped open and she stood staring at Cathy.

The stone house sprawled over a large acreage, thoughtfully landscaped from the gated front entry with the words *Esse Quam Videri* over the arch, around to a sprawling deck sporting an outdoor kitchen and Jacuzzi, even down to Pine River at its edge. Windows lined the front on two floors. The tasteful décor within was exquisite, with original artwork sprinkled throughout. Andi could do things that defied the imagination with any raw material. She would have contended that it was the rest of the world that simply did not see clearly.

Harry stood beside Cathy, quivering now and then. Visits to Andi were right up there with chasing squirrels; there was so much land on which to run and a house with wonderful nooks to explore.

"The morning's got a bit of a chill, cuz."

Andi looked at her watch. It was six-thirty. "Ah, of course."

Andi grabbed her by the hand, pulling Cathy through the door. She closed it behind her just as Harry slipped through. Andi pulled her through the living room and the library/music room, past the small, enclosed chapel with *Amo Dommina* engraved above the door, and into the kitchen. She let go of Cathy's hand as they approached a rocking chair she had brought in especially for her cousin years ago. It stuck out like a sore thumb in a kitchen that suggested an indefinable sense of Old World beauty and up-to-date sensibilities, and, as such, was a clear demonstration of Andi's love for her cousin. Andi referred to it as a Lazy Boy on skis. Cathy described it as her happy place.

"I got to thinking that too much at once isn't – usually, at least – a good thing. What kind of mother am I if I ignore this fact? I was thinking perhaps they're just as happy as they can be with the way things are now." Cathy accepted from Andi's hand a flavored hot chocolate of some sort, topped with real whipped cream and drizzled with caramel. "Except for a little surprise here and there. Every so often something just showing up out of nowhere."

Andi scrunched one eye.

"Maybe a lot of money would take something away rather than give it."

Andi tilted her head to one side and smiled. "It doesn't seem to be hurting you."

Cathy laughed. "Nor you. Nor your kids, though they've grown up with it, so maybe it's different. Maybe if you've never worried over something, it doesn't impact you in the same way; it doesn't hold the same import because you've never had to think much about it.

Mysterious possibility doesn't surround it. It doesn't have the same pitiful effect."

"It's not possible that you're over-thinking this, is it?"

Cathy shook her head. "I need more time to think it through." She held up her hot chocolate. "You got me a new pink cup."

"I accidentally knocked the other one off the counter after you left last time. Otherwise, you know, it sits at the back of the cupboard where it can do the least possible harm. I don't know why you won't consider a color that will show even a remote sense of style. I get a headache every time I look at it."

Her cousin's aversion to pink had begun sometime during their pre-teen years. In all probability, it had something to do with a science experiment gone wrong. Maybe it was something else. Should she ask? Um, no. There are, after all, chapters in life that are best left closed; a policy to which both she and Andi wholeheartedly subscribed. It could be, after all, simply a matter of personal taste, though such a thing was hard to believe. At any rate, Andi's opposition to pink would never keep Cathy from liking it. Andi's eyes wandered the room, looking anywhere but at the cup.

Cathy knew her cousin believed her fondness of the color was more fervent than necessary. Andi would have preferred red, cranberry, plum, even mauve; anything but pink. Poor girl.

"When one can't afford crystal, one should insist on color. To cheery colors worth the headache." Cathy toasted her cousin.

"You can afford crystal now."

"Sorry. I've always bled pink." Cathy would never apologize.

Andi closed her eyes and breathed through her nose until the color returned to her face. "So, what in the world did you dream up for an excuse to have had everyone stop the world to come to supper?"

"I told them the truth. That I had managed to save more money than I thought..."

"Good one," responded Andi dryly.

"And I wanted to make some changes to the house. That I hoped it wouldn't hurt them too much to have their childhood home renovated. They, of course, were thrilled about the extra I'd saved..."

"No need for them to be distracted by zeros."

"Cam wanted to do the work himself, but it would be too hard on his family, being so far away. I convinced him to refer me to someone capable nearby."

"He probably thought he'd save you money."

"No doubt."

"He's probably already worried about cost over-runs."

"He should trust me. I *am* his mother."

"Just like you always trusted him."

Cathy rolled her eyes. "The teenage years are in a class by themselves. People who've been in both the race *and* the pasture are obligated to look out for those with the life experience of a gnat just entering their stud years."

"I have no idea how you mixed so many metaphors. Did you hurt yourself?"

"Still, I'm right." Cathy lifted her cup in a toast. "To the teenage years: when rock and roll seems profound."

"To the teenage years: when every minute past curfew gives you more proof of an abduction," Andi added, lifting her cup.

"When every girl that looks at your son is a tart and every boy that looks at your daughter deserves to be shot at high noon."

"Kamikaze prayer time." Andi gave a short laugh, taking a sip of her hot drink.

"Does it ever end?" Cathy murmured. "Speaking of teenage years, I have another visit to make: a student from the early days of my Sunday school class. I hear she's PTA president in Hudson. Maybe I can fit it in day after next."

They both held a strong dislike for PTA meetings and, during their children's school years, had both attended them without fail. It was a strange fact, though, that their association with the association brought them more trouble than the organization would ever have believed.

"PTA? I'm so there." Andi yawned audibly.

"Yes. You. Are." Cathy gave her a stern look.

"Remember the ruckus we caused by complaining about the lack of modesty in the 6th grade talent show?" Andi put down her drink to wipe a few crumbs from the counter.

"First of all, it was you, not me who complained. I was always the picture of decorum when it came to dealing with people who were given copious amounts of time during the day to say anything they chose to my children. Secondly, in your defense, I still can't believe it ended in a shouting match between the school psychologist and the music teacher."

"Ah, Cath. Those were the days." Andi's lips formed a crooked smile.

Cathy raised her eyebrows at Andi. "Sometimes I think you enjoy watching the trouble you make."

"Only if I think it's deserved."

Cathy got up and poured herself more cocoa. "I do think that my neighbor might consider moving if the price was right. I could use the space to enlarge my garden after their house was demolished. Or maybe expand my garage from a single to a double. What is this? It's divine!"

"Raspberry hot fudge. A double garage! Don't go crazy." Andi paused. "A pool wouldn't hurt."

"A pool? Me? I don't think I'm the pool type. I'm more the..."

"Double garage type. I know. Exercise could help your arthritis, Cathy," Andi persisted.

"And that sounded maternal."

"There are no return tickets from the motherhood. It's in the invisible agreement you sign the first time you look into your baby's eyes."

"Hey now. That was not fair. Now I'm thinking of babies' eyes." Cathy crossed her arms and squeezed her eyes shut tight for a second. "Still, I think I'll keep the house small enough to clean by myself."

"And the kitchen. Please. A good layout doesn't mean lifting a pan off the stove, dishing it up at the table, and putting it in the sink all without moving from your chair. Little Ben could be salvaged, of course; maybe build a play house for the grandkids or a little guesthouse and put him in there."

Cathy stretched her legs out in front of her, kicking off her shoes. "I love your thinking. That stove has seen more than its share of our lives. It definitely has to stay. A guesthouse! It could possibly salvage my nerves as the grandkids grow and multiply. I'm sure I could get some Senator to believe the government should pay for it."

"Maybe it could be placed on a supplemental policy." Andi laughed.

Cathy looked up at the ceiling. "Alexio Kastellanos. That was the name Cam gave me. Ever heard of him?"

"He built my deck, including the outdoor kitchen and sunken whirlpool, and my chapel room. Need I say more?"

"Good to hear. I've an appointment to interview him at his office in an hour. I'm having a little trouble locating Hap Skalinski. Do you think you could look him up on your machine?" Cathy looked at her watch.

"It's called a computer. My, you're branching out. No more post office scavenging?"

"Do me a favor and pretend you didn't notice. It's hard enough for me to suggest without your noticing I did." Cathy paused, shaking her head. "The last time I tried to understand the thing, the crick in my neck lasted for eight days."

"I'll help you."

"You'll help me and then you'll leave and I'll have downloads multiplying like rabbits, like last time. No thank you. While you're at it, would you mind looking up the directions to Trudy Brown's address?" Cathy rummaged in her purse. "Here it is." She pulled out a scrap of paper. "24 Park Drive."

"Hudson, you said? You really should use a machine yourself."

"I believe the expression is 'when pigs fly'."

# Chapter 8

*Honestly, Kari, I sometimes wish it wasn't there; but it is. Let's say it together, shall we? "Whatever you do, work at it with all your heart, as working for the Lord, not for men." And, yes, that does apply to practicing the piano and doing homework.*

A bell tinkled as Cathy pushed open the door to the Corn Hut. With a maximum capacity of 45, it was one of two restaurants in Pine Point. A counter seating eight anchored one side of the diner. Booths lined the other wall and the back. The speckled linoleum floor was peppered with tables.

The diner was the second undertaking of Ernie and Amelia Flynn, the first being the Java Hut, a tiny drive-through coffeehouse. That coffeehouse, situated between Pine Point High and Harriet Harper's Hair Haven (which had been built intentionally and infuriatingly across from Dick's No Nonsense Cuts), had been a raging success. It was more than Amelia had expected from Ernie's crazy idea and enough for her. She preferred a life of steady plodding and no surprises. The most adventure she had ever expected, or wanted, was when Ernie had popped the question not three months after their first date.

It had taken six months, 181 straight days of reasoning, pleading, and sweet-talking for her to relent to Ernie's latest endeavor. To say the Corn Hut's prosperity was a surprise to her would be an understatement. To suggest that she was proud of her husband's good fortune would be underselling the result.

She, however, did her best to keep her mouth shut on the matter lest Ernie take the least inkling of approval as a green light for another venture. As proud as she was, she was already looking forward to the day when she could sleep in and, if she was feeling adventurous, go to the beach. She had been in denial since the day she'd said 'I do' that the man she married would never be content sleeping in or going to the beach. He would be content climbing a mountain or, for now, opening businesses left and right.

Her mother, a librarian, had warned her. "Amelia," she had admonished, "you love books and peaceful living. That fellow has never known a story that wasn't in high def and Surround Sound, much less enjoyed a quiet evening."

But Amelia hadn't listened. She had thought she could change him. She, of course, was wrong.

Lisa, one of the waitresses, looked up from adding a bill at the counter and nodded her head toward a back booth.

Hector Valentine was sipping a soda and examining a menu.

"Heck," Cathy greeted him.

"Hello, Parade Committee Chairwoman!" He stood as she slid onto the amber-colored vinyl bench opposite him.

"Call me Cathy."

"I don't think I can do that. How about Chairwoman Covington?"

Cathy sighed as she grabbed a menu from behind the napkin dispenser, glanced at it, and put it back.

The waitress came to the table. "Are you ready to order?"

"I'll have the French Dip with house fries and a diet cola." Cathy smiled.

"You?" Lisa turned to Hector.

"I'm not quite ready."

Lisa cleared her throat and tapped her pen on the order pad. Anyone who had been served by Lisa at least once knew that she did not tolerate uncertainty well, and most of Cathy's former Sunday school students knew she grew impatient in the absence of creative thinking, which meant that just now Heck found himself uncomfortably situated.

"Oh, I guess I'll have a grilled cheese and lime Jell-O. And a chowder. Wait. I mean fries. No. And a cup o' salsa on the side."

Lisa looked at Cathy, who looked back as they both tried to smile.

"Lisa, would you do me a favor and put my soda in a..."

"Pink cup. Got it."

"You need to call the meeting to order." Heck nodded knowledgeably.

"Since it's just the two of us, why don't we keep things less formal for now." Cathy's voice didn't allow dissent. Raising six kids gave you skills you could use all over the place.

Heck got down to business. "I handle the bands."

"I'm glad to hear you're set to do that, Heck, but don't you think we should round up some more volunteers first?"

Hector gave her a blank look.

"I handle the bands," he repeated forcefully.

Ashley Andrews and her four-year-old daughter, Adele, stopped at the table. "I read in the paper you were voted Parade Committee Chairwoman. Congratulations!"

"Thank you." Cathy tried to sound agreeable.

"Are we going to have a Kiddie Parade this year? They didn't have one at the parade last year and we were so disappointed, ya know what I mean?" Ashley dropped her eyes to her daughter and back to Cathy.

The parade planning list rested on the table in front of her and, of the ten headings desperate for action, not one, not even a subheading, was a Kiddie Parade.

"There's not enough manpower," Heck interjected. "Kiddie Parades take a lot of time that we don't have. You've got your motorized wagons that stop halfway through the parade and have to be either repaired quickly or pulled by some kid that's already upset, and then there's got to be a first aide responder. Nancy Howard is a nursing assistant, and she did it for three years, but she said she was too busy last year. Then there's the dog stuff someone has to pick up after. Plus, the tiny kids that start crying, missing their mothers. Kiddie Parades are a recipe for a headache and a half."

He was rather more aggressive than necessary, in Cathy's opinion.

Adele was pulling at her mother's hand.

Cathy spread her hands. "As you can see, we're short volunteers, but if you'd be willing to work on the Kiddie Parade, we'll put every ounce of support behind you."

"I don't know. I've never done anything like that before, ya know what I mean? Plus I've got Adele and such."

"Adele's welcome to come with you to our meetings."

Heck gasped.

"We don't do that," he whispered behind his hand.

Cathy looked at him and raised her eyebrows questioningly.

"We don't have kids at our meetings," Heck repeated more loudly.

Ashley took a step back.

"We aren't concerned with that right now." Cathy pinched the bridge of her nose. "We could really use the help. Can you help us?"

Cathy gave Ashley a guilt-inducing look that every mother grows to recognize, but which Ashley, as a young mother, had not yet learned. Cathy felt bad about pulling it on her, but this was no time for ethics.

"I suppose," Ashley said slowly, "As long as I can bring Adele..."

"That's terrific!" Cathy beamed.

"We're having a meeting right now." Hector sighed.

Ashley looked like she felt trapped. Welcome to the club.

Cathy took a deep breath. "Don't worry about joining us today. Why don't you see if you can find some friends to help with the Kiddie Parade? Then give me a call and we'll move from there."

Ashley looked relieved. "I can do that."

As she walked away, Hector pumped his fist in the air. "Wow. We've already doubled our volunteer force!"

Lisa brought their orders to the table and motioned to Teddy Hornbach, a former parade committee chair. "Hornbach paid for your lunch."

"Great!" Hector waved.

"Not yours," Lisa snapped.

Cathy nodded him her thanks, prayed to be put out of her misery, and bit into her sandwich. She spied Mrs. Kipton out of the corner of her eye. She was sitting alone at a table for two, having a bowl of corn on the cob chowder with crackers. Cathy excused herself and went over to the table.

Heck frowned his disapproval as he took a bite of his grilled cheese.

"Mrs. Kipton? May I sit for a minute?"

Mrs. Kipton motioned to the chair across from her, dabbed her mouth with her napkin, and put down her spoon.

"It's nice to see you having a relaxing lunch," Cathy said.

"I'm on break from the bank."

"Do you come here for lunch often?"

"Not very."

"I'm having the best roast beef sandwich." Cathy offered the friendliest smile she could muster.

"That's nice." Mrs. Kipton took a sip of water.

"Diet soda makes me burp, but I have a weakness for it," Cathy continued.

Mrs. Kipton almost smiled.

Cathy took that as the most encouragement she would receive. "We are looking for volunteers for the parade committee this year. Have you ever thought of doing anything like that?"

"No."

The door of the diner slammed as five teenagers jostled in. Lisa called to the cook for three large orders of fries before they'd decided where to sit.

"I'd love for you to be on our committee. Maybe you could help with a few things here and there?"

"No one's ever asked me."

"I'm asking."

Mrs. Kipton looked down at her lap, then at Cathy. "Thank you. I will."

Cathy jumped out of her chair, nearly knocking it into the family behind her. After a quick apology to them, she shook Mrs. Kipton's hand. "I'm so, so glad; so very glad. I'll call you with our next meeting time."

"I'll answer the phone," Mrs. Kipton replied.

The meeting lasted one hour and two minutes according to Hector's notes, which, with an air of self-sacrifice, he'd insisted on taking until a volunteer secretary could be found. The parade date was confirmed with City Hall via Heck's cell phone. He would contact the bands to get the parade on their calendars. He had been telling the truth when he said he handled the bands. That was all. He handled the bands.

Cathy would call around for more volunteers and put an announcement in the local paper about accepting parade entries at a discount. She would submit a short essay about Logjam Days to the city papers in hopes of eliciting additional event sponsors. She would contact the local business that made trophies to explore the options for band and float awards. She would also contact the police and fire departments with the parade route. The rest of the to-do list she'd received from last year's committee chair continued for two more pages. What was the point of reading those two pages with no more volunteers on the horizon? She laid the list on the table. She was looking around the diner as Lisa returned with Hector's check.

"Amelia said to tell you you're scaring away the customers," she mumbled to Cathy.

"I thought Amelia didn't care about the diner." Cathy gave Lisa a meaningful look.

Lisa looked over her shoulder, then whispered, "That's her story and we're stickin' to it."

Cathy looked around again. The diner did seem to have cleared rather quickly.

"Sorry, Lisa." Cathy put a fist to her lips and gave the waitress a hopeful look.

"Oh, no. Not me. I've got enough on my hands being vice president of Motocross Mamas."

"I won't ask then." Cathy recognized a definite no when she heard one.

Cathy stopped by Hornbach's table to thank him for paying for her lunch.

"I'm so grateful for you," he said. "I'll be praying for you."

"Thank you." Cathy shook his hand.

"I believe the expression is be ye warmed and filled," she added under her breath as she walked out the door.

# Chapter 9

*I suppose Jesus had the disciples shake the dust off their feet to show that they were not part of what the townspeople chose. God holds us responsible for doing our part, class, but it's the other guy's responsibility for what he does with the information. No sense in beating a dead horse.*

After a few minutes of research on the PTA and the Trudy Browns of the world on Andi's computer, which Cathy described as more boring than an accounting class in a beige classroom, Cathy and Andi stopped for strong tea and scones at a small café in Stillwater. They strolled through some antique stores and the downtown, noting only by their hunger pangs that an entire morning had passed while they had examined things they remembered from their childhood. Cathy crossed her arms and began tapping her foot as Andi continued perusing the merchandise. Why in the world would these things be labeled 'antique' when they had only recently been introduced to the buying public? What was wrong with people?

They sped over the St. Croix bridge, anticipating their arrival just outside of Hudson in time for a very late lunch and the friendly investigation of Mrs. Trudy Brown, wife and mother of two, owner of a stylish home, community activist, and PTA president.

Hours later, Cathy looked at her watch, raised her eyebrows and cleared her throat. Both women were in need of a good stretch and yearned more for a comfy chair and a Twinkie than a chat with one of Cathy's former students; one who, in Cathy's memory, had been concerned more with appearance than substance during those growing up years. They had both passed tiredness and were growing easily irritated.

Andi ran her hand through her hair as she turned left. "Highly unusual, getting lost in Hudson."

Cathy gave a short cough.

"But I'm telling you, Cathy, with all these little curvy twists and turns and trees blocking any view but that of an expert marksman NRA member..."

"I thought you were an expert marksman NRA member."

"Obviously the wrong example, then; I have no idea which way Barker, Packer..."

"Park Drive."

"Park Drive is."

"I don't suppose it would have anything to do with missing the last exit to Hudson in the first place and driving half-way through Wisconsin before..."

"Half-way would be the Dells – ish."

"You know, they say that not knowing where you're driving is a sign of Alzheimer's."

"I knew exactly where I was going: Hudson. I think it had something to do with the iced latte I was drinking and the song you were trying to remember the words to."

Cathy relented with a small smile. "The search for those words could've taken us to Tomah, at least, if you hadn't hit upon 'no ear may hear his coming'."

"Who sings *O Little Town of Bethlehem* this time of year, Cath?! Really. Who?!"

"Christmas isn't a day, it's a gift." Cathy paused for a minute. "And you can be quite proud of yourself for recalling the third verse."

"Does the word 'seasonal' mean anything to you?"

"I can't help what jumps into my mind and won't leave." They drove for a while in silence. "Have you thought how you'll decorate the small tree this year?"

Andi ignored the question.

"The large tree in the foyer?"

"Not answering," Andi replied.

"I loved what you did with the outdoor garland last year."

Andi slapped her hand on the steering wheel. "And now you've succeeded in putting that in my mind where I will obsess about it until I can manage to eradicate it sometime in the middle of the night a week and a half from now. Thank you very much."

"See? It's hard once something jumps into your mind." Cathy looked out the window, hiding her smile.

They drove through yet another neighborhood of manicured lawns, hanging baskets overflowing with color, and houses painted in muted colors. All but one.

Cathy turned her head and peered at the house. "Wait. Pull up here. Maybe she can help us."

Andi glanced out the window. "Oh yes. She looks like a real fount of information."

Andi pulled over to the curb and Cathy pushed herself out of the passenger side, quietly shutting the door behind her with a click. An older woman, probably twenty years her senior by the lines in her face and her thinning hair, sat in a woven plastic rocker by the steps of her house. She was knitting what appeared to be an afghan of enormous proportions.

"Hello!" Cathy called as she made her way up the sidewalk.

The woman looked up. "Whacha want?"

Cathy looked around uncomfortably as she made some idle chit chat with the woman who clearly wasn't used to it.

"My friend," Cathy pointed to the car, "and I are looking for an address. We thought perhaps you could help."

"Yer interruptin' my peace."

"Yes. I can see that now."

The woman was putting aside her knitting. How sharp were those knitting needles? Cathy smiled, then frowned in an effort to hide the smile, then wondered if she had ended up looking slightly deranged. The woman frowned back.

"Well? What address're ya lookin' for?"

"Um. I can't believe it. I forgot." Cathy held up a finger. "Just a moment, I'll be right back." She hurried to the car and poked her head through the open window.

"Address?!" she hissed.

Andi looked at her as though she'd lost her mind. "*You're* asking *me*?" She scrunched her eyes shut. "It was ah twenty-two, no, four, twenty-four Backer... "

Cathy snapped her fingers. "That's it! Thanks."

She hurried back up the walk.

"24 Park Drive," she said proudly.

The woman picked up a long needle lying next to her in the chair and pointed. "No wonder yer lost. Yer stupid. It's two blocks thataway."

"Ever in your debt." Cathy extended her hand for a handshake but quickly pulled it to her side as the woman tilted her head and frowned suspiciously. Cathy hurried down the walk and jumped in the car, calling out the window, "Thanks again. If you're ever in Pine Point..."

But the words were lost to the wind as Andi squealed away from the curb.

"You're kidding. You're actually squealing the tires?"

"That lady scared me. Did you see her cat in the window?"

"What cat?"

"IN HER WINDOW. It had to easily be the size of a coyote."

"What was *in* that latte?"

Andi began humming.

"No. Not another song." Cathy shook her head. "We're not getting punchy. It's only," she checked her watch, "7:00 in the evening."

Andi rolled her eyes.

"Besides, we're here. Look. Park Drive. Uh. There. There on the left. 24."

Andi pulled over and Cathy opened her door before the car was in park. "Well?"

"I'm tired. Just let me take a little catnap. I've driven like 2,000 miles today."

Cathy raised her eyes heavenward and plunged down the walk. She was back inside of two minutes.

Andi opened one eye. "You did not talk to Trudy Brown, PTA president. I know for a fact I didn't even start breathing slowly and evenly, not to mention begin dreaming about Christmas garland."

"She's not here. She's at..."

"If you say a PTA meeting, I'll shoot you where you stand."

Cathy slid into the passenger seat. "I'm not standing."

Andi looked at her incredulously. "That's not possible. The school year is nearly two months away!"

"I told you this girl always was a go-getter. Apparently, she has a planning session complete with a speaker every summer. How lucky are we? The school is three blocks 'thataway'." She did a good imitation of the woman who had given her directions before.

"I'll remind you that we mix with PTA like oil and water. What do you say we forget about it?"

"Having driven this far? Trudy's sister answered the door. She and her husband are visiting. Guess what her sister's married name is."

"I..."

"You'll never guess. Dowling!"

Andi was silent for a moment.

"Is it *that* Dowling?" Andi perked up momentarily.

"I don't know. It would be interesting to find out, though, wouldn't it? By the way. You'll never believe this," Cathy continued. "That woman, the one with the cat..."

"Let me guess. She thinks people like you should stay on their own side of the street."

"Hm. Some things go without saying. But no, that's not it. She told me she's..."

"Don't say it."

"Our age."

They drove the three blocks in silence.

The media center at the school held about twenty parents in addition to a few school personnel and the evening's speaker. Clearly, Trudy meant business.

A woman called the meeting to order. Her make-up was perfect, her bleached blonde hair expertly highlighted, teased, and sprayed in place. She wore white pants with a white and powder blue waist-length suit jacket, and two-tone kitten heels in the same colors as her jacket. Her fingernails were polished pale tan. She looked at the small crowd and immediately frowned.

Cathy leaned over to Andi and whispered, "This seems to be my day for getting frowned at."

"Welcome to our planning session for the coming school year! Our push for new members, *PSEO, GO!*, as we called it in the mailing, must be working; I see we have some new members here. We love to have new members! Welcome. Would you like to introduce yourselves?" The woman extended her hand to Cathy and Andi.

Andi whispered, "No."

Cathy stood. "Trudy! I'm Cathy Covington, your former..."

"Why, Mrs. Covington!" Trudy Brown's bright smile diminished with every syllable. "What are you doing so far from Pine Point?"

"I wanted to visit you, Trudy." Cathy looked around at the group. "I'm her former Sunday school teacher," she volunteered with an innocent smile.

What remained of Trudy's smile froze.

"Perhaps we can talk after your meeting."

"Would you like to wait outside?"

"We're fine here, dear. We'll just sit and listen." Cathy settled into her chair.

Trudy nodded and began the meeting again. A woman near the front of the room looked back at them with a curious gaze. "Trudy, you didn't get the other visitor's name."

"Oh yes," Trudy sighed. "You are...?"

Andi stayed in her chair. "I'm Andi Clemens. Just along for the enlightened conversation."

The entire group turned and gaped at Andi until Trudy pounded her gavel on the podium.

Andi whispered to Cathy, "She doesn't like surprises, does she?"

Cathy gave a short laugh. "Never did."

Following a short business meeting, Trudy introduced the speaker. Dale Carbon sported short, spikey hair and a diamond earring. His topic, the problem of censorship in school libraries, appeared to be one about which he was very passionate. As he closed his presentation, he asked for questions and Cathy raised her hand.

"No one needs to raise their hands. Just call out your questions." Mr. Carbon sniffed.

"Got a Bible in here?" Andi interjected before Cathy could continue.

"Wh..."

"I just wanted to look something up while you all carried on." Andi got up and looked around. "It's probably in your reference section, isn't it? Otherwise, I guess it would be with your History books."

The speaker scoffed audibly. Some of the parents frowned at him. Others frowned at Trudy. Some squinted at Andi, who walked out.

"Well?" Andi drove through the streets of Hudson, trying to find the highway.

"*Well?* Well, after you sauntered out, all hell broke loose." Cathy covered her eyes with her hand.

"Hell in the public schools? Imagine that," Andi smiled in the now-dark car. "Serves them right for cutting out Jesus and Easter in favor of Darwin and Earth Day."

"One or two ladies thought you had a legitimate question, a few thought you were a Bible-thumping idiot, the school secretary seemed pleased with you, and most of the others seemed more than a little uncomfortable that some law was being broken."

"Did you defend me?"

"There wasn't time for me to say anything. No one raised her hand..."

"Just as Dick Copper or Bobbin, or whoever he was, said they shouldn't," Andi interjected.

"Dale Carbon. And it seemed to me that everyone was talking at once. I wonder what their children's manners are like? I feel sorry for the teachers. So, I just started looking around for a Bible. Couldn't hurt, right? Put the question to rest?"

Andi chuckled.

Cathy sighed heavily. "I finally gave up. Maybe I was looking in the wrong spot. You would've thought the speaker would've tried to help me. He didn't seem interested."

Andi looked fondly at her cousin. "You do innocent so well. You are the Charlton Heston of innocent."

"Don't say that name. You might get us in more trouble," Cathy murmured.

"Is Trudy Brown going to go to Sunday school in Hudson?"

"Trudy Brown, it would appear, prefers to sleep late and then have a leisurely brunch on Sundays in Hudson. She seems to think I should stay in my Sunday school room, though she didn't put it quite that nicely. I'm guessing she prefers the ACLU to the NRA, though I suppose it was lucky for me she wasn't carrying a gun. I'd forgotten what a temper she has. I suppose one should not peeve a PTA president."

"Tsk, tsk. I don't remember the alphabet being this exhausting. Pretty soon we'll all have to L-I-E D-O-W-N and take an N-A-P," Andi groaned as they sped on the highway toward home.

# Chapter 10

*One of the many reasons we memorize scripture, Netta, is that what we put in our memories slips out into our behavior. Why do you think there's so much money in advertising?*

"Here's what I think." Cathy and Andi walked through the Farmer's Market. It was a glorious summer day. The clouds were mere wisps in a sky of such deep blue that it made your heart ache. "If we're ever to get to Kendrick Bogstrom, we're going to have to meet him where he works. I can't nail him down at home for love nor money."

"You've gone to his apartment, then? I thought you were hesitant."

"I didn't want to waste my time. He's one of those that it would just go in one ear and out the other. That's the way he always was: looking straight at you, but never listening; nodding without the foggiest notion of what he was agreeing with. But I don't like being thwarted, so now, of course, I'm doing it for all the wrong reasons."

"That's how half the stuff in this world gets done." Andi sneezed.

"Bless you. I've gone to his apartment three times. He's never home. I've tried to call. Everyone seems to carry a phone these days. He certainly should get my calls. "

"Do you suppose he's not answering when he sees your number?"

Cathy stood stock-still by some sweet corn. The vendor approached them, but Andi shook her head.

"Why did that not cross my mind? Though why he would recall my phone number is beyond me. It was just the one summer when I called on a few Saturday nights to remind him about Sunday school." Cathy began muttering to herself. "You'd think when they get to thirteen every cell in their brain having to do with times and dates wouldn't wash away, but it does. At least, for most of the boys. And a few of the girls. Ack! See what cell phones have done to civil society?" Cathy looked at Andi. "He wouldn't do that to a Sunday School teacher, would he?"

"While it's hard to grasp, anything's possible." Andi smiled indulgently as they continued strolling through the produce. "But don't rush to blame cell phones. He could have a land line with a caller ID."

A man with a bag slung over his shoulder did a double take as Andi passed him and ogled her as they continued on their way.

"The field of communications is promoting chaos faster than two year olds at a birthday party," Cathy said more loudly than she intended, causing the man to snap his head back ahead.

"Thanks," laughed Andi.

"Yes. Well. What was that you were saying about how half the stuff in this world gets done?"

"Where does he work, anyway? Kendrick."

"Delta."

Andi paused by some jars of honey. "Airlines?"

"No, Dawn, Andi. Of course airlines. He's a male stewardess."

"You mean a flight attendant."

"Isn't that what I said?"

A woman with a miniature dog, to which she was talking baby talk, muscled her way in between them, heading for a farm stand from Hugo.

Andi picked up some lace and examined it. Handing it to the vendor, she pulled out some bills and change while the woman nervously placed the lace in a flowered paper bag, and took a picture of Andi taking the bag from her with her cell phone. "I have been in the mood for a little escape. Why don't we do a little digging and see when he flies next?"

"Already did. He's new enough to be on reserve."

"Okay," Andi replied slowly. "I know a purser over there. I don't know if he can help us, but he does owe me a favor."

"Really?"

Andi stopped at a booth where the vendor was selling unroasted coffee beans and several kinds of beans he roasted himself. She bought two pounds of green Colombian while chatting up the coffee geek whose breathing seemed to become suddenly fast and shallow.

"Want to try?" Andi looked at Cathy. "You can use my roaster."

Cathy shook her head. "The last time I tried it, the burnt coffee smell lingered the season. I'll stick with Grammie Mae's. And I'm not a middle school boy. I can't be distracted that easily. You were saying the purser owes you."

"It was a bit of a delicate situation. I'd rather not do a retrospect."

"You don't have to tell me now. I'll just ask you sometime when you're tired."

"Play fair."

"You know me better than that." Cathy laughed.

"At any rate, any plane trip will seem shorter than the drive to Hudson."

"And we'll get a snack!" Cathy added optimistically.

The two women wandered over to a string of stands that offered green beans, lettuce, and five varieties of peppers. A young woman was running the pepper stand, and a man was watching the other two; they appeared to be working together. The man was going about his work, whistling. The vendor, who had been looking over some papers, set them down to help a customer. Cathy glanced at them, then edged closer to get a better look. The papers appeared to be a sublease agreement.

"Hm. That's interesting." She nudged Andi and nodded to the papers. "Can someone really do that?"

Andi studied the stack, and discretely pushed the top page over slightly.

"Can they sublet a space?" Cathy persisted.

"Shhh," Andi pointed to one of the names at the bottom of the page. "Dowling?"

Cathy shook her head to clear her thoughts. She let out a sharp laugh and scrunched her eyebrows. "I've heard of branching out, but an inner city landlord renting out farmer's market stands?"

Cathy grabbed a few heads of lettuce without examining them, and got the vendor's attention.

"How's business?" She handed him some money.

"Great!" He swallowed as he gazed at Andi.

"I've always wondered how a person even gets in here. It's so full year after year," Cathy said.

The salesman nodded, still staring.

Cathy drummed her fingers on the counter.

"The vendors jockey for a booth because this place gets a lot of traffic," he agreed, recovering from a momentary daze.

84

Andi had been looking at his booths. "I recall some woodwork and flowers and books in these three stands last year."

The merchant lifted his eyebrows. "You have a very good memory."

Cathy began to laugh hysterically.

Andi gave her an annoyed look. "I just notice things," she said. "You weren't here."

"You're right. The wife was sick last year, and I couldn't care for both her and the stands. My daughter pitched in."

"With different items?"

"A different location." He nodded his head toward the entrance. "Over there."

Cathy, still choking back her laughter, made a sound rather like the moan of an injured moose. Andi ignored her.

"That's a great location over there," Andi noted. "Why did you move?"

"Like I said, the wife was sick. She usually handles the paperwork, including renewing the lease. And with the confusion of things at home, we lost it."

"But you got some spaces after all," Cathy noted, wiping a tear from her eye, having, with some effort, recovered from her hysteria.

"Barely. The spaces were all rented out. Some guy came in and swooped up the strays. I got a letter from him in March, making a sublease proposition I couldn't pass up."

"I imagine there's a waiting list of vendors. That's unusual; giving up a coveted space like that." Andi waved a fly away from the lettuce.

"It sure is. When he contacted me, he said he'd decided to take his product online and wouldn't need the booths."

"Wouldn't one usually use the space to advertise and increase online sales?" Andi persisted.

"I wasn't gonna argue. There weren't no other spaces available, Ma'am. Not at this market. And, like I said, I got a good deal."

"What makes it so good?" Cathy stepped forward.

The vendor leaned in. "This guy, the guy subletting to me, he buys all my produce, every last lettuce leaf."

"I don't understand." Cathy swatted at the persistent fly.

"It's part of the agreement. He buys all my stuff. I have the cash for today's stuff in the bank right now. The only thing he asks is that I resell it for him and reimburse him for the investment."

Andi frowned slightly. She asked softly, "So it gets sold twice. The second time at a profit?"

"That's the crazy thing. This guy, he don't want no profit. Just says I resell the same as always and he takes the sales at the end of the day." The man laughed. "Says it's his penance for changin' his mind about the site in the first place."

"He loses some of the money if you don't sell out every day," reasoned Cathy.

"Not him. If sales are down by more than four percent, I'm in it for every last nickel. But it's not often I don't sell out, Ma'am. I've been the top seller here for eight years."

"He sounds like a saint anyway," Andi commented.

"Hey! Saint Paul! Sure enough!" The vendor laughed until he had to grab the table to steady himself.

"What keeps you from pocketing the money and walking away?" asked Cathy.

"Nah. I've always lived by a handshake. I have to sign somethin' for the sublet, but the rest is on a handshake. Besides, I'd lose part of the season if I walked. No, this is too good a deal."

"What is the name of his product site?" Andi dug around in her purse.

The salesman scratched his head. "Ya know, I offered to put a sign up for him; but the conversation got sidetracked. Now that you mention it, I guess I never got the name of it."

"So do you have an address for this guy?" The fly landed on Cathy's shoulder, then took off as she blew a puff of air at it.

"Why?" The salesman frowned.

"I might be interested in finding out if he has any other stands to sublet," she offered weakly.

"There ain't nothin' else here, Ma'am. And I, myself, am already wonderin' what I'll do for next year. This guy still has his name on the lease."

"Can he legally do that?" Andi furrowed her brow.

The man shrugged his shoulders. "I'm not doin' nothin' to risk losin' this deal."

"Still, I'd like to check it out, and maybe I'll take one of your orange peppers from your other stand there." Cathy handed him a bill.

"Keep the change," Andi quickly added.

"What are you doing?" Cathy whispered.

"You can afford it," Andi said between her teeth.

The vendor smiled, signaled his daughter to bag a pepper, and gave Cathy the address.

As they walked to Andi's car, Cathy looked down at the slip of paper in her hand. "What did we just do?"

"You're the one who's mad at Dowley. We're just... curious."

"Dowling," Cathy corrected her. "That sublet arrangement does seem... unseemly."

"We couldn't help ourselves. Sometimes one question just leads naturally to another."

Cathy stopped in her tracks and looked at her cousin. "I couldn't agree more."

The two women slid into Andi's car. "However," Andi put the key into the ignition, "I'll remind you my memory is fine; just a bit unreliable when it comes to names."

"I'm sorry, Andi, I just," Cathy tried very hard to hold a bubble of laughter at bay, "when he said the thing about your memory..."

"Never mind," Andi interrupted. "We have a different concern here." She looked at Cathy and Cathy returned her gaze. "I believe another one of those projects I mentioned when you started this is materializing before our eyes."

"Um." Cathy bit her lip.

"Hmm," her cousin responded.

# Chapter 11

*Welcome to our Middle School class, sixth graders. Since this is your first Sunday in my class, I'll point out the cocoa bar in the corner is for everyone's enjoyment and the sarcophagus in the corner is where I keep the bones of Middle Schoolers who misbehave. Any questions?*

Contemporary furniture filled the spacious living room. A doorless chrome wardrobe stood against one of the beige walls, one shelf holding pictures of a boy at various ages. Another shelf held a few pictures drawn in the style of preschool abandon, one Mother's Day card, and a graduation cap. An electric guitar was propped against the back of the wardrobe floor.

"Can I get you some more coffee?" asked Mrs. Mehan.

"No thank you," Andi replied.

"Love some!" Cathy said at the same time.

Mr. Mehan uncrossed his legs and folded his hands in his lap.

"So the last time you visited James was..." Cathy left the question hanging in the air.

"About two months ago." Mr. Mehan nodded toward the kitchen where his wife was refilling Cathy's coffee cup. "She'd like to go every week, but when we visit she comes home so depressed, it takes more than a week for her to be functional again. She puts on a good front, you know, but I see what it is for her when there isn't anyone around to put on for. After the last visit, I put my foot down. I said, 'Nibsy, we can't keep on like this. That boy doesn't care squat about anything, and it's too hard on you. No more visiting for a while.' Oh, she carried on, but she knows I'm right, of course. She hasn't said a thing about it for a couple of weeks. This visit will set her to crying after you leave."

"We're sorry, Mr. Mehan," Andi offered.

"Mike," he said.

"Mike."

Cathy leaned forward. "Mike, we'd like to talk with some of James' friends."

"Friends," Mr. Mehan spat the word.

Mrs. Mehan came back with Cathy's coffee and sat down. "His friends," she answered, "Yes. I'll find some names and phone numbers."

She left the room again the soft scraping sound of opening and closing drawers echoed down the hallway. James' mother came back with a few slips of paper. Her eyes were red, but dry. She handed the papers to Cathy. "They usually hang out in this neighborhood, I think."

She scribbled a couple of street names on another sheet of paper and held it out. Andi took it.

Cathy began to say something, but Mrs. Mehan continued talking. "He had a girlfriend."

"Nice girl," Mr. Mehan inserted.

"Her name is Tiffany. I put her address on there." She gestured to the paper Andi was holding. "They're not seeing each other now..."

"She broke up with him," Mr. Mehan explained.

Mrs. Mehan stared at the floor, the ensuing quiet like a funeral parlor.

Cathy and Andi looked at each other.

"I thank you both for your time," Cathy said.

Mr. and Mrs. Mehan saw them to the door. "You were such a good Sunday School teacher," Mrs. Mehan said with a weak smile. "James always seemed a little less moody after one of your classes."

"He liked the war stories," Mr. Mehan added.

Cathy smiled. "The boys always do."

"I'm sorry he brought drugs to class that time," Mrs. Mehan offered.

"We took care of it." Cathy shook her head and pressed Mrs. Mehan's hand into her own. "He did seem a bit alarmed as he watched me empty it all into my coffee grounds and stir." Cathy chuckled. She stood for a moment, reflecting. "Good thing Pepper Delany made the coffee that day. She always forgets to put in a filter. I believe her love of gossip distracts her."

"He said you threatened him with a machete," Mr. Mehan recalled. Mrs. Mehan's intake of breath was audible. "That was fine with me at the time," he qualified.

"Threaten? I never threaten my students."

Andi reached over and hugged the parents, and the cousins walked out to Andi's car.

"I'd send some muffins for him, but they don't allow that sort of thing," Mrs. Mehan called to them.

Cathy waved to her over her shoulder.

"I'll believe you didn't threaten him as soon as I'll believe Mrs. Mehan will ever take down that shrine in the living room." Andi pulled her car door shut.

"What? Oh, I think when the Mehans say the word 'threat' they really mean 'empty threat.' I was merely speaking their language; a matter of semantics." Cathy looked out the window. "As far as the 'shrine,' maybe parents could use more of those. Might remind them to pray for more than a good parking spot."

As they drove away, Andi turned on a CD and tapped the music's rhythm on the steering wheel with a manicured fingernail. The jazzed-up, wired orchestral music of one of Andi's favorite groups filled the car. She turned into the drive-through of the Java Hut. "Want something?"

Cathy shook her head.

Andi gave her a sympathetic look. "Discouragement doesn't suit you. C'mon now."

Cathy sighed audibly.

"You can't do more than what you can do, Cathy," she consoled her.

"Obviously."

Andi ordered an iced green tea soy chai, took the drink from the barista and pulled out again. She turned into the parking lot of Lakeview Park and rolled down the car top. The two women sat in the car and looked out at the water, placid under the summer sun. The leaves of six-year-old trees along the curbside fluttered imperceptibly as sunlight filtered through them, landing in geometric shapes on the car. Andi slurped her chai tea and looked at her cousin out of the corner of her eye. Cathy didn't laugh or make a smart remark. She just kept gazing toward the lake.

"Are you ready for tomorrow's secret destination?" Andi batted her eyes.

"I would be more ready if you would tell me where we're going."

"Knowing where you're going? Where's the fun in that?" Andi laughed. "All I'll tell you is that we'll be seeing Kirby Bergstrom..."

"Kendrick Bogstrom."

"And we'll be staying overnight."

"I'll pack my slippers." Cathy rolled her head from one side to the other, crunched up her face, then forced a smile with her eyes still shut, ending up with a grimace. Opening her eyes, Cathy turned to her cousin. "I hope you remembered to forego first class. No sense in spending more money to fly on the same plane to the same destination."

Andi looked heavenward. "By the way," Andi threw her chai cup from her position behind the wheel and turned her palms up as it swished into the trashcan by the curb. "There's a," she pulled a slip of paper from her bag and read, "Hap Skalinski on the 2007 alumni listing of Metro State."

Cathy's eyes regained a hint of their usual sparkle. "Address?"

Andi handed her cousin the slip of paper. "It's probably outdated."

"What a helpful thing to say." Cathy smoothed the paper.

"I live to serve," Andi replied.

Cathy glanced at her watch. "Ugh. I didn't realize the time. We need to get back. I still have to get my things together, and I have a parade committee meeting in exactly one hour."

"Aw, heck," chuckled Andi.

"More than you imagine." Cathy rolled her eyes as Andi revved out of the parking lot.

Cathy waved to Lisa as she walked through the door of the Corn Hut. She chose a large table in a back corner of the restaurant, sat down, and spread some papers in front of her.

Lisa placed a Diet Coke in a pink cup in front of Cathy. "I thought you might like that," she said over her shoulder on her way to the next table.

"And that's why you get the big tips." Cathy smiled.

"That, and great legs," Lisa called.

There was a commotion at the door as Ashley Andrews entered with Adele. Lindsey Mayberg, the young university graduate who had just moved into the upstairs apartment of the duplex that was Ashley's home, followed her as did two other young mothers, their children in tow. They made it across the diner, knocking over only one person's coffee and stepping on the toes of two others.

Cathy jumped up and pulled an adjacent table nearer so that the children could sit there and color on the paper place mats without spilling someone's water. The coffee had been wiped up and the crew had settled into their places by the time Heck arrived. Mrs. Kipton followed, pulling open the door Heck had just walked through without a thought for anyone behind him.

The assembled team ordered and Lisa deftly served them without mixing up a single request. Cathy chatted with each one in turn.

The Kiddie Parade committee had posted and handed out flyers around neighborhoods, and at churches, pre-schools, parks, and restaurants. They reported they were already being flooded with calls from parents, grandparents, and one eager third grade girl.

"We're mulling over whether we should set an age limit, ya know what I mean?" Ashley raised her brows as the others nodded in agreement.

Cathy looked down at the pages in front of her. The single-spaced type listed all that was left to accomplish before parade day. "You're doing a wonderful job. However, there's still a lot to be done. I'd like

94

to hand out some responsibilities today to each one of you. Please contact the name I give you, find out availability and needs of the person or organization and we'll go from there."

"We have our hands full with the Kiddie Parade," one of Ashley's friend's face went white.

Heck motioned to Lisa with one hand. "My corn paella isn't piping hot like I like. Enough said?"

Lisa swept his dish from the table and walked off.

"Chairwoman Covington, don't you think we should get the meeting underway?" Heck muttered under his breath. He had managed to take a seat next to Cathy.

The sound of a dish being slammed on the counter resounded from the kitchen.

"I already have. The Kiddie Parade details are moving along nicely." Cathy smiled at Ashley and company. "Weren't you listening?"

Heck pulled a pen from his shirt pocket and started writing.

"Honestly, Heck, I don't know that we need meeting notes." What was needed in the two months between this meeting and the parade itself was action, not meeting minutes. The Kiddie Parade was a go, but the rest of it, the main event, was stalled out.

The look Heck gave her prompted her to backpedal. "However, you never know when they'll come in handy."

She could not afford to lose the committee member who was rounding up the bands even if he did have an inflated opinion of himself, God pity wife number two.

Heck nodded importantly.

They all looked up as Denny Jorgenson and Carl Stein walked over and pulled up some chairs.

"Ashley said you was wantin' some committee members," Denny said. Denny was Ashley's younger brother.

"Here we are!" Carl declared, sneaking a look at Ashley's new neighbor.

"Wonderful!" Cathy squared her shoulders as the hint of a smile crossed her face. New residents and curious flirtations were a great combination. "We're dividing up some of the work right now. Mrs. Kipton, would you be willing to take over parade publicity?"

Lisa came to take the latecomers' orders.

Mrs. Kipton took a sip of her ice water. She twisted her napkin and looked down at her lap, her expression growing increasingly anxious.

Ashley jumped up to wipe up water Adele had knocked over. One of the other kids started whining for the Corn Hut's milkshake flavor of the day.

"Or, if you would be willing to keep a record of income and spending, I would be much obliged." Cathy bit her lip.

Mrs. Kipton nodded, back on solid ground once again.

"Denny and I will do publicity!" Carl volunteered, looking directly at Lindsey Mayberg this time.

"I'd like to do one other thing if it's okay," Mrs. Kipton murmured.

"By all means!" Cathy raised her hands in the air.

"I'd like to hand out water to the parade entrants." Mrs. Kipton's face was full of hope, like she was asking for a favor.

"And I'll take care of water acquisition," Lindsey offered, looking back at Carl.

"Let's hear it for the aqua acquisition division!" Carl quipped.

Sure enough, this committee was becoming a genuine force to be reckoned with, just like committees all over the world. The person who had come up with the idea of committees in the first place ought to have been tarred and feathered before he was allowed to inflict his damage on the rest of mankind.

Lisa brought her another pink cup of Diet Coke. "This one's on me," she whispered, "That look of gratitude you're givin' me will carry me through 'til quittin' time. That bad?"

"An alternate reality." Cathy exhaled while the others talked about where to get the best deal for bottled water and Heck furiously scribbled each idea for posterity.

# Chapter 12

*The verse "You will be ever hearing but never understanding; you will be ever seeing but never perceiving" simply means that sometimes a person is unable to see the truth because he's made up his mind to the contrary. That being said, no, Dan, I didn't believe the Cubs would ever win the World Series.*

"Kendrick Bogstrom!" Cathy greeted her former student as he walked through the aisle, appraising the passengers and attending to requests.

Kendrick stopped mid-breath. He appeared to be looking at the back of her seat.

Andi leaned over and whispered, "I didn't realize a greeting could be so dumbfounding."

"Give him a minute. He's just processing," Cathy whispered back.

"Excuse me, we need help here." A portly man a few seats ahead of them gestured frantically.

Kendrick moved ahead and explained that OSHA regulations did not permit him to push some overstuffed luggage in the overhead rack. He continued making his way toward the front of the plane as the traveler pushed and heaved until his carry-on was crammed overhead. Kendrick did not look back at Cathy again.

The two cousins were each lost in paperbacks they'd brought when Kendrick came down the aisle offering a variety of drinks.

Cathy requested a glass of water. "Thank you, Kendrick. How do you like your job as a stewa…"

"Flight attend…" Andi whispered.

"Flight attendant?"

"Thank you, Ma'am." Kendrick stared at Andi.

Andi stared back, furrowing her brow. "I believe you know Cathy Covington?"

"Sure." Kendrick nodded, not taking his eyes from Andi's face.

"We miss you at Sunday School." Cathy touched his arm. Kendrick kept nodding, then continued down the aisle with his drink cart.

Andi looked at Cathy in disbelief.

"I told you." Cathy looked around to see if any snacks were forthcoming.

"I can't believe that. Here, let me out. I'm going to check something." Andi slipped out of her window seat and into the aisle. She stood there for a moment, looking at Kendrick.

He glanced over his shoulder, turned from a passenger he was helping, looked Andi up and down, and hurried back to her. "Can I help you with anything? Anything at all?"

Andi raised her eyebrows, then looked down at Cathy. Kendrick's eyes followed hers, then gazed back at Andi as if Cathy's seat was empty.

"No, I don't want anything, anything at all." Andi huffed. She squeezed back into her seat and tapped her fist to her chin.

Cathy leaned over to her. "Don't work yourself up over it. You'll bruise yourself. We must admit there are things in this world that defy rationality."

A flight attendant made her way from the back of the plane, offering some snacks. Cathy was about to select something when Andi told her she'd have to pay for it.

"You're kidding."

"I told you we should fly first class, but you insisted on coach," Andi reminded her. "Things have changed a bit since our college trip to Greece."

The off-hand reference brought broad smiles to both of their faces. That trip had been the trip of a lifetime. Cathy had not traveled outside of the U.S. since then. Andi had taken many trips, but had never again known the pure innocence and hope and desire of the four weeks she and Cathy had spent around Athens and the tiny village of Polythea, what they knew as Meliki. They were young and fun-loving and ready to indulge in the world's offerings then. In the warm days of felicity and exuberance, they wholly believed they lived some of the most carefree of days ever lived in history. In fact, they did.

Of all their explorations, though, one was best. One was the spot where still, on quiet days, each in her own way, would return in memory. Their favorite place had not been the Parthenon nor any other of the ruins of the large city, though they had loved to tour it. It had not been the small room with its Greek décor they shared, nor the Mediterranean food made and served with various methods in changeable venues. Their favorite spot, rather, had been a hill where a little church, dedicated to the memory of St. Louis, stood. From their simple perch, they could see the brilliant blue of the Ionian Sea. It was there, as they lazed under the Mediterranean sun, that they talked and laughed and cried and dreamed of lives full of adventure.

"I guess I'll have a bag of peanuts." Cathy counted out a few dollars and change.

"Enjoy." The attendant took Cathy's money.

"That much for this tiny bag of peanuts?" Cathy shook her head. "I should have gotten a jar for that price."

"At least we're flying in the same plane to the same destination as the people up front who are enjoying more than salted peanuts and juice about now." Andi pulled a magazine out of her bag.

Kendrick moved spryly back through the aisle attending to travelers' requests.

Cathy signaled for a pillow. He walked past her to the man seated just ahead of her.

As the two women disembarked, they passed Kendrick who nodded courteously to Andi.

"I wouldn't have believed it if I hadn't seen it with my own eyes," Andi commented as they hailed a taxi.

The cousins spent the day wandering around Fisherman's Wharf. They enjoyed clam chowder and hot pretzels. They lingered nearly an hour, watching the sea lions along Pier 39, while Cathy sipped an iced coffee as delightedly as if it was unique to the area.

Before they returned to their hotel, they stocked up on chocolate at Ghirardelli Square and spent the evening dining from a room service menu and watching a movie in their room while savoring chocolate truffles and drinking decaffeinated tea, Andi's spiked with Mountain Dew.

"San Francisco is pretty at night." Cathy sighed as they made their way down the tarmac after their return trip. "But I'd hate to live all stacked on top of each other like they do."

"And I'd hate to fly half way across the country to spend the evening in my hotel room."

"After a day of walking around? My legs ached so much they were pulsating. Besides, you did get in a swim."

"Yes, there was that, considering I have only two pools at home."

"At home you wouldn't have had a visit with that nice young man next to you."

Andi scratched her temple and, tilting her head, looked at Cathy.

"You have no secrets. I saw you from the balcony of our room."

"You may have seen me, but you did not hear his proposition or you would not have called him a nice young man."

"Ah. Sorry. There you go, suffering in silence again. I should have gone with my first inclination and not wasted my time. Kendrick Bogstrom hasn't changed a bit."

"Now you know. Plus you got to see some Fisherman's Wharf attractions, so it wasn't a total waste of time."

"Yes, now I know. Kendrick Bogstrom will never see me even when I'm not twelve inches from his face; San Francisco boasts a trap tourists love to be caught in; and too many truffles followed by one glass too many of fresh orange juice for breakfast make for a very long plane trip home."

They picked Harry up from Christy's house and Andi dropped them both off at Cathy's door. Cathy found a message taped to it and pulled it off as she put her key in the lock. She scruffed around with Harry for a few minutes, let him outside to sniff around the backyard, and dialed a phone number. "Lisa? This is Cathy Covington. I'm sorry I missed you."

Lisa's voice was all business. "R'member that time six years ago?"

Cathy closed her eyes. "The past is sometimes best left firmly tucked in bed. No getting out for bedtime stories or drinks of water."

"You said somethin' like that then, too; that it would be buried underneath the oak of all the good things I would do in the future."

"That's right."

"I never paid you back for gettin' me out of that predicament."

"Not necessary."

"I'd feel better if I did." Lisa paused. "Okay. Here's the deal. I talked with the Motocross Mamas, and we're willin' to help plan the parade on two conditions."

Cathy grabbed a kitchen chair and sat down, patting her heart. Who was she to prevent the payback of a good deed?

"First, we get to lead it on our bikes."

"Done." Cathy's neck ache began to fade and she scooted to the edge of her chair.

"Second, we meet with you and nobody else. No one on the committee gets to know we're helpin' until parade time, especially Heck."

"I completely understand." Through the window, she spied a red squirrel taunting her from the bird feeder. The next minute, the crack of the BB gun filled the phone lines.

"You get it?"

"Next time. Go on."

"No extra little committee meetin's unless it's somethin' important."

"I couldn't agree more." Cathy replied with as serious a voice as she could muster to cover her giddiness.

"That's it."

"Deal. And, Lisa? Consider yourself paid up and then some."

"You got that right." Lisa hung up.

"And that," Cathy whispered to Harry as she grabbed her BB gun, "is not only an answer to prayer, but," she took aim and fired, "a fine example of reaping what you sow." The squirrel fell and her bird feeder swung free in the breeze.

# Chapter 13

*We might think of baptizing as what we do with a seed in a garden. It's completely buried, the seed coat is stripped away and it acquires nutrients from the earth; just as sin is canceled and the Holy Spirit is given. The result is more productive than we'd ever dream of from just looking at the pitiful size beforehand.*

The two women stood outside a duplex in North Minneapolis. Slabs of the neighborhood sidewalk jutted up like snowdrifts, dipping, then leveling again. Cathy had stubbed the toe of her shoe twice and nearly tripped once already. The boulevard grass, straw-like in its thirst, showed patches worn to dirt that was hardened like cement. Every day of the week so far had promised rain, but had delivered warm and humid instead.

Cathy eyed Andi's purse and Andi nodded and patted it as she would a holster.

"I remembered my cell phone, too." Andi pasted a smile on her face. "But just so you know: if something goes south, honey, I'm running."

Cathy blurted a laugh. "At least drag me by the hair after you. You run faster than I can."

"Deal."

"What do you think they meant by 'They're your kneecaps'?"

"Are you serious? Those guys we were talking to are as trustworthy as a Mexican penny."

"Peso."

Andi looked at Cathy over the top of her sunglasses. A police cruiser turned the corner onto the street. Andi flagged him down, and walked to the curb to talk with them. Upon her return to the duplex sidewalk, Cathy looked at her questioningly.

Andi waved her off. "It was more for them." Andi nodded her head toward a group of young men a block and a half down the street. "I want them to know your car is being watched."

"But that's why I drove my '87 Mazda. I can't imagine anyone bothering it."

"Dear, dear Alice. You're in la la land."

"I think you mean 'wonderland'."

"Exactly."

Cathy squared her shoulders, walked up to the door, read the names listed and rang the downstairs bell.

"Thank heavens for small favors," she murmured, looking through the window at the narrow stairway to the second floor.

A young woman came to the door, opened it a crack and peeked out, then opened it another inch.

"Hi." Cathy cleared her throat. "Miss Tiffany McCraig?"

"Yeah?" Tiffany was small and shapely, with fair skin and deep green eyes. Her dark red hair would have fallen lushly to her waist if it had not been braided in one thick rope down her back. Little tendrils escaped, framing a pretty face.

"I'm an acquaintance of James Mehan. May we come in?"

After a moment, Tiffany opened the entry door, and Cathy and Andi walked through it into a tiny foyer and through the open door into the living room of the duplex.

The living room was furnished with worn furniture. Delicate antimacassars decorated the arms of two chairs and the back of a couch. A knitted woolen afghan in muted shades of green was spread over the arm of the couch, in front of which a large braided rag rug of varying colors was laid. Through an archway, Cathy spied an old-fashioned percolator resting on the burner of a small gas stove in the kitchen. A pot, carefully painted with an intricate scene of a stone house on a green hill, held a daisy plant. It sat in the middle of a dark caramel-colored gate-leg table placed in front of a window there.

"He's in prison." The girl followed them into her home and shut the door, locking it behind them.

"He is, indeed. My name is Cathy." Cathy extended her hand. Tiffany shook it hesitantly. "He was in a Sunday School class I taught when he was still in school."

A suspicious frown flitted across Tiffany's face.

Cathy continued, "I'm in the neighborhood today on the outside chance someone can give me an idea of how he's been since he left that class. Oh. By the way, this is my cousin, Andi."

Tiffany looked at Andi, then down at the floor.

Andi offered her hand. "Thank you for inviting us in."

Tiffany looked up. Andi pulled a warm bottle of sparkling mineral water from her bag and held it out to Tiffany, who took it.

"Thanks."

"What do I get?" Cathy looked at Andi.

Andi eyed Cathy and pulled out a tepid soda.

"Do you have anything else?" Cathy squinted into the opening of Andi's bag.

"Do I look like the beer man at the ballpark?" Andi responded impatiently.

"Well I didn't mean..."

"These were in case we got dehydrated."

Cathy took the soda, opened it, took a gulp, and offered some to Andi.

"I'm fine. Really." Andi rubbed the corner of her eye.

Tiffany took a sip of her water, a small smile forming around her lips.

"I was talking with some boys, men, I guess, down the block who said they were friends of his," Cathy gestured.

Tiffany made a guttural sound. "They hang together, those guys, but if you ask me, they're trouble."

Cathy and Andi glanced at each other, and settled back into a couple of chairs.

"According to James' friends, you were his girlfriend for a while."

Tiffany took a long drink from the bottle, stifled a burp, then looked at the two women. "We were tight. It coulda worked, but James, he don't stick with nothin' for very long. I finally got tired of it and told him to leave."

Cathy drew her feet up underneath her and studied Tiffany. "He no doubt needed to hear that from you."

Tiffany's eye narrowed.

Cathy explained, "He needed to hear that from you because he hasn't had many people draw boundaries with him."

The girl picked up a small statuette of a dove from the end table near the couch, stroked it with her thumb, and returned it to its place. "You mean he's gotten away with a lot."

Cathy nodded.

"You mean I drew a line in the sand." Playing with a pinkie ring on her left hand, Tiffany volunteered, "The thing is... In another lifetime..."

She started over. "He's mister macho on the outside, but somewhere inside he wants ta do right. He's just got too much pride. That pride, it's like a cement wall."

"You loved him," Cathy noted.

"Yeah, I did. And he loved me. But..." Tiffany shook her head.

Andi got up and peeked out the window. A black car pulled up behind Cathy's car.

"Cathy, Cathy, Cathy." Andi's words tripped over each other as she pointed out the window. "How about we all go for a quick burger?"

Cathy raised her eyebrows questioningly at Tiffany, who nodded, and they headed out the door. As she passed out the threshold, Tiffany locked the door with one hand and grabbed a shillelagh with the other. Andi smiled broadly.

When they had bought some burgers and fries and settled in a booth, Cathy leaned forward. "So, Tiffany, how did the two of you meet?"

Tiffany's face grew slightly pink. "He actually he found my dog and brought him back for the reward."

"I didn't see a dog..." Cathy tilted her head.

"He died a couple months ago," Tiffany interrupted. "He was old. I'd had him forever." The girl's voice quavered momentarily. She shook it off. "Anyway, Nixon was an Irish Wolfhound." Tiffany laughed at the women's curious expressions. "I know. How do you lose an Irish wolfhound, right? He just ran off one day. I can't think what got into him. James had seen the flyers I'd put up in the neighborhood. I had a basement apartment then, two blocks from the duplex I live in now. So when he saw Nixon trotting down a side street clear across I-94, he lured him into his car with a candy bar. Great for a dog." She muttered under her breath with a short laugh. "He brought him back to see if it was the dog on the flyers. I was offering a fifty dollar reward."

Andi leaned over toward the girl sitting opposite them. "I'm betting you got to keep your fifty."

Tiffany smiled and nodded.

"He got all pal-sie with Nixon all of a sudden. He said he thought Nixon would miss him if he didn't see him again. He asked if he could come with us the next time I took him for a walk. He came every day after and we just, we just hit it off. We spent a lot of time together. He and I, we laugh at the same things. He asked if I wanted to live together, we found the duplex I'm in now, and things were great for a while." Tiffany stopped and shrugged her shoulders.

"Do you have family nearby?" Cathy nibbled on her fries.

Andi nudged Cathy's knee under the table. Out of the frying pan and into the fire.

After a couple of hours with Tiffany, and having received an invitation for a return visit, the two cousins drove out of the city.

"She could have talked all day about James, couldn't she have?" Cathy remarked.

"He was a fool to let her go."

"She has an interesting story, herself. She seems older than her years."

"She's had to be. What a mother."

"Yes," Cathy murmured, thinking it over. "So many things fall to the mothers and when they don't keep the spring fresh, the whole river runs foul."

"Except for people like Tiffany. She's a fighter of the best sort."

It was true. Both Cathy and Andi had seen it played out over a lifetime of general observation. Above all other effects, a person's family background influences them for good or evil. Families where selflessness is unknown and where love is lacking create despair and anger. Good families, strong families, set a course for life's travels and provide safe harbor both. They provide the stitches that hold countries together, though social engineers would dream otherwise. There are those, however, who, without the security and goodness provided to the majority, manage, of their own will, to be good and strong on their own; perhaps with slight unavoidable variation. Those people, the ones who defy circumstance, give hope to the rest of us that God's grace and good efforts, small or large, really are more powerful in the end than evil of any sort.

"I felt quite safe in company with the two of you," Cathy laughed.

"I liked her shillelagh, but it wouldn't fit in my purse quite as efficiently. I'm feeling the heat. Would you like a DQ?" Andi had a wicked gleam in her eye.

"Don't even," Cathy replied, in a voice that held a world of meaning. "Besides, we need to stop by Britty's convenience store."

Andi gave a short laugh. "Another note?"

*"As water reflects a face, so a man's heart reflects the man."*

"Will she even understand what that means? Again, I'm thinking she's not so acquainted with Proverbs."

"Well then. When she reads this, she'll have read a dozen words from it." Cathy sighed. "Odds of Tiffany darkening the door of the church?"

"Two to one."

"And we still have our kneecaps intact!" Cathy grinned.

After they had pulled out of the convenience store lot, Cathy suggested they track down the address they had for Hap Skalinski. Andi read directions from a dog-eared map and they eventually pulled up to a house overgrown with weeds in the front yard. The neighborhood had obviously been overtaken by landlords looking to make money from renting to college students the likes of which either did not know about property upkeep or shared their landlords' lack of consideration for it. The two women stepped up to the door and knocked. Loud music blared from the back of the house.

After waiting a few minutes, Andi trudged through the Creeping Charlie to the back, peeked around the corner, and returned. "Major party going on. You interested?"

"Woot, woot," Cathy replied without excitement.

About twenty college age kids were standing in groups, lounging, or refreshing their drinks from a keg on the back deck.

Cathy walked over to one of the partiers. She had to raise her voice over the music. "Could you tell me where I might find Hap Skalinski?"

The young man cupped his hand to his ear.

"Hap Skalinski!"

He shrugged his shoulders and pointed toward the deck.

Andi had already made her way up the stairs and was examining the clapboard underneath some peeling paint. A group of college boys had begun to gather around her. Cathy came up behind them and nudged into the group. They didn't notice. Andi turned around, then flinched. The group of admirers was still growing in size. She breathed a sigh of relief when she spotted Cathy.

"Carpenter ants." Andi pointed behind her.

Cathy raised her eyebrows pleadingly.

"Do any of you know a Hal Swisky?" Andi asked the group.

Cathy shook her head quickly.

"Harold Swinzel?" Andi tried again.

"Do you know Hap Skalinski!" Cathy called over the music.

The boys turned toward her in surprise.

"She's with me," said Andi.

At that, they all looked as though they wished very much that they could answer in the affirmative.

"He might've lived here a while back," one boy finally responded. "I've been here the longest of any of us that lives here – five years. Never heard of him."

Andi shook his hand. "Thank you, Mr. ..."

"Gavin. Todd Gavin." He blushed.

"Mr. Gavin then."

"Hey! You want the landlord's phone number? He might know something," volunteered an admirer who sported a profusion of dreadlocks.

The others nodded exuberantly as though they had come up with the idea. A sudden expression of pity crossed Andi's face. She shook each one's hand, asking their names in turn, and nodding as though the guy she was speaking with was the most important person in the world.

Todd, who had gone into the house to find the phone number, came back out and handed Andi a slip of paper.

"Which number is it?"

"Heh, heh. That one." Todd pointed and brushed Andi's hand in the process. "The other number is mine. Want a beer?"

"Thank you, no." Andi made her way down the rickety stairs of the deck.

Cathy grabbed a corn chip from a bowl and munched on it on their way back to the car.

"I told you it was an old address," said Andi as they slid into the car.

"Yes, but you got to go to a college party and wasn't that fun?"

"College boys are the same as I remember."

"Some things never change, though I do recall being more noticeable when I was their age."

"You turned plenty of heads back in the day before moisturizing was a necessity. And now at least you don't have to wonder what kind of college boy germs are crawling along your hand." Andi slathered on hand sanitizer.

Cathy pulled out the address she had gotten from the farmer's market vendor and held it up. Andi made a face.

"I'll take that as a yes." Cathy laughed.

"We were there for what? Ten minutes? And now you're misreading a facial expression as well as a college boy."

"When in Rome." Cathy shrugged.

"The 'visit to Tiffany' is getting more complicated than I'd anticipated. I'm fine with dropping a verse off for little Miss Immodest; I'm fine with crashing a college party in search of Hal or Hap or whoever, but adding the motorcycle repair guy's landlord to the mix is a bit much."

"At least it's not in Hudson."

They located the street, driving slowly down the block, peering left and right for the building number. Cathy finally pulled over and parked. "It has to be this block."

Andi looked out the window and sighed loudly. "Why are we here, again?"

"Curiosity!" Cathy beamed an innocent smile.

"Killed the…" Andi murmured under her breath.

They stood before an empty storefront and looked around. The block seemed to have been tossed aside like an old tire. There was a deserted gas station on the corner with the pumps removed and no sign. Interspersed between a few empty lots were a few other inexplicable structures. An untenanted stand that appeared to have been intended as a place to sell watermelons or sweet corn stood in the middle of the large parking lot of a small warehouse. Several other buildings dotted the block, but their former use was anyone's guess. Cathy looked down at the address for the third time, then handed the slip of paper to Andi.

Andi walked half a block down, looking at the numbers of the buildings where numbers still existed. Cathy crossed the street and did the same.

"Aha!" Cathy waved to Andi.

Andi came over as Cathy peered into the window of a vacant building. Andi removed her sunglasses and scrutinized what she could make out of the room within.

"This makes no sense," Andi murmured.

"The thing is, if the vendor is sending checks, there has to be mail delivery here."

A feral cat eyed them suspiciously from its place against the side of the empty building.

"Do you see anything that would suggest regular mail delivery?" Andi shook her head.

Cathy shook her head, too.

Some litter skipped down the street under the influence of a sporadic breeze.

Andi looked around.

A siren began blaring somewhere in the distance.

"Let's get out of here. This place gives me the creeps." Andi headed to the car.

"You always were easily influenced by your surroundings." Cathy slid into the driver's seat.

They had driven a few blocks when Andi suddenly turned to her. Startled, Cathy veered out of her lane momentarily. The car behind her laid on the horn and whizzed past.

"The vendor didn't actually say he mailed his payment to this address, did he?"

Cathy gave her a 'have you lost your mind' look and returned to looking through the windshield without comment.

"What?" Andi put her palms up.

"You act like there's a tarantula hanging from the dome light just to ask about where he mails his profits?" Cathy scratched her head. "No, he didn't say anything about it." They drove another block in silence. "And now that you mention it, I didn't see what address was listed on the contract, did you?"

"I did not."

Cathy pulled onto the freeway. "I guess I just assumed he mailed the day's sales, but maybe Dowling gets the money from him another way. Maybe he just picks it up from him." Cathy craned her neck over her shoulder as she switched lanes.

"Maybe our lettuce and pepper guy just took the return address from the initial letter mailed to him," suggested Andi.

"Maybe we need to go back to the farmer's market."

"Is this Dowling really worth it? I've never wasted my time on foolish men and I don't intend to start."

"You know how it's hard to sleep when something is bothering you? Well, I figure if I'm ever going to get a good night's rest in the future, I need to satisfy myself that this is not as strange as it looks to me at this moment."

"You're doing things for the wrong reasons again."

"You said that's the way half the stuff in this world gets done, but it's your turn to buy a pepper. Next time I spend ten dollars for a vegetable, I want the stir fry thrown in."

# Chapter 14

*The Israelites – children, babies, the whole works – were trapped with a powerful Egyptian army behind them and the sea in front of them. It was a hopeless situation, all right. But faith is not a matter of what things look like. Because life can turn on a dime, we must trust the One who sees what we can't. Oh, and the One who not only makes seas, but parts them.*

"Are you sure you don't want me to pick you up when you get back?"

Cathy and Andi were standing in line at a ticket counter in the Lindbergh Terminal to check Andi's bags. Kendrick Bogstrom was nowhere in sight.

"No. I'm not sure how long I'll stay. I'll take a taxi. Who knows? Maybe I'll take the red eye back."

"Lovely thought." Cathy tried to stifle a yawn.

Andi gave her a crooked smile. She lifted her suitcase on the counter, shelled out some bills and turned, nearly running into a family who stood close, gazing at her. The mother was the first to awaken from her temporary daze, and, with an apologetic smile to Andi, she quickly nudged her husband and kids to move.

Cathy glanced over her shoulder as they made their way to the shortest security checkpoint line for Andi's flight. The husband was making an accounting to his wife who appeared to feel rather foolish, herself. The children continued to stare in Andi's direction.

Andi hugged her cousin and set her bag down on the conveyor belt.

"Give Phil my love," Cathy said into her shoulder.

"I'll give him that and the letter full of advice you wrote to him, too." Andi chuckled.

With a hint of a smile, Cathy shrugged one shoulder.

"You're incurable." Andi fondly kissed her on the cheek.

"You'll be back when?" Cathy backed up against a stanchion to make room for other passengers.

"Two, maybe three weeks." Andi called as she shrugged out of her suit jacket, placing it beside her bag, and passed to the other side of the machine as a man in the next line began to choke.

The line came to a standstill as security watched her. She caught their collective eye, raised her eyebrows with a slight smile, grabbed her jacket and bag, and waved to them. A man bent down to collect the change he had dropped.

Surfing the radio dial as she started home, Cathy finally gave up and switched it off.

She prayed aloud for a while, a habit she had indulged since childhood. Decibel levels didn't matter to the Lord. Sometimes hearing her own voice helped her feel an additional connection. The occasional exclamation without words she sent straight to the skies was another kind of prayer in itself. Now that the kids were grown and out of the house, there was less of that, though. Of course, invariably her voice could not keep pace with her thoughts and after a time she would lapse back to prayer the silence of which betrayed the colorful conversation taking place.

There are some who limit prayer to specified times. There are those who do without an occasional joking manner, word of complaint, or thanks for something seemingly benign, but the confines of such a connection leave it short-circuited. A relationship, a real relationship, has room for all sorts of respectful expression. There is no reason to pussy foot around with someone who knows everything. No reason to hide thoughts or actions. No reason to hide doubts. No reason to hold back when amazed or thankful or overwhelmed by love or stress, either one. Prayer, beyond action or assertion, is illustrative of the depth of relationship. It also clears the path for heaven's directives.

Cathy glanced at her watch, flipping through a list of names and addresses lying next to her in the car. She exited onto a wide boulevard. Humming *The Magnificat,* she squinted at the street signs in the glare of the afternoon sun. After a few miles, she turned onto a street that led to a series of townhouses.

Pulling into a driveway, she parked and stepped up to the door. She knocked rhythmically and heard what she guessed was the door to the attached garage close a second before the front door opened.

"Dillon!" A persuasive smile radiated from her face like the sun.

"Mrs. Covington!" Dillon exclaimed at the same time.

"I… what… please. Hello. Come in."

Cathy hesitated. "It appears I've caught you at a bad time. Were you going out?"

"Oh! No. No. I."

He did not continue.

Dillon opened the door wider, and Cathy stepped into a very clean home. There was no stray newspaper nor sweatshirt nor speck of dust anywhere. The kitchen sink and counters were as clean as a hospital. The floors were not only swept, but polished. Her eyes roamed around the room and rested on a letter left on the kitchen table. Dillon snatched it up, and folded it, stuffing it into the pocket of his jeans.

"I just felt like a little visit," Cathy offered, filling the silence. "Rather impulsive of me, I guess."

Dillon stared at her for a minute, blinked, shook his head as if to clear it, then shuffled over to an espresso machine and flipped it on. "Care for some espresso?"

Cathy sucked in her breath, then smiled bravely. "Love some."

He opened cupboard doors to reveal empty shelves except for a partially used bag of Dunn Brothers Ethiopian coffee. He opened the refrigerator and grabbed an unopened carton of creamer. A chocolate cupcake with a small candle in it was the only other item resting on the shelves within.

She slid into a chair at the small kitchen table. The panes in the window sparkled.

Dillon reached into another cupboard, took down two mugs and filled them. He set a black one in front of himself and a pink mug in front of Cathy.

She gave him an inquiring look as he seated himself across from her.

"I... I always remembered how you had a pink cup in Sunday school. I saw one when I was in New Mexico awhile back and bought it just to remember." Dillon blushed.

"Dillon! I'm touched."

"You can keep it. I won't be needing it."

"Absolutely not. I love the thought of this pretty color reminding you of Sunday school! Besides, pink cups apparently being next to contraband in Minnesota, a state where beige is revered, you dare not lose it. Those were some classes, hmm?"

"Some classes. Your class was my favorite. You made everything seem so real."

"It is real. Actually, that's why I'm here. I miss seeing you. A person never graduates from Sunday school, you know."

Dillon gave her a tired smile. His blue cotton shirt was unbuttoned and he wore a white T-shirt underneath. "You said you'd always be watching us."

Cathy laughed. "And see? You can't get rid of me that easily. You were going somewhere when I came just now?"

Dillon gulped some of the hot coffee. He set his cup on the table and appeared to warm his hands. His eyes darted toward the garage and then back at Cathy.

"You might as well turn off your car until you need it."

Dillon's chair scraped across the floor, and he squeezed through the door to the attached garage. He came back in, coughed a few times, and drank a glass of water before returning to the table.

"So what are you doing these days, Dillon?"

"Actually, I'm a manager at the Kensington."

Cathy whistled low. "Nice place. How do you like it there?"

Dillon paused for a moment. "It's not a bad place, I guess."

He lapsed into silence.

It was unlike the Dillon Cathy knew. He had been a nice boy; compliant, thoughtful. He had always seemed to possess a sensitivity greater than some. He did not appear to have changed in that regard. As a student, he'd made interesting contributions to the class. Although he had never seemed at a loss for words in those days, it was apparent she would be carrying this conversation. She didn't mind. She would bear the entire thing, if necessary, until she felt it was no longer required. The thing about bearing each other's burdens wasn't just a dear little suggestion. "What are the people you work with like?"

"Mostly nice co-workers. Interesting guests."

"No doubt. And this," she looked around the room, "this is one nice townhouse."

"I've been here for about three years."

"It's very nice. Great neighborhood. Easy to find or I would have gotten lost, I'm sure." Cathy paused. "Though there's no place quite like Pine Point." She laughed.

Dillon barked a laugh. It seemed that a hint of animation came to his face for the first time since she'd walked through the door.

Cathy looked around again. Expensive drapes hung at the windows in a living room with two dark brown damask chairs and an end table. The table held a forest green pillar candle. A hunting magazine was in the attached magazine holder. Through a hallway, she caught a glimpse of a bedroom. The bed was stripped.

Cathy gamely sipped her espresso, promising herself an ice cream cone on the way home.

"I love the photography on your wall." She examined a large picture of an old man reading in a wooden chair next to a tree whose branches tangled in the sky.

Dillon turned his head and looked at it with her. "I took that two years ago while I was hiking in the Appalachians. It's been a favorite of mine."

"You have talent."

"Talent needs money to be of much use financially, though. I…" Dillon paused as though he was trying to decide whether to continue.

"I've no doubt someone would buy it, Dillon. My doubt is whether you'd want to give it up."

He smiled weakly. "I thought so, too." He stared into space for a moment. "Six months ago I took out a second mortgage, invested everything I had, and signed a contract to finance a photography business."

"Dillon! How exciting!"

"I wrote the check. It was cashed. Then the company vanished into thin air."

The ensuing silence felt like a two-foot snowfall on a weak roof. Cathy looked at him blankly.

"I gave him all of it and now, instead of a photography studio I have a double mortgage, no savings, and an empty contract. The space I was shown was a set up. I had planned to pay off the second mortgage within five years. Now I'm not even holding out hope of holding onto my home. I contacted the attorney general, but it doesn't sound good."

Cathy swallowed. "But surely you identified him?"

"Yes, someone named Buford." He paused for a minute. "I don't know if that's his real name, now, I guess. It was part of a company called Primary Properties. I brought in the papers. I thought I'd done everything right, but apparently, there's not much for the AG to hang his hat on. In their words, I believe, it was 'an extremely believable counterfeit operation.' At least that's what I was told. The truth is, Mrs. Covington, it's a hopeless situation. The one thing I liked doing can't be useful to me, and I've lost everything, including my life's savings." He leveled his gaze at her. It was a sudden defiant look that told her if she argued his point she would not like the consequences.

Cathy ignored it.

"Hope and its counterpart are only states of mind. As for your assessment, no one can say the first until he's dead and the second until he's retired. You still have a job. And talent. And talent, my dear boy, is what brightens up this drab world whether it makes money or not. You never know, Dillon. What seems written in stone one day can be blown away like dust the next. Believe me. I know."

Dillon looked doubtful.

"Really. My own life is one long example of leaving some of God's gifts wrapped."

It sounded like something a Sunday school teacher would say; one of those sentences that took you by the hand and pulled you forward into the unknown.

"Let's see." Cathy ticked off fingers as she counted. "You've lost your money and may lose your house. Homeless is a scary word. Then again, you have your health which, though you don't value at this age, you will value sometime a few decades hence. And – yes, you have your eyesight, which allows you to take those beautiful pictures. Of course, you still have your camera. You may or may not have friends. No, no. Scratch that. At least you have me, though, granted I'm not twenty anymore. Still. And a job. Yes, as I said before you have a job. Hmm. I don't know if you have God anymore, though I know for a fact He still has you. So, yes, you have God who, as you recall, can make something out of nothing if He decides to; though He often lets us stumble along when we'd just as soon He give us a hand out or, to be quite honest, a jackpot to make things easier. What else? Family. Intelligence. Freedom. Choices."

Cathy paused to take a breath and looked over the table at the desperate man.

Dillon sighed. Whatever poison had inflated him a moment before, deflated in that one breath. He stared at the table.

Cathy gave him silence to think things through while she wandered about in the midst of her own thoughts. The choice before him was one of allowing the known and subjective present to crush the unknown future. It was not completely true of Dillon, but in as much as it is true of every person, this was true of him. It is in the nature of people to think that, contrary to their observation of others, life should be fair to them.

People want no trouble, only delight. They desire to boast wisdom and an interesting life without enduring the hardship through which such things are won.

Taken to a greater degree, human nature seems to want heaven and hell at the same time. It wants to behave with all sorts of self-indulgence, yet be paid for its lack of effort with glittering rewards. It wants to eat as much and whatever it wishes, yet to stay slim. It desires to put forth little physical effort, yet to boast the fitness of an athlete. It wants to dismiss hard work in favor of sitting in the sun or canoeing down a river or going to parties, yet to enjoy affluence. It shuns being inconvenienced, yet desires the admiration of others. It wants the benefit of God's goodness without God.

Human nature wishes heaven's rewards now, not at some future time. It says 'why can't I have all of my heart's desires now,' not comprehending the dwarfish nature of its dreams. It wants the bliss of heaven to coexist with mortality. Lacking a clear understanding of paradise, it thinks up some small perks and would take the worthless nickel now in exchange for the diamond mine later.

It is a choice daily before each person: to live as though today is all there is or has been or will be, or to live with the belief that the length of a lifetime is just a speck in eternity.

After a few minutes, Cathy broke the extended silence. "You know, Dillon, you certainly keep this place ship shape."

Dillon looked around as though seeing it through her eyes. His gaze returned to his old Sunday school teacher sitting across from him sipping hot espresso on a warm day, a tiny bead of perspiration at her temple.

Dillon stood suddenly. "Mrs. Covington, would you like to go out for supper? My treat."

Cathy raised her eyebrows.

"Okay. I do have enough for a night on the town," he admitted sheepishly.

He went to his bedroom and was quickly back, adjusting a tie around his neck.

"We'll go someplace nice," he said holding out his arm and heading for the door.

"I can't think of anyone I'd rather have dinner with just now. Let me take my car, though. I'll follow you. And, Dillon," she added sternly, "Don't you ever again imagine God doesn't hear your prayers."

A smile slowly spread over Dillon's face. "Yes, Ma'am."

Gray was blending with periwinkle, resulting in a fuzzy blanket of sky by the time Cathy pulled into her driveway. Harry bounded to meet her as she walked through the front door and switched on a light. Cathy scruffed around with him until he nearly knocked over a lamp, then she let him out the back door. She splashed fresh water into the teapot and set it on the stove.

"Well, Lord," she paged through the newspaper, looking for the crossword puzzle, "thanks for the nudge, though I would have appreciated a few more specifics before that visit. I *do* believe You got more than Your share of exclamation points from me today. I *don't* believe he'll be giving up on things again anytime soon. I *do* believe he'll turn up at Sunday school on Sunday. Who knows? He may just do what he threatened, and move back to Pine Point."

# Chapter 15

*Did you see the beautiful sunrise this morning, class? Ah, just as I suspected. Well, you missed a majestic sight in the eastern sky. But in the western sky was another gift: a rainbow. God gave us a greeting of the new day in front of us, and the promise of all the days following it, behind us. Sometimes there's more blessing than our eyes can take in at once.*

Harry barked frantically, calling Cathy to the door. She opened it to Alexio Kastellanos. He stuck out his roughened hand, his eyes sparkling. "Mrs. Covington."

"Please come in." Cathy led the way to her kitchen as he hung back, glancing over the size and layout of the house. Alexio paused to allow Harry to sniff his shoes, giving the dog's head a generous scratching. Harry trotted behind them and settled under the table, alert for a falling crumb.

Alexio's eyes roamed over the tiny kitchen as he pulled out a chair and settled into it. "Nice dog. I bet he takes care of you as much as you take care of him, eh?"

Cathy inclined her head. There was something different about this guy. Somewhere along the line she guessed he'd experienced something that changed him from a scrappy contractor to one who allowed nickel and dime jobs to seep into his successful business.

"Mm. Coffee smells good, Mrs. Covington."

"Why thank you. I like to put cinnamon in it. I hope you don't mind."

"My wife does the very same. I can't even taste it anymore."

Cathy filled two pink gingham-patterned cups and set them on the table. A smile tugged at Alexio Kastellanos' lips as he took his first sip. If his buddies could see him now, drinking from a pink cup, he'd never hear the end of it.

The kitchen light had barely flickered before Cathy was halfway down the stairs to the fuse box. She was up again in an instant, the light restored. Cathy pulled up a chair opposite him and, after taking a sip, set her own cup on the table.

The builder appeared gruff on the outside, but she suspected he had a marshmallow-soft center. He pulled out a steno pad and rolled a pencil over and under his large, callused fingers like a baton twirler. "Ya gotcherself a little wiring trouble?"

Cathy gave him a half nod and smiled slightly.

"So, a new house, you said? No renovation?"

"No, I think not. As you can see, there's not a lot worth saving."

A look of concern flitted across his face. "Memories count," he replied with a friendly smile, "We can fix this up so you can knit or watch your soaps or scrapbook to your heart's content. Maybe even invite a few ladies for tea. I'm sure your son or daughter would approve of a change here or there."

Yep, marshmallow cream. Why couldn't they all be like that? She nodded. "We'll keep the memories, just not the house. However, we need to save the Ben Franklin stove there." Cathy pointed. "I'd like to put it in a little guest house, if possible."

He jotted it down and glanced out the window. "A guest house?" Alexio Kastellanos sighed. "First, we should probably talk about a price ceiling."

Cathy shifted uncomfortably.

Alexio looked at her sympathetically. "Really, Ma'am. We can work with what you have. A simple nip and tuck to the existing structure and you won't believe you're in the same house."

Cathy lifted her chin. "I'm afraid you're a bit mistaken, Mr. Kastellanos."

She cleared her throat.

"More coffee?" She refilled her cup.

Alexio held out his cup. "It's best to face facts squarely, Mrs. Covington."

"Please. Call me Cathy."

"Okay. Cathy. Money can add up pretty quick when you're building. We need to do the figuring before we sketch it out. Understand? I'll cut costs where I can, but we need to know up front, so we don't run out of money before the work is completed."

"What a helpful thing to say, Al. Can I call you Al?"

"Call me anything but lazy."

"What you said about facing facts squarely."

"Yep. Face 'em dead on."

"You are absolutely right. Being poor is not a crime unless it's a result of laziness, and even in that case it's more base than criminal. Nor does it make you undignified. I've always said so, and it was something I taught my children. On the other hand, being rich isn't a crime either nor should you be accused just for having more money than others do. Money's a silly thing, really. It has very little to do with a person, yet everyone treats it as a matter of merit or demerit, depending on their politics. No reason for me to pussy foot around, you know? Why should I cover anything up?"

"Exactly."

"When circumstances change, one shouldn't pretend they haven't."

Al nodded. "Right you are."

"A person isn't defined by how much money she has. No need to be shy about it."

Al smiled slightly. "You're absolutely right. The ones with friends and family: them's the rich ones."

He leaned his bulging forearms on the table and grasped his cup more tightly as his eyes began to glaze over.

"And besides that, there's no law against spending your money as you see fit. You can give it to a food bank or you can buy flowers. You can buy an obscenely expensive cup of coffee or you can buy a New York cheesecake. Although, homemade is always better, don't you think?"

"Absolutely." Al nodded, glancing at the counter for said cheesecake and, failing that, looking up at the ceiling as if the Almighty might send him an exit strategy.

Cathy tapped her fingers on her cup. "There're a lot of things, and I add parenthetically, the best things, in this life that money can't buy."

"Lots."

"But, on the other hand, there're a lot of things that can't be gotten without it. Who cares what you do with your own money? I mean, really, Al, it's no one's business. If the heavenly Father sent me the proverbial cattle on a thousand hills and dropped it squarely in my lap – although that would be a bit heavy, wouldn't it?" Cathy sprinkled her words with laughter. "But if He did, He wouldn't want me to wring my hands. He'd expect me to scream with gratefulness and then get up out of my chair and start milking them!"

Al looked worn out.

"And there's nothing wrong, not a blame thing wrong, with buying what you want if you can afford it; as long as God approves, of course," Cathy continued. "It's not like I skipped the tithe. I do think I spread it around intelligently enough; though I thought poor Mr. Bingham was going to have a heart attack, not to mention the Bible College president who actually did end up in the ER; but that's not *my* fault. All those fundraising dinners came back to roost, no doubt," she finished under her breath.

Cathy looked at Al and Al looked helplessly back.

"Before I give you a cost ceiling and a list of things I'd like, may I show you around the property?"

"You're the customer."

They rose from the table and she linked her arm in his as they went through the back door. Harry budged ahead of them, frisking around the yard. She showed him her garden and the property lines. They walked to the front yard and sat on the front step. It was a two-minute tour.

Cathy stared ahead, unseeing, for a moment. Then she turned to Al. "I've recently come into some money."

She scratched the side of her head with one finger. "It is amazing, really, but I won't bore you with the details. The thing is, Al, that money is now no object. We could fly with your wife to France and back this afternoon, and the cost to charter a private jet and enjoy a meal at a fancy restaurant would be of no consequence. I could buy a large home on each coast and I wouldn't feel it. I could even go so far as to suggest something about financing a run for the Presidency, but I can't for the life of me think of anyone we'd dare put there, so let's just forget about that."

"Some things are best forgotten," agreed Al, a small smile forming on his lips.

Cathy paused, rubbing her hand over the top of her head, overwhelmed all over again.

Al began to giggle. Cathy looked over at him. Sure enough, there was a brawny man sitting beside her – giggling. She began laughing quietly with him.

"For land's sake, Ma'am! What're you so sad about?"

Cathy laughed out loud now. "I don't know."

Al abruptly stopped laughing. "There *is* one problem." He was all business. "This piece of property won't hold two dwellings. Most cities wouldn't allow it."

"You're forgetting you're in Pine Point."

"Ah. Right. However, you'd still be losing your garden space and every other blade of grass besides. You want to look for a new location?"

Cathy thought for a moment, then let out a deep breath. "No, Al. I'm tied to this place by an old grief and those wonderful memories you mentioned."

Cathy glanced over to see Harry nibble on a fern. He was the antipathy of the family's two former dogs, Dan and Ann, who had died within a week of each other. Sociable, clean, obedient, and loyal, they had been perfect in all the ways dogs can be perfect. She caught the dog's eye and raised her eyebrows. Harry glanced her way and relieved himself on some rhubarb. He trotted back and lay down at her feet. "I had been toying with the idea of asking one of the neighbors if they'd be interested in selling. It's possible they might consider it if presented with the opportunity."

"Do it; the sooner the better. And in the meantime, let's make that list. If they sell, we'll really have something to work with and if they don't, well, we're in Pine Point, like you said."

Cathy pulled a list from her pocket and read it aloud to him, answering his questions as they went. "Do you think we could start right away? Is there any way to have the whole thing done by Thanksgiving?"

Al looked at her and blew air loudly out of his lips, thinking of his other jobs lined up like boxcars on train track.

"Tell you what. You look into the next-door property, and I'll draw up some plans. It's possible I could double the work crew if you're willing to pay for it."

"Willing."

"Do you have a cell phone number where I can reach you if you happen to be out of the house?"

Cathy shook her head. "Don't care for them."

"Uh huh. Well then. If you're free, let's meet next," he looked at his watch, "Tuesday and figure out what to do. I can hire extra men, but I can't make any promises. And Cathy?"

"Yes?"

"You have my word we'll give it one hundred and ten percent."

They both stood and Cathy stuck out her hand and smiled at him. Al Kastellanos' eyes sparkled as they shook on the deal, and Cathy felt her spirit begin to dance, happy and free.

# Chapter 16

*I believe the Pharisees started out with good intentions. It's just that they focused so much on rules, they forgot about being open to God's Spirit. That is why we temper justice with mercy and why, Trudy, you will apologize to Phoebe for what you just called her.*

Cathy had bought a jar of raw honey and a round loaf of sour-dough by the time she made her way past the booths of fresh produce, homemade juices, and other variety of wares to the pepper vendor. He wasn't there.

She walked the length of his stands, then browsed nearby for ten minutes before approaching the woman tending them. "Excuse me? I bought a pepper here a few weeks ago."

The young woman smiled. "I remember. Your friend told my dad to keep your change. I thought it was funny."

"She's a real comedian." Cathy scratched her nose.

"She looks like a model. No, better than a model. She looks, she looks, I mean, I can't even describe it. That woman is drop dead gorgeous."

"Don't let *her* hear you say that. I'm looking for your dad. Is he around?"

The woman shook her head. "My ma had to get all checked out today at the hospital so he went with her."

The girl began kneading one hand with the other.

"How is she doing?"

"We think she has it licked."

"You have all three stands yourself? That's a big job."

"I've been doin' this with my dad since I was little. I used to hang around, handin' him the bags to put produce in, but I've been around this stuff so long, I could open my own booth no problem. I'll be ready for a long soak in a hot bath when I get home, though."

Cathy picked up a pepper and rolled it between her hands. "Actually, he gave me an address, but I think he must've confused the street numbers."

The young woman scanned the crowd, then examined Cathy. "Look, I know the arrangement he has with that man looks sketchy. My dad's pretty innocent about some people. He takes everyone's word at face value. He thinks everyone is Ward and June Cleaver. But this is our livin' we're talkin' about here."

The girl wiped the palms of her hands on her jeans. "I tried to talk to him about it, but to him I'm still his little girl who doesn't know much. There's no reason to press him about the details when he won't believe me anyway. He's got too much on his mind, what with my ma and everything."

"I just..."

"He didn't mix up nothin.' That address he gave you? It's from the contract. It's the only one we have. My dad might've signed this deal, but he wouldn't intentionally pull the wool over nobody's eyes." She scanned the crowd again. "Just... just don't make trouble for us with those men. If we lose our stands, we lose our livin'."

"Is it the address where you send your day's profits?"

The vendor looked at Cathy, unsmiling. "You want that pepper or not?"

Cathy handed her a ten. "Keep the change."

The comment lifted the young woman's countenance. She grinned, shook her head, handed Cathy the change, and went to help another customer.

Cathy wandered through the market, keeping an eye on the pepper stand. The variety of people who wandered through a farmer's market was a like a little microcosm. Without Andi near her, Cathy observed it all to her heart's content without attracting anyone's notice.

A little woman, considerably less than five feet tall, with more wrinkles than Cathy had ever seen in her life, was doing a brisk business selling a variety of jams and jellies. People called her by the name of Amanda, and seemed to feel like they were part of a well-loved and dependable club. She seemed to know how to make each customer feel beholden and needed at the same time. Once a shopper became a customer, Cathy doubted they would ever feel free or interested to buy their jam anywhere else.

A man wearing sandals, whose hair touched his shoulders, wandered from stand to stand and was not above lifting merchandise into his canvass bag when other customers distracted the vendors.

There were people who seemed to know each other by sight and some by name in the market that became a little community to those who desired it.

Cathy watched several of the extremely picky customers handle produce as the sellers cringed. What they considered being selective and knowledgeable was neither to those who did the selling.

There were harried women who flew through the market somewhere between work, home, and a myriad of other responsibilities. One of them paid for a dozen ears of corn and then left the merchandise on the counter as she raced back to her car.

There were those for whom shopping was more of an event than a necessity, who browsed through each aisle and enjoyed the samples.

She watched it all and, while entertained, felt confirmed in her gratefulness that the one waiting for her at home was a dog.

Near the end of the sales day, a man walked straight to the pepper stand and approached the girl from the side of the stand. They appeared to have a brief conversation. The saleswoman seemed a bit tense while he leaned against the side of the counter. She turned her back to him and pulled out a large envelope into which she hurriedly placed the day's receipts. Cathy started over in his direction as the man nodded and walked away.

By the time Cathy was within a few yards of him, the man was getting into a tan sedan. Cathy hurried to her car, threw her purse and packages into the passenger seat, and squealed out of her parking space. She spotted the sedan three cars ahead as it turned onto a main thoroughfare. One by one, the cars ahead of her peeled off until she was directly behind him. Pulling a pen from her purse, she jotted his license number on an old gas receipt that she'd left in the cup holder.

A red squirrel darted in front of her car, and Cathy reflexively jammed on her breaks and swerved to avoid the fatality that she would have celebrated had she been in her own backyard. She straightened her car and searched the road ahead of her. The sedan had vanished.

Back at home, Cathy paced. Harry supportively paced with her. They reached the back door, turned and walked the small perimeter of the living room, down the hallway, and back again to the kitchen and its screen door.

What was it that bothered her about this Dowling guy anyway? There were plenty of people who pulled tricks for money and they weren't just the ones walking Hennepin Avenue at night, either.

Justin was no Boy Scout. No doubt he deserved some of the trouble life gave him, but he was effectively hogtied by this guy and had no decent way to fight back. That he'd managed to start his own business was admirable. That he'd kept it going was even more impressive. And that his landlord would bring the boy's efforts to the brink of closure just to wring more money out his rental property was, to Cathy's way of thinking, obscene. It seemed a form of slavery, something akin to credit card companies with high interest rates or countries with high taxes.

Like the dilemma Dillon faced: people who pretended to offer one thing, all the while covering up completely different intentions, kind of like an adjustable rate interest.

The problem wasn't just that they tarnished the reputations of honest businessmen. It was that they enticed optimism like a flirtatious cheerleader and then doused it without a backward glance. While it might not be quite like the unforgivable sin of quenching the Spirit found in scripture, it was still core rotten.

She might not know how yet, but the man or men or whoever it was had to be stopped.

She'd just reached the middle of the kitchen, when she whirled, yanked the broom closet open and in two more steps, kicked open the screen door. She took aim, and the crack of the BB gun pierced the air. Not counting the menace that had run out behind the sedan, today it was Cathy: 1, red squirrels: 0.

Harry danced at her feet until she gave him the go ahead, then he raced out of the house to bury the fatality.

A tomato sandwich wouldn't cut it for her tonight. Maybe she'd feel better with some sort of commotion around her.

Cathy sat down at a table by the door once inside the Corn Hut. The place was packed. Lisa brought her a Diet Coke in a pink cup and sat down across from her.

"Is all well in parade land?" Lisa rubbed her calves.

Cathy took a sip of her pop, leaned back in her chair, and folded her hands. "Two of them are working on publicity, Lindsey Mayberg is doing design selection and button sales, Mrs. Kipton is keeping the finances in order, and the Kiddie Parade appears to be up and running. Heck keeps putting me off when I ask about the bands, but then again…"

"…that could just be Heck," Lisa finished.

A fleeting smile crossed Cathy's face. "I've got a possible idea to pad the entries, something admittedly folksy and quirky, but it's a bit early to comment yet. How're the other pages coming along?"

Lisa pulled two sheets of paper from the pocket of her uniform and slid them across the table. Cathy studied them.

"I see there's no messin' with the Motocross Mamas." Cathy grinned.

"We figure it'll be runnin' on automatic by parade day."

"Do you have anything else for me to filter to Mrs. Kipton?"

Lisa pulled out some receipts with notations for each and handed them to the parade planning chair. "That Kipton woman doesn't mess around when it comes to numbers."

"Numbers are her thing." Cathy nodded.

With a sense of finality, Lisa slapped the table with her hand as she rose from her chair. "Now that's what I call a committee meetin.' The corn on the cob chowder is extra good today. Ernie accidentally spilled in extra bacon."

"Corn on the cob chowder it is." Cathy slid her menu back behind the napkin dispenser.

The sound of a bug's demise by a bug zapper just outside the door mixed with the tinkling of the bell as Mrs. Kipton entered. She did not look unpleasantly surprised when Cathy invited her to join her at her table, though Cathy could never be certain how Mrs. Kipton was feeling.

After they had talked parade business, the conversation turned to bank matters. For the first time in all the time she'd known her, it was Mrs. Kipton who talked without much prompting, and Cathy found herself actually interested in the workings of the world of finance.

Cathy mentioned her house renovation plans which led to a general discussion of phony business addresses; although later Cathy couldn't, for the life of her, recall how she had maneuvered the conversation to make that leap.

"So you're saying that giving someone a bogus address isn't necessarily illegal?" Cathy bit into the cob shaped corn bread that accompanied her chowder.

"I'm saying," Mrs. Kipton said sternly, "that a shell corporation..."

"Is that the same as a dummy corporation?"

"No. But neither of them are illegal. There are various reasons for hiding a company's true identity and using an alternate one instead." Mrs. Kipton dabbed one corner of her mouth with her napkin. "If my company wanted to buy this diner but the owner didn't like me, said company could do it under another name. The deal is still legal as long as everyone signs the papers."

"Would you say..." Cathy began, but Mrs. Kipton looked at her watch and rose to leave.

"I really must get home." Mrs. Kipton straightened the cuffs of her sleeve. "It's a rare supper out for me, but with my husband at a late work meeting, I thought I'd throw caution to the wind." A hint of a smile crossed Mrs. Kipton's face. "However, I'd rather be home when he gets back. You know, you could look up more information on your computer."

Cathy sighed.

# Chapter 17

*God gave Israel the Promised Land, but it wasn't wrapped with a bow sitting on the breakfast table. He expected them to go after it. Yes, Kaily, I suppose He could have used the expression 'go for it.' Now do me a favor and stop writing love notes to Jack.*

Cathy pushed a rebel log back from its precarious place in the Ben Franklin stove, then quickly sucked on her finger to soothe the resulting burn. She sat down on one of the boxes nearby and looked around the kitchen. Nearly everything was packed up. Al and his crew would be starting at daybreak on Monday, and she needed to have it all out by then.

It was 6:00 AM. Mentally reviewing a list of the day's appointments, she walked over and poured herself a cup of the still brewing coffee. As she replaced the carafe, the coffee maker stuttered to a halt. She flipped the switch back and forth. She pulled off the carafe, setting it on the stove, unplugged the coffee maker, turned it upside down over the sink, and shook it. Cathy plugged it back in and flipped the switch again.

"Seen your last day," she muttered. "It would seem I'm moving to my temporary address in the nick of time."

As she passed by the refrigerator, Cathy pulled out a piece of pizza to go with the molasses-covered toast she'd already made. Balancing her toast on the pizza in one hand and cup in the other, she dropped into a chair, kicking off her slippers. She sipped her surviving cup of Cranberry Hazelnut flavored coffee ground fresh the previous day at Grammie Mae's Confectionery. She took four bites of pizza and tossed the remainder in the air, where Harry jumped up and caught it.

Cathy rubbed her temples and inhaled a few extra minutes of peace. She anticipated a day that would surely feel like a white water rafting trip by the time it was over, and knew with certainty that a sixty something, pudgy, slightly out-of-shape woman would not endure it well.

She opened her Bible and read a chapter, just like she'd done every day since she had learned to read; a chapter a day without skipping a book or jot or tittle. After nearly sixty years of it, a person could get a pretty good idea of the history of Israel, Jesus' life, the myriad of ways people messed up, and the marvel of mercy, among other things.

However, she was in the part of Joshua that allotted property to the tribes just now. Accounts such as this had been far from a favorite, she, herself, not being a census taker, an accountant, or a king; but she would not waver. She would read it because it was part of the book which gave her her best direction. This particular property allotment was important to the people who lived then. After all, she would be excited if she was going to be a property owner for the first time. Besides, dry reading was sometimes necessary in order to better understand the more interesting stuff. It was pretty simple, really, just like the rest of life. Pour a solid foundation and pretty soon you have a house.

Cathy closed her Bible and stared out the window as a new thought occurred to her. Property, indeed.

Whistling for Harry, she gave him the remainder of the molasses toast and a pat on the head, slid on some shoes, grabbed her purse and headed for the door. He whined, then barked.

"Not today, old fellow," Cathy told him. "We'll take a little drive later, okay?"

Cathy tucked the key to a storage locker, an address with a hand drawn map, and two 100's into an envelope addressed to Dan and Kenny and placed it on the counter as she left. The two boys from the college class at church had agreed to move her things. Dan was getting married soon and was looking for every bit of extra income he could find. Kenny was going to be his best man and had a truck. Hopefully they wouldn't break much.

It was 11:30, and as Cathy peeked out the curtains of Martina's house, relief flooded over her. Martina's car was just coming down the street and not too soon, as far as Cathy was concerned.

"Juan! Anita! Martin!"

Rumblings from another part of the house led Cathy to the kitchen where she found them balancing on an assortment of couch cushions, pillows, and an orange crate stacked on four kitchen chairs.

"Ah, Mrs. Covington! We liked the Moses story you told us. See? Martin's the death angel! He is going to fly over the houses of the Israelites." Anita grinned.

Three-year-old Martin did not look very happy as Anita and one of his older brothers were about to throw him over some houses built from Lincoln Logs scattered over the floor.

"Ah ha ha." Cathy hurried to rescue Martin, accidentally destroying an Israelite house with her shoe in the process. "Your mother is just driving up, so you had better put the cushions and chairs back," she instructed, as she grabbed the orange crate and set it outside the back door.

Cathy, carrying Martin on her hip, returned to the living room to find Joseph frowning at the Bible.

"God's mean!" He looked up at her in alarm.

"Why do you say that?"

"He said all the Israelite boys and men have to be crucified." Joseph's face was all despair.

Cathy choked back a laugh. "Phonics, Joseph, phonics. You have the right number of syllables, but the word you're referring to starts with the 'sur' sound. Ask your mother to help you sound out words this week, and that particular word today, okay? But I am proud of you for reading the Bible I brought. Why don't you keep it?"

Cathy opened the door as Martina walked up the steps, her arms full of bags.

"Hello." Martina came in and dropped the bags next to the couch, its cushions just replaced by three angelic children sitting on them. "Have you been sitting here all morning while Mrs. Covington told you stories?"

The children smiled. Cathy smiled. Martin wriggled out of her arms and began running around the room making the noise of a siren.

Cathy hugged Martina. "You'll bring these beautiful children to Sunday school with you tomorrow, won't you?"

"We will be there. Thanks for giving me a lovely morning off. You've no idea what a gift it is!"

"I have an idea," Cathy said under her breath as she let herself out.

Cathy looked at her watch. After her morning with Martina's children, she visited three more former students, received two promises to come to Sunday school and one non-committal response and still had to meet with Casey at 4:30.

After dropping a note off at Britty's convenience store: *The Lord is near to all who call on him, to all who call on him in truth. He fulfills the desires of those who fear him*, she hopped onto the interstate. She supposed her efforts, which she'd privately begun to think of as 'operation: stealth scripture,' were closer to fruitless than helpful, but Cathy had never had the capacity to let hope go: certainly not to let it go easily, and rarely to let it go at all. Besides, someone like Britty, with more passion than depth, needed direction by whatever means it could get to her. Sure, she'd never win a Nobel Prize, being undoubtedly more interested in finding a prize in the bottom of a cereal box; but the Lord didn't count liabilities the same way people did.

She parked in front of an expensive-looking restaurant, ran her fingers through her hair, freshened her lipstick, and got out, handing her keys to the attendant. "I won't be long, dear, just a cup of coffee, probably."

He gave her a broad smile and nodded.

A doorman held the door for Cathy. She patted his arm and asked about his children.

A gold-colored, diamond sunburst pattern radiated from the center of the floor's dark carpet in the restaurant composed of a large space with four smaller, cozier rooms anchoring each corner. Rich, dark woodwork framed the interior. The tables were covered in white hand-blocked linen; a few deep coral linen tablecloths punctuated the room like happy splashes of surprise.

Cathy was seated at a table next to the kitchen at her request.

Katie breezed out the swinging doors and motioned for a waiter to bring Cathy a cup of coffee. "Mom! Someone told me you were here. Is everything alright?"

"Actually, I'm in the market for your pecan banana bread. Do you have some loaves on hand?"

"I'll send one home with you."

"No, no, Katie. I'm going to buy them and I need more than one. I'm making some visits this evening and need to bring something with me."

"They're baked fresh every morning. Are thirty loaves enough?" Katie laughed.

Cathy laughed with her. "I won't need quite that many."

A sous chef stepped out to consult with Katie.

Cathy wrote a number on a slip of paper and handed several bills to the waiter who brought her coffee. "Can you have someone bring the order to my car?"

He looked questioningly at Katie who gave him a distracted nod and concluded her conference.

"It's been a busy day." Cathy blew on her coffee.

"Have you been thinking of what you'll do with the house yet?" Katie stopped a dessert cart and lifted off a mandarin orange cheesecake drizzled with dark chocolate to set before Cathy.

"You're spoiling me." Cathy sipped her coffee.

"You make it hard to look after you. This is the least I can do. A double garage might be nice. Of course, that could get expensive."

"Mm hmm," Cathy closed her eyes and savored the cheesecake.

"Of course, anything having to do with a kitchen runs into money, too, but the investment is never lost. I can inquire around."

Katie paused. "No, never mind. Kitchens are too pricey. Unless – would you like a new stove?"

Cathy put her hand on Katie's. "No need. I've hired a nice man to do all of that work."

Katie leaned her chin in one hand and bit a fingernail. Cathy swallowed a last bite of cheesecake. "You know, dear, I think I'd like for you all to see this little remodel at the same time. A kind of fun surprise, don't you think? So if you and the others don't mind, let's just keep in touch by phone until I call to have a big family dinner to celebrate its completion, hmm?"

Katie tilted her head, a slight frown crossing her face.

Cathy hurried to explain, "I don't want anyone tripping over any tools."

Katie squinted at her mother.

Cathy gulped the rest of her coffee and rose to leave. "Thanks, Katie. They love you for more than..."

"The food. I know." Katie walked her mom to the door and gave her a goodbye hug.

It was nearly 10:00 by the time Cathy, with Harry at her side, returned to her house from her evening stroll. She had stopped at every house on the block. The basket she had carried on her arm, loaded down with loaves of pecan banana bread, was now empty. She sat on the front step and looked at her dog who looked back supportively. "One more trip, ol' boy and you and I will crash for the night."

They strolled around the perimeter of the yard and Cathy began to quietly pray. "Thank you, Jesus, for the deck. Thank you for a place to sit and just *be*. Thank you for my garden and the way it provided for us."

They entered the house through the back door. Cathy stood for a time in the quiet, absorbing it. She unconsciously nodded her head. She then walked slowly through the house, stopping first in the kitchen.

"Thank you, Father, for enough food." Her voice broke momentarily, but she continued, "Thank you for the experience of cooking for a family. Thank you for the Ben Franklin stove and the warmth and reassurance it has provided, especially on hard days. Bless Andi for giving it to me. Thank you... thank you for the years I had with Perry. Thank you for Dan and Ann and the way they helped the kids grow up and the company they provided.

"Thank you for the laughter and goodness of visits in this living room. Thank you for the couch cushion money. Thank you for books to read. Thank you for my piano and for the music witnessed here. Well, *most* of the music.

"Thank you for the races up and down this hallway and for the squeak in the floor that let me know when someone was coming home late.

"Thank you, oh thank you, for these bedrooms, for safety, for good nights' sleep and for times with you when sleep wouldn't come. Thank you for teen-age posters and whispered secrets between the kids, for clothing enough even if it wasn't exactly what they wished for, for a place of relative privacy and camaraderie both.

"Thank you that no one killed themselves running up and down these basement stairs. Thank you for the experience the boys had making two extra bedrooms down here and thank you that Alden's fingernail grew back. Thank you that I learned what to do when a fuse blows.

"Thank you for a big and glorious life... big and glorious... in a small and humble house."

Switching off the last light, Cathy softly closed the front door. She stood on the step, facing out. A light breeze rippled a strand of gray hair that had newly sprouted. A persistent star winked on in the seal-skin gray sky. It appeared that Cathy studied it for a moment, then she and Harry walked to her car without looking back.

# Chapter 18

*No, Stevie, I don't think we can adequately imagine what heaven will be like; or, more accurately, a new heaven and a new earth. I can imagine pristine lakes and rivers, colors in the spectrum not yet visible, a sky full of things that out-play science fiction, grand feasts, great humor, and everything I've ever wanted and more. But, no, I don't think we can think of it all: not in our wildest dreams.*

Cathy was standing near a very large pile of dirt, her pants rolled up to just below her knees. Her face was smudged, her tennis shoes blackened, and her hair was matted with sweat.

"If you had a cell phone, I could've called you and avoided this picture which will surely stay in my memory long after Alzheimer's sets in. What in the world?" Andi walked gingerly across the property.

Cathy looked up and wiped a line of sweat dripping down her cheek. "I thought I'd save money by moving some of this." Cathy motioned to the demolition in her yard, spreading into her neighbor's property.

Andi shook her head in disbelief. "Did you forget that you waved farewell to 50 a while back?"

Cathy picked up a large board and pitched it into a large dumpster.

"Cathy, you're being ridiculous. You can afford to have this done by someone..."

Cathy tossed an armful of shingles over the top of the bin.

"Someone young-"

Cathy glared at Andi and threw a shingle in her direction, hitting her on the toe.

"-er. Ow!" Andi bent down, picked it up and threw it into the dumpster. "At least someone with a bit more muscle, though that throw wasn't half bad." Andi grabbed a nearby wheelbarrow and started loading pieces of wallboard into it.

Cathy lobbed a pair of work gloves in her direction.

By the time Andi's shirt was drenched in sweat as well, Cathy said, "I just can't see having someone do such a mindless task for me. It's like having someone vacuum your floor for you or write your speech."

"Or make your bed?"

"Exactly. I mean, I'm not a princess nor am I a nursing home resident."

"My fingernails haven't had this much dirt under them since I planted the blue spruce. You know, that one near the walking path in the west gardens."

Cathy nodded. "Never did learn the Latin, but yes, I know the one. You're getting blurry."

Andi walked over to Cathy and grabbed her by the shoulders. "Sit," Andi commanded as she pushed Cathy onto the soft dirt. "Let me get you some water. The time for a break passed at least an hour ago."

Andi returned from her car with two bottles of Gatorade, several bottles of water, and two aspirin. "One for you and one for me. You get to chew yours."

"I'm cooled off now, cuz." Cathy took a swig of Gatorade. "No worries."

"None at all." Andi looked heavenward. "By the way, there's a house missing." She swept her arm in the neighbor's direction.

"Yes. I may have forgotten to tell you that when you called while you were out east. They could barely contain their excitement when I made them an offer. Seems they've wanted to move to Alabama for years now, but hesitated putting their house up for sale." Cathy leaned toward Andi and whispered, "T'wasn't in the best condition and they're past the age for upkeep."

Andi raised her eyebrows.

"Okay, yes, they have more high school reunions ahead of them than I do."

"Everyone has more high school reunions ahead of them. We don't go. Remember?"

"I'm not the one to blame for that. I just can't stand watching those worn out jocks hit on you all night."

"Not to mention the wealthy nerds." Andi tilted her Gatorade toward Cathy in a gesture of agreement.

"There are some days when a wealthy nerd seems rather appealing." Cathy cracked an apologetic smile.

The two women laughed so hard, Harry trotted over to find out what was going on.

"Ah! Where has he been?" Andi wiped tears from her eyes.

Cathy ruffled her dog's fur as he sprawled next to her, his tongue hanging from the side of his mouth. "If my guess is right, he's been sitting in the shade of the Jeep over there." She nodded toward her left. "He's been thrilled with all the commotion, frisky as a pup; but when everyone leaves except his ol' master, he plops in the shade."

"So your neighbors were out like a shot?"

"Like a cannon." Cathy glanced at the nearby lot. "That property looks smaller without a house on it."

"Maybe you should ask the ones next to it, see if *they've* wanted to move to Alabama."

"Actually..."

"You're kidding."

"Not Alabama. He's wanted to take it on the road. They just bought that Winnebago in the driveway. See?" Cathy pointed. "She confided she'll make him settle in a condo in Miami after he gets it out of his system. They leave tomorrow. We demo day after next. Oh, and don't worry. I'm donating the good salvage to a place in St. Paul that – does something – with it."

Andi shook her head as if to clear it. "Anything else I should know about?"

Cathy paused. "I bought the block."

"YOU..."

"Except for Mrs. Serling's property. She's such a dear. I'd miss her holiday cookies. Besides, she doesn't have any wanderlust at all."

"I leave for a simple month-long visit to see my son in Quantico, and you buy a city block."

Cathy shrugged her shoulders. "It's a short block. And this *is* Pine Point. Besides, people don't seem as sentimental about their homes as you'd think. This way, I can build whatever size house suits me and gain the privacy to plop down for a rest in the middle of my morning constitutional."

Andi rose to her feet and began to walk around, looking down the street. She pointed. "That one there?"

"Yes, yes. The yellow with the while picket fence. She's a dear ol' gal."

"I hope you don't plan on us clearing *all* the demolition."

Cathy laughed. "No. I just wanted to do my own. You know, pride of ownership and all that. Besides, we've got to get the concrete poured before the weather turns." Cathy looked around. "Nearly done, I'd say. Actually, Al insisted I leave it, but I just couldn't. Won't he be surprised? Would you like to see the plans? They're in my Jeep."

"Your Jeep? What happened to your Mazda?"

"Sold it to the neighbor girl. She's in 7th heaven."

Andi gave her a blank look.

"I won't have to listen to any tires squealing. They're moving closer to the high school."

Andi squinted.

"You *know* I've always wanted a Jeep."

Andi stretched out her hands and pulled Cathy to her feet. "I should have known when I saw it sitting there. I can't see Alexio Kastellanos owning a banana yellow Jeep. I was just coming to ask if you wanted to remain in the room you put your stuff in, or if you want the bigger one closer to the bathroom."

Cathy smiled at her cousin. "I knew you wouldn't mind if I transferred some things while you were gone. The one I'm in is fine. The rest of it only took one storage unit out on Highway 10. I had a garage sale..."

"A garage sale?"

"...and got rid of some stuff. I don't need much room."

Andi stopped in her tracks, looked around at the neighboring houses and back to Cathy.

"Okay, okay. I don't need a big *bed*room."

"And I wondered what you'd do in a mall."

"You *know* I tend to get lost in malls, but I must admit, I'm finding property rather intriguing just now. I'm making an offer on the building Justin rents, as well as the dry cleaners down the street from him. Well, actually, Casey is making it for me. I prefer to keep my name out of it for now."

"I need to sit down."

"Andi, dear, chill. Casey's put his stamp of approval on all of this. He thinks the city properties, particularly, could provide a nice little additional amount of income."

They climbed into Cathy's Jeep and she pulled a set of blueprints from the back. Andi helped her spread it over their laps and examined it.

"It's a nice little thing, Cathy." She hesitated. "Are you sure you don't want a little more room?"

"I want it small. See?" She pointed. "There're two bedrooms, a laundry room, and a spa upstairs."

"Elevator. Love that." Andi looked closely with an eye for implicit details that would result from those included in the blueprint.

"The kitchen, living room, bathroom, and library slash music room..."

"A necessity," the cousins said to each other in unison.

"...are on the first floor."

"You should consider carved stone for one of the kitchen walls."

"Done."

"The basement looks comfortable." Andi laughed.

Cathy tilted her head toward Andi with a broad smile. "Two words: Grandkid heaven."

"I see you're expanding to a double garage just as you'd said. My, I'm impressed."

"Cousin," Cathy imitated puppy dog eyes to Andi, "you'll help with interior design, won't you?"

"I'd be seeing it in my head anyway. Of course."

Cathy pulled out another blueprint. "Here's the guest house."

Andi looked it over for a few minutes. "Ah."

"Don't you like it?"

"It's bigger than your house."

"It needs to be." Andi was missing the obvious.

Andi was silent for a while. "What are you going to tell the children – you know, the grown ones with opinions as numerous as poppy seeds in a muffin – when they see all this?"

"No idea. Suggestions?"

"It would take at least two strong cups of coffee and a long massage for me to come up with even the hint of an explanation. What are you going to do with the rest of the land?" Andi looked around them.

"Well…"

"Yes?"

"That's where you come in. I thought you could also design…"

"Yes! Yes! Yes!" Andi leaned over and kissed Cathy on the cheek.

"This won't get in the way of the Collins wedding, will it?"

"I'm doing consulting, not the actual work." Andi shook her head.

"Make sure there's a place for a big garden, will you?"

"And a small herb garden off a breakfast terrace."

Cathy squeezed her eyes shut. "I just want a cottage on a large, quiet, peaceful piece of property, not a showcase."

"Okay. One pine tree and a potted plant coming right up." Andi sighed, sticking out her bottom lip.

"Maybe a little more than…"

"I'll have the landscape plans ready within a week." Andi climbed down from the Jeep and nearly tripped over Harry, who jumped into the back. "Just now, though, I need a good soak after all this work. Let's go back to my house."

"There is a time and a place for whirlpool jets, after all!" Cathy started her engine.

# Chapter 19

*I don't believe God puts a box around us, class. We do that to ourselves. No, God expects us to journey without having to have it mapped out, to live fearless lives, and to talk with Him about it all without having our hands held at every turn.*

Bubbles swirled gently around Cathy and Andi as they submerged to their necks, sighing in unison.

Shadows were beginning to lengthen and the sky promised clear stargazing. An unseasonably warm evening breeze stirred the leaves and grasses as the outdoor sunken whirlpool massaged the cousins' tired muscles.

"I ran into little Stevie Cartwright when I visited Casey last. You know, there are a lot of businesses in that building," Cathy commented.

"It would be embarrassed not to have them since it's called the International Trade Building."

Cathy gave her cousin a half-smile and batted her eyes. "Actually, t'was Providential. He was on his way to lunch, so I joined him, and we had a lovely time together."

"Did you call him Stevie?" Andi smiled a mischievous grin.

"He was dressed in what I'm guessing was Armani, so – tempting – but no. He lives on the other side of town now, but admitted he hasn't gone to church since he left for college. What is it about college, anyway?"

"The ones who prefer dessert, skip dinner once they're out of the house?"

"Or their faith is so weak it wouldn't last one day in the desert, much less forty." Cathy tilted her head back in search of an early star.

"It's puzzling how a seminary ends up becoming a socialist think tank and calls itself a university. No wonder the kids get confused." Andi twirled a lock of her hair. "Which is why America must now find better alternatives."

"Only if you have a lot of spare change. Anyway, he's getting married the summer after next, and agreed it would be good to come back again. He actually seemed a little excited to return; it seemed almost like he was returning to visit to a hometown. He's bringing his fiancée to Sunday school this coming Sunday."

Andi squinted a frown. "Would you say that long engagements are for arranged marriages?"

Cathy shook her finger in her cousin's direction, and Andi shrugged. Cathy scratched her temple in thought. "Maybe they should have a brunch buffet for the adult class. I'll call Kyle. He loves any excuse to cook for a crowd."

"Kyle? Is he the one that makes the roasted white chocolate mousse with a hint of vanilla and nutmeg?"

"The same."

"Ask him to throw some more together and send it to me. Oh. And a dozen of the square truffles that melt in your mouth. I'll send him a check."

"Will do. Back to the brunch buffet. He can put it in the Taste That the Lord is Good room just off the kitchen."

Andi rested her arms on the edge of the Jacuzzi, and snorted a laugh.

"Don't blame me. That name is what happens when there's too much punch and fruitcake at a ladies' group meeting. You know," Cathy momentarily stretched her legs in front of her, "if Emma Peebles was a heathen, she'd be the kind that dances on the table with a lampshade on her head."

"What is she like as a saint?"

"Oh, she dances on the table with a lampshade on her head. She just makes certain there're no men in the room. And she can remember it the next day."

They both laughed, then Andi grew serious. "Tell me about the rental purchases, Cath."

"Well, this thing with Masotic or Dowling, or whoever it is, has been getting under my skin more every day. I went down to county records, and asked questions. Then I read over as much of the public record as they could provide. There are a number of properties owned by something called Primary Properties. Reading that name really stirred me up."

"Why?"

"No need to go into everything just now; only that while you were gone, one of my former students had mentioned a Primary Properties that sold him a bogus property, the deal of which propelled him to near bankruptcy. And while I know the Lord says vengeance is His and to leave the repaying to Him..."

"An admittedly difficult thing for you to swallow just now, it appears." Andi looked up at the velvety sky.

"There's a time and a place for everything under the sun; also Bible authority."

"I'm glad you're not the one who wrote Ecclesiastes. Your way with words leaves something to be desired."

Cathy shrugged, nodding in slight agreement, and continued. "It appears Dowling is behind most of the transactions. Masotic must be an associate. Those records and my hunches suggest he's built up a bit of a business buying run-down properties, but he doesn't seem to care to fix them beyond what is barely necessary. Then he rents them at a price the buyers can barely afford, but lower than they can get someplace else. He probably targets those who can't get a loan to save their souls and to whom other landlords won't rent, and he gets them between a rock and a hard place."

"I get the picture. You know, Cath, that's not illegal. As long as he stays one step ahead of the building inspectors, he's golden."

"But there's something more that bothers me. I can't quite put my finger on it, but it seems to me that, besides the rental business, some of the financial deals he's involved with appear to take place without anything of substance to back them." Cathy shrugged her shoulders. "I mean, it's just a suspicion at this point."

"And we know that you are never unnecessarily suspicious of anyone," Andi tilted her head. "Contracts built on promises. Hm. It's happened. So am I to understand that you're buying up those rental properties you were talking about?"

"Only a couple. You can't expect me to rescue everyone."

"And the empty promises: the contracts made out of air; someone should really look into that," Andi said quietly.

"My sentiments exactly. I mean, I could be wrong. I'm no businesswoman."

"Depends on your definition of what business is."

"I'm no financier."

"Yet."

"I'd love to be wrong."

"But what if you're not?"

"Nobody messes with my Sunday school students and gets away with it," Cathy replied darkly.

"And don't forget the thing at the farmer's market."

"Oh! That's what got me down to the city records in the first place! Didn't I tell you?"

Andi raised her eyebrows. "Apparently our phone conversations were more one-sided than I realized."

Cathy tilted her head. "Well I can't be expected to think of everything when I'm on the phone."

"I'm learning that you certainly had plenty to distract you."

Cathy heaved a loud sigh and nodded. "It's been... I don't even know how to describe it. It's like a maze. Anyway, I went back to the farmer's market..."

"Did you get stir fry thrown in?"

"I did not. However, I saw mister pepper vendor's daughter hand someone a manila envelope with the day's receipts in them at the end of the day. This, after she admitted to me that the address her dad gave us before was on the contract, but that they didn't use it for anything."

"That looks pretty fishy."

"Fishy enough that I followed the car of the guy with the manila envelope."

"You followed his car. What are you turning into?!"

"I couldn't help myself! What was I supposed to do? Let him get away?"

"Cathy, what in the world did you think you were going to do once you caught up with him?"

Cathy paused. "I guess I didn't think that far. See? That's why you need to look into this whole weird thing with me. You can do the thinking ahead while I act on impulse." Cathy thought a minute, recalling some past experiences with her cousin. "Or vice versa."

"So what did you do once you followed him to his destination?"

"Well, it didn't work out. An obnoxious squirrel ran in front of my car, I stepped in the brakes..."

"You did what?"

"It was an automatic response. Anyway, I lost him."

"From one tap of the brake?"

"More like a screech, but yes." Cathy nodded. "But!" She held up her index finger. "I got a license plate number which is what initially led me down to look at those records. Once I got there, though, I forgot to look for it."

Andi shook her head once, as if trying to understand.

Cathy shrugged. "There was so much to try to understand and more papers to look through than I'd have dreamed and I just – forgot."

"It probably would have been in a different part of the building anyway," Andi comforted her, "Or another building entirely."

"It's a puzzle." Cathy sighed. "Now if we knew more about the workings of governmental agencies..."

"Of regulatory entities..."

Cathy nodded. "We'd have a better idea of how to put everything together in a way we could understand it."

The women sat silently for a while as the heat from the tub and the cool air met in a steamy haze over the whirlpool.

166

Finally, Andi broke into their thoughts. "I have a friend in the city, Chief Jasper to the thin blue line, but he lets me call him James."

A slow smile spreading across her face.

Cathy screwed her mouth to one side.

"What? I was just thinking of the last time I ran into him. It had to be in the last three months. We're both board members for – oh never mind what for. He's very nice to me whenever I see him."

"Oh Andi, Andi, Andi. Thou hast either the innocence of a child or..."

"Never mind the 'or.' We might need to report something."

"I'd rather just explore for now. If we find something worth talking about, we go to the troublemaker first. Give him a chance to reform."

"Oh Cathy, Cathy, Cathy. Thou hast either the innocence of a child or..."

"Never mind the 'or.'"

"James does strike me as a very patient man." Andi laughed. "He'll hold back if I ask him to."

Cathy placed a few fingers over her mouth.

"But," Andi said sternly, "don't you get in bed with the devil in the name of mercy."

"Absolutely not."

Andi pushed herself up to sit on the edge of the Jacuzzi, dangling her legs in the water. "I need a swim."

Andi looked up at the sky in which clouds suddenly seemed to be forming out of nothing. The leaves on a grouping of nearby poplars made a whispering sound as a slight breeze dodged in and out of their branches.

"I'll stay here." Cathy shivered in the now cooling evening. "Maybe I should consider an indoor pool. This is Minnesota, after all."

"You could have both, like me. Heaven knows you have enough room, now." Andi tilted her head and raised her eyebrows.

Andi walked over to the nearby pool and dove in. The water rippled slightly. Cathy watched as she swam five uninterrupted laps and jumped out.

"You done?" Andi shook water from her hair.

"Like a lobster." Cathy grabbed a towel.

After quick showers, the two curled up in soft leather chairs in the study. Cathy held her blueberry herbal tea in her pink cup, and Andi began pouring something into her half-filled cup of green tea.

"Mountain Dew at this time of night?" Cathy raised her eyebrows.

"You say that as though I'm twelve."

"If you were twelve, you'd be able to sleep tonight."

Andi gave her cousin a kind smile.

"You'll still sleep after this atrocity?"

"Like a baby."

Cathy sighed and gulped her tea. Harry wandered into the room, sniffed the cello, and lay with his head between his paws underneath the Steinway.

"That dog looks positively thoughtful." Andi sipped her tea.

"He's probably thinking of Al and the boys. He's thrilled to see someone dig up dirt as much as he does."

"Perhaps they'll inspire him to greater heights – or depths."

"Wonderful. That's all I need. Speaking of boys, how do two widows nail an apparently well-established businessman?"

"I say we continue the investigating you've already started. We explore as many of his investments as we can find, and we follow the money."

"We wouldn't know what we were doing."

"No one alive was born knowing what he was doing."

The two women looked blankly at each other.

"A visit with Casey wouldn't hurt." Andi shrugged.

"Couldn't do any harm." Cathy nodded. "Besides they have a charming little coffee shop nearby."

"How singular."

"And on our way we can stick our heads into a department store three blocks over."

"You're actually going shopping?"

"I'm waiting to lose twenty pounds."

"You always say that."

Harry got up with a half-hearted stretch, walked over to the fireplace, and settled himself in front of it.

"I have a former Sunday school student working there. Name's Alison McCormick. She works behind the perfume counter, I think."

"Lovely," Andi replied in a tone Cathy couldn't interpret.

"She had real potential, I thought. She paid attention, seemed to understand the lessons. She's really a great girl," Cathy said softly, shaking her head in puzzlement. Cathy poured herself another cup of tea.

A soft September rain began to tap lightly on the windows as Cathy, Andi, and Harry gazed into the fire.

169

# Chapter 20

*They did indeed burn incense. Actually, in this passage, it might've smelled like dinner cooking from the sacrifices being burned. Jesus said that the sacrifice God loves even better is a merciful heart. Yes, Kari, I believe God likes perfume, but I don't believe I'll weigh in just now on the church's allergen policy. Here's your question: What's more important to God: mercy or money? Here's another one: What's more important to you?*

Cathy and Andi strolled along the perfume counter, picking up testers, spraying sample cards and sniffing. A customer made her purchase, and a tall, elegant-looking saleswoman, appearing to be in her late twenties, approached them then broke out into a surprised smile.

"Mrs. Covington?"

"Hi, Alison," Cathy said cheerily. Noting Alison's admiring glance, Cathy continued, "This is my cousin, Andi Clemens."

Andi gave Alison an irresistible smile and nodded. "I'm pleased to meet you."

"Hello, Ms. Clemens. Wow," she turned back to Cathy, "How long has it been?"

Andi turned as a man tapped her on the shoulder and asked her about a bottle he had in his hand.

"Longer than I care to count." Cathy tugged her ear. "That's why I'm here. We're missing you in Sunday school."

Alison looked down at the counter, then shook her head slightly. "I miss being there."

Cathy tilted her head and studied the woman. "What keeps you?"

Alison looked squarely at Cathy. "I just don't feel like I belong anymore, I guess."

"Not belong?"

"I try to tell myself to get back, but…" Alison's voice broke. "Excuse me," Alison pointed to a woman with bleached hair, a leopard-print wrap top, and brown leather pants. "I'll be right back. Don't go anywhere."

"Ya'll have some o' that thar movie star perfume?"

Andi leaned over toward Cathy and whispered, "I love transplants. She's serious about those heels, isn't she?"

"I'd need a ruler to even guess," Cathy whispered back.

Alison left the customer with a selection to consider and came back over to Cathy and Andi.

"I think we were somewhere at not belonging, though I can't fathom why," began Cathy.

Alison shook her head. "It's me. It's all me."

"Ah. '80's retro."

"Gotta love a decade that wasn't afraid to tease." Andi lifted an eyebrow.

Alison looked confused.

Cathy explained, "Hair. Big hair in the '80's. She's just entertaining herself. Go on."

Alison shrugged her shoulders. "As I got older, I just realized more and more how far I was from who God wanted me to be. Excuse me."

She went to wait on a customer.

The transplant sidled over to the cousins.

"'Scuse me. Ma name's Dorthea Tucker," she said to Andi.

"Lovely name, Dorthea. I had a great aunt with that very name," volunteered Cathy.

"Why, hi. Ah didn't see you standin' thar."

Andi closed her eyes and touched her hand to her forehead, while Cathy smiled benignly.

"I's just wonderin'," she continued, again turning her attention to Andi, "what kinda perfume y'all war?"

Andi sighed. She scratched her hairline with her fingertips. "I'm sure you'd rather wear what pleases you than what pleases me."

A slight frown crossed Dorthea's face.

"I think she means she's sure you have great taste, yourself," Cathy stated hurriedly.

The woman nodded her head and turned back to the bottles on the counter, lifting up each one and inhaling deeply.

Andi said quietly, "It happens every time. You'd think a girl could look at perfume without ten questions. I'm not wearing a white coat."

"I appreciate your sacrifice," Cathy replied dryly.

Alison returned and began speaking as though there had been no interruption. "I just got so discouraged with myself. And I know God is forgiving, but I just, I just couldn't stand the thought of letting Him down so much. I guess I finally just gave up."

A customer at the jewelry counter behind them held a bracelet in front of Andi's face. She nodded dutifully.

"Like Peter in the boat? He said, 'Go away from me...'"

"...For I am a sinful man," finished Alison. "Exactly."

"You and a fellow named Justin ought to have a conversation," remarked Andi.

Cathy tapped her fingers on the glass counter.

"And Jesus was out of there in a heartbeat, right? And Peter had nothing to do with Jesus or the church after that."

Alison laughed.

A lady at the opposite side of the counter held a bottle high in the air and raised her eyebrows inquisitively in Andi's direction. Seeing it, Andi shuddered imperceptibly, gave her a tired smile and nodded.

"You're right, of course; but it doesn't take my unworthiness away."

Andi looked at her for a moment. "If God doesn't set a limit on confession, you will?"

"We don't live in a state of failure, dear. We live in a state of forgiveness," Cathy said.

"What church y'all go to?" Dorthea had again edged closer the three women.

It took Cathy a moment to see Dorthea was speaking to her. "Why, the Christian Church just over in the southeast corner of Pine Point. Stop in and check it out on Sunday if you'd like."

"I'd like 'at. Last church I's at gossiped about me. A few folks was all it took for me to not want to step foot in again. Can you imagine?!"

Cathy shook her head and Andi nodded.

"But you know, whether you do what they say or thar operatin' on bad information, it hurts just the same."

Andi said, "It's like a knife thrust in your gut and twisted, isn't it?"

"Just like," Dorthea answered with a surprised look.

Having just been asked by another customer at the jewelry counter for a recommendation, Andi nudged Cathy with her foot.

173

She whispered under her breath, "Get me out of here. I feel like I'm in the monkey exhibit at the zoo."

Dorthea asked, "Y'all go ta that thar church, too?"

"I'm a member of a little Christian church in the country. It's slightly more liturgical."

"Can't say I'm familiar with 'at."

Alison said, "One's more beautifully scripted, the other is less formal with somewhat more latitude in their worship."

Dorthea gave her a blank look. Cathy wrote down directions to both churches and handed them to her.

"I'll take this," said Dorthea, shoving a perfume bottle marked with a number toward Alison.

"Nice choice," Andi commented.

Dorthea gave her a broad smile, took her purchase, and pulled out her cell phone as she walked away.

"I'm surprised to find you here, Alison. I thought you were studying to be a doctor," Cathy remarked.

"I got my degree in biology, but failed my MCATs."

"Can you take them more than once?"

Alison looked at the floor and then back at Cathy.

"As soon as I move out of the state of failure," Alison said softly, with a short laugh.

"Bad case of amnesia," Andi remarked as Alison went to help another customer.

"Discouragement can be fatal, alright. She just needed a nudge, though."

"It's curious how a relatively good person like Alison finds herself wallowing in unworthiness and people living lives not remotely as moral don't even think about such things."

"Well, some, you mean."

"Yes, some," Andi replied. "Some do."

"And it keeps them from moving ahead. They get locked into their own self-disappointment and can't imagine God overcoming it."

"Or being willing to."

The two cousins were silent for a minute, thinking of the sadness of the big wide world filled with some not understanding their unworthiness, some unable to move from its grasp, and only a relative few who both understood it and accepted the hand out of it.

Andi took a deep breath. "I believe God loves perfume," Andi commented as they walked away. "But not the cheap stuff."

"I couldn't agree more."

Andi looked at her watch. "If we hurry, we can catch Casey before he leaves for lunch."

"Maybe he'll invite us to go with him," suggested Cathy longingly. "My stomach's been growling for the last half hour."

"If he does, I'm going to propose that new French American place on the corner."

"Please, please, please don't let it be another Entitea."

"Please, please, please order something other than American," added Andi sternly.

# Chapter 21

*David was a wonderful musician and an amazing warrior, both, showing that machismo – sports, for instance – and music are not mutually exclusive. It also means, Tom, that you sing right out in our Sunday school program next week. God does not care how you sing. He cares if you sing.*

It was the edge of twilight as Cathy and Andi entered the music hall. Sparkling lights illuminated the vast lobby and flashed on the front wall of windows which echoed the light back on the crowd. The carpet, in swirls of coral and teal, softened footsteps as they passed through the doors and down the stairs from the skyway. Voices murmured, rising and falling, as men and women in semi-formal attire milled around, visiting and laughing in polite tones before the concert.

People throughout the room cast long glances at Andi as she studied the building's architecture with familiarity, though not with affection. It was a matter of taste. She had always thought the Hall, one she frequented with regularity, should have been so much more; should have better expressed visibly the beauty of its purpose. Her main contention was with the lobby. She had no quarrels with the auditorium itself, and the music within surely redeemed much of the rest. Cathy and Andi would have gone anywhere, though, to listen to good music: to a school auditorium or park or home or a city street; and the Hall was much, much more than these. A chamber of ticket stations was located at the east corner of the room. Next to them a wide, curved staircase led to balcony seating. Along the lobby's entry wall stood a too-short counter of coral corrugated metal, from behind which two attendants were serving drinks and coffee. As they edged toward it, Andi turned to her cousin.

"I can't hold back any longer, Cathy. You look terrific! Now aren't you glad you splurged on that dress?"

Cathy requested two cups of hot water from the bar. She rummaged through her purse and pulled out two tea bags, handing one to Andi. Andi dropped a twenty in the tip jar as the man behind it grabbed a towel to wipe up three spilled drinks of patrons nearby who had been distracted by Andi's approach.

"The pale gold suited me better than black, present company excepted, of course, though neither has much vibrancy." She squirmed. "I feel like a salamander." She played with her earring. "Besides, I've plenty of church dresses that I've worn innumerable times before to concerts. They were perfectly fine. Your season tickets don't discriminate." She dipped her tea bag up and down. "Did I mention the lack of color?"

Andi, in a sleek, silk black dress that fit her as though God, Himself, had been the designer, gently blew on her tea. "Those earrings are the perfect cut, if I do say so myself."

"A rather extravagant gift, but I do love them. Thank you again."

"And you have tiny little pale pink sparkles on your shawl."

Cathy's mouth formed a small smile. "Those, and the reason we're here, are the only things that keep me from hailing a taxi this instant."

"The music?"

"Okay. My pink sparkles and my Sunday school student and the music are the only things that keep me from..."

"Mozart? Haydn? Dvorak?"

"Okay. My pink sparkles and my Sunday school student and the music and the emphasis on the works of the Masters..."

Andi began to speak, but Cathy held up her hand. "Okay. I admit. There's nothing like a night at the orchestra."

Cathy looked around, then caught Andi's eye, nodding her head toward a pillar.

Andi turned and looked over her shoulder.

"I can't be sure, but I think that's Trudy Brown's sister," Cathy whispered. "The last time I spoke with her she was wearing a lime green sweat suit."

"The one who's a Bowely?"

"Dowling. Yes.

"He's rather old for her."

"Maybe she didn't marry him for his youth," Cathy answered.

Their eyes traveled from his balding head to his growing paunch.

Andi nudged her. "Let's go see if he has a sparkling personality."

The two women crossed the room and introduced themselves.

Cathy said, "I believe I spoke to you at Trudy's house."

The woman nodded her head slightly. "Oh, yes. This is the woman Trudy mentioned at our last visit, Paul."

The woman spoke to her husband as though she had a bad taste in her mouth.

Paul Dowling turned, took one look at Andi and choked on his drink. He pulled a handkerchief from the jacket of his tux and dabbed his mouth and collar. He stepped closer to Andi and grabbed her elbow. "I'm in real estate and investments."

He lowered his voice. "If there's anything you ever need, *anything*, you give Dowling a call," he purred, not taking his eyes from her face.

"Thank you, Paul, is it?" Andi smoothly extricated her arm from his grip.

He pulled a card from his pocket and handed it to her. "Here's my number. Call anytime. I mean it."

Cathy flashed a disbelieving glance at him, then smiled at Mrs. Dowling whose return smile was as genuine as the fur over her shoulder.

"So what kind of investments..." Cathy began, determined to take advantage of the situation.

Mrs. Dowling interrupted her. "I wish we could stay and visit, but it appears the doors are open."

She pulled Mr. Dowling away with visible effort.

After they left, Andi let out a breath. "His breath nearly sank me to my knees."

Cathy sympathetically waved to clear the air in front of her. "He did seem to be more in love with his drink than his wife, and she didn't really wish they could stay and visit, declarations to the contrary."

Andi handed her the business card. "Please take this. I'll be too tempted to call that taxi you wanted earlier if I have to hold it another second."

Cathy laughed as she took the card and turned it over. "It's not often you have someone you're suspicious of give you his address."

"Speak for yourself." Andi took a deep breath of clear air.

"Perhaps Mozart will help," offered Cathy as they made their way to the auditorium.

"Perhaps? A pox on thee for thy doubtful language."

The concert did what good music always did for Cathy and Andi. It touched the part of them that wasn't touched any other

179

way. Its forcefulness was straight from the earth's core and alternating sweetness was knitted of some kind of goodness from heaven's constellations.

During the intermission, Cathy leaned toward Andi. "I think if everyone attended a concert once a month, the need for Prozac would be cut in half."

"If everyone listened daily to classical music, the police force could be cut in half." Andi was about to continue when an usher handed her a note. "Ah. The maestro has invited me to a little post-concert refreshment backstage." She looked up at Cathy. "I'm sure he would love for me to bring you along."

"No doubt." Cathy laughed. She fiddled with her earring and looked around.

Andi mused, "It's been awhile since I last visited with him. I wonder if his arthritis is acting up again."

"Maybe I'll see Juliet backstage. We can kill two birds with one stone!"

"It's illegal to kill songbirds, isn't it?"

"Not in Pine Point. There it just confirms one's boorishness to the populace."

"He always has wonderful coffee," Andi remarked.

Cathy reflected for a moment. "Cranberry juice? Does he have that or herbal tea or something?"

She posed a face that spoke eloquently of the blessedness of a decent night's sleep, making Andi laugh.

"I'm sure there will be something for you."

They sank back into their seats as the musicians filed in to begin the last half of the concert and the sound of a crinkled a cough drop wrapper from the row behind them was drowned out by applause.

The backstage area was filled with musicians carefully returning their instruments to their cases and chattering. Conversations on all matters of topics, personal and professional, ping ponged through the space. Cathy and Andi gingerly made their way through the happy chaos, down one of the hallways and toward a room out of which an inviting light shown and around which people were gathered in groups, talking.

Cathy grabbed Andi's arm. "I think I saw Juliet back there. Is that your friend's suite?"

Andi laughed. "I suppose you could call it that." She pointed distinctly. "Now you're sure you can tell where to go? Your sense of direction is..."

"Maternal," Cathy accused, making a face.

Andi held up her hands.

"I'll catch up with you in a few minutes." Cathy veered left, walked a short distance down another hallway, and stood near a violist tucking the soft cloth of her case around her instrument for the night. "Juliet?"

A heavy-set blonde dressed in concert black looked up. "Why Mrs. Covington! This is a pleasant surprise. How did you like the concert?"

"I loved it as I always do. You were splendid. The music simply soared tonight, didn't it? It must be such a pleasure to produce such lovely sounds."

Juliet smiled and nodded, standing to face Cathy.

"These surroundings suit you. I'm so happy for you, Juliet. And it didn't come without practice, did it?"

Juliet laughed. When her parent's exhortations to practice her viola had not helped, her old Sunday school teacher's hounding her to do so did.

"I remember when you were in our little chamber orchestra at church, and those surroundings seemed to fit you, too."

"The one you conducted." Juliet appeared pleased at the memory.

"I miss seeing you there. Are you attending church somewhere else?"

"I've been busy."

It was an excuse that was, by now, beyond boring to someone who had heard it more times than she cared to count. Cathy crossed her eyes and directed her annoyed smile at the floor. Looking up again, Cathy gestured to the scene around them and resolutely continued, "Schedules certainly can get full, can't they?"

"Yes, yes. I'm a very busy woman now." There was a note of condescension in Juliet's voice. She said it in a tone that suggested a simple older woman like Cathy would have no understanding of the pressures of life.

"Perhaps you'll find a Sunday some day when you can come back. The Sunday school misses you. And you know," Cathy added, with a glint in her eye, "that little chamber orchestra might like a guest conductor sometime. I've always preferred arranging music to conducting it, and would welcome a break."

Juliet seemed intrigued. "There might be some room in my schedule next Sunday."

"So soon? Then we'll consider ourselves fortunate to have you there. Rehearsal, as you recall, is an hour before Sunday school."

How could someone so talented be so transparent in her misplaced motives? Such talent would be found sorely wanting

182

when offered to a God for whom it cared little. However, she was determined to do her part, and let the other guy face his own music, so to speak.

Having said goodbye to Juliet and leaving her with the agreement to see her on Sunday, Cathy started toward the room she had seen before.

Halfway there, she felt her earring fall. Losing it was unthinkable. Besides the pair being the first fine jewelry she'd ever owned, aside from her wedding ring, not to mention a treasured gift from her cousin, she was planning to wear them to the Collins wedding. She stooped to look for it in the now dim backstage area. How far could it have rolled? She wandered down a hallway, then back again. Finding that unsuccessful, she got to her hands and knees and crawled around, finally locating it near a curtain pulley.

Cathy got to her feet, brushed off her dress as well as she was able, and squinted, searching for a lighted room. She turned, wandered a little way, and then turned again. She retraced her steps, but found herself more confused than when she'd started. God had given her many things, but a sense of direction had been left off the list. It was an inconvenience to be sure, but it didn't overly trouble Cathy. There were worse things, like being self-important. But then, arrogance in a person wasn't God's fault.

She continued to walk around, looking for someone who might direct her. She spied a janitor carting some garbage out what she assumed was a back entry, but he was too far for her to catch up with or to call. Cathy stood for a moment, distractedly thinking about back alley dumpsters.

She sighed and sat down on a nearby box. Cathy straightened, alert momentarily at a sound. She listened hard, but heard nothing.

The space was quiet, and its vacuousness felt a little unsettling. Funny how a hall could be filled with magnificent sound one minute and emptiness the next.

Maybe that's what she was trying to do by looking up her former students. Most of them had some degree of heaven's music in them at some point. She had seen it in their eyes as they listened in class. She had heard it in their questions, even if those questions had sometimes led them not only off track but off the map. Maybe she was trying to call back the past sound from the current emptiness.

Everyone had heaven's music ingrained in them, whether a note or a symphony. It was a matter of decision whether to acknowledge it and, when acknowledged, whether to allow it to expand through honest searching and prayer or to diminish it through inattention.

But here was the question that plagued her: was this search of hers helpful or futile? Did it really matter if she tracked down her wayward students? Most of them certainly would be just as pleased to not see her as to have her knock on their doors. Still. One visit might remind them of some good thing. It might tweak their curiosity in returning to a little church about which they'd forgotten. It might encourage them to utter a prayer. And she might never know.

People want to know efficacy immediately. They say to themselves 'I will keep working only if I see the results I desire' without a thought for future results that will be seen only by another, not themselves. In so doing, they diminish themselves to being a rat in a maze looking for a reward.

Cathy shook her head. It was always the same. Impatience for results was like a hunger pang borne from emotion; one best mastered. Appearances didn't tell the whole story. History offered unprejudiced judgment, and eternity alone proffered the final objectivity.

Sometimes a person had to admit that walking in the dark was as much of a duty as receiving accolades for success. Heaven knew Abraham only saw Isaac and some grandkids, never an actual nation; and Moses didn't set foot in the Promised Land. She'd just keep going and trust her little efforts would somehow, somewhere, someday make some sort of good difference to someone. It was part of what is called walking by faith, not by sight.

Cathy heaved a long sigh, then looked around her. Nope. Not a clue where her cousin was. She wished for something to wet her whistle: maybe cranberry juice with a little seltzer. Now that she was thinking of it, a pastrami sandwich with a variety of cheeses, a little mustard mixed with a dollop of garlic cream cheese, and something crunchy would hit the spot. Add a fruit salad or maybe fresh spinach with strawberries and a nice sweet dressing. Chocolate. Anything chocolate would be a wonderful conclusion. Cathy's stomach rumbled loudly enough that it would have been embarrassing had anyone been around to hear. No one was.

Half an hour later, she heard Andi's laughter, got to her feet, and walked toward it: it came from a completely different direction than she could have imagined. She arrived at the door just as Andi was leaving. Andi was holding a small bottle of cranberry juice in her hand.

"Here." Andi handed Cathy the bottle. "What took you so long?" she raised one eyebrow.

"Oh, just musing over the unplayed notes." Cathy sighed, looking longingly through the door at a beautiful buffet as Andi walked out.

# Chapter 22

*I checked with the property committee, and while they didn't want us to light a bonfire in the wastebasket, I don't believe roasting a grasshopper on a bamboo skewer over a lighter should bother anyone too much. Good grief, Francie, stop screaming. A few grasshoppers roaming around the room won't hurt you. You had the lead in last year's school play. Pretend you're John the Baptist like the rest of us.*

"Are you sure this is legal?" Andi followed Cathy down the alley behind a string of storefronts on 24<sup>th</sup> Street.

"I cannot in my wildest dreams imagine a law against taking what someone else has thrown away. Throwing something away, after all, indicates they don't want it anymore. I furnished the basement of my house with things people left on the curb, for pete's sake."

"You have a point, Cath. The Doberman at the last place put me a little on edge."

Cathy looked around. "Well, we're not at the last place. Or the place before that. We're here. Besides, I *am* purchasing these two properties – at least a little temporary ownership. The owner no doubt has more than he can stand in surplus paper."

"Then why are we dressed in black?"

"It goes better with our bags," Cathy innocently replied, holding up a garbage bag.

"And here I thought you eschewed the color even at the orchestra."

"It's not a col..." Cathy's voice drifted off as she squinted at the building for a minute. "Here it is. I think. Where is the starlight when you need it? I don't recall it being this dark at the last place. What in the world are you doing?"

Andi hoisted herself over the edge of a large bin and disappeared. Andi's head popped out of the top. She held something in her hand. "Look what I found," she sang, waving a manila envelope. Andi examined the address more closely. "It looks like something from the bank. What do you suppose..."

"Here. Put it in the bag. We don't have time to diddle."

"Diddle? What are you trying to do to the English language?"

"I think that word must have been from my graduate statistics class," murmured Cathy, looking into a bin.

Andi bent down, intent on her sorting. "I am so glad we wore these latex gloves. Otherwise I'd have to kill myself when we got home."

Cathy leaned over the side of the bin nearby, grasping for a bank statement.

"N... n... no, no, no," Andi gasped, just as Cathy slid head first over the top and landed in a heap of wet garbage.

"You sounded just like a machine gun." Cathy righted herself and wiped something green from the side of her face.

"And you look like a Caesar salad. Which has been sitting on the counter. For at least a week. Oh no, I feel like I'm going to..."

"Stop gagging, Andi. We don't have time."

Andi promptly threw up over the side of the garbage bin. Cathy observed Andi for a moment to see if she was okay. Andi looked back at her and made a face.

"Now there's something new. Throwing up *out of* the waste basket," Cathy remarked.

Andi's face was white, but she went back to piecing through the papers that surrounded her like water in a tub. "Just don't say anything about – salad – for a while, okay?"

She burped and swayed momentarily.

"That reminds me. I loved that new restaurant."

Andi sighed. "You ordered American."

"I don't speak French. Besides, the thought of a snail on a plate…" Cathy stopped abruptly and glanced at Andi who had closed her eyes and was concentrating on breathing. "I loved the maître d'. Fred's such a friendly fellow."

Andi opened her eyes and got back to searching. "They tend to be that way when you give them an obscenely large tip."

"He promised me he'd go to Sunday school on Sunday."

"I admit, he did seem to hold a rather unfathomable affection for you the minute he saw you walk through the door."

"He told me I reminded him of his Aunt Renee. He said she makes killer brownies." Cathy wiped the face of her watch with her shirt.

"How's the Monopoly game going?"

Cathy smiled. "Very well, thank you. I mean I haven't put up any plastic red hotels or anything, but I'm having fun. And once we sort through the stuff we're getting tonight, maybe I can gain a little insight into how best to help Mr. Dowling become the boy his mother intended."

"Or not."

"Or not. The thing is, if we can find proof of some questionable dealings, we can use it as leverage to make him lay off of those former students and behave himself."

"Ever the optimist," Andi murmured.

For a while, the women plowed through the dumpsters in silence, alternately picking up papers and envelopes and either tucking them into a bag or tossing them aside.

"It's 11:00. I'm done with sorting through my side. You?"

"As a doornail." Andi threw her leg over the side and climbed out.

"That would be dead. Dead as a doornail."

"Okay, I'm that, too." Andi stifled a yawn.

"A little help here? I can't make it out." Cathy puffed her cheeks and fell back into the bin.

Andi took a deep breath, made a painful face, and held out her hands. Cathy had nearly grabbed them before Andi pulled back.

Cathy sank back down. "What did you do that for?"

"Besides due to the remnants of garbage covering every inch of you, you mean? Raindrops. I can see them. Can you see them?" There was a slight sound of panic in her voice.

"Big deal. Raindrops. They're hardly noticeable. Can you please?" Cathy pulled herself up and forced her arms to rest along the edge of the bin again.

Andi reached across the edge of the dumpster. They grasped each other's forearms as Andi pulled Cathy out, slipping backward as she did so. They both landed hard on the now wet and muddy pavement.

The cousins moaned in unison.

They lay there for a minute before Cathy said, "I think I'm beginning to understand your concern about the rain. One more. Just one more bin. Down three doors. Dry..."

"Cleaners. I know." Andi groaned. "You are going to owe me big time for this one, cuz. Nearly as much as the Dairy Queen incident."

"We agreed to never bring that up again."

"I'm just saying..."

"Would a weekend at one of those fancy spas..."

"...Not nearly enough."

The raindrops were becoming a steady sprinkle. Both women looked up.

By the time they had searched the final bin, it was pouring rain and they were soaked. The two women found their way to Cathy's Jeep, threw the garbage bags into the back, and drove home.

"Shower and Jacuzzi," Andi ordered as they stepped through the door, dropping the garbage bags at the entry, where Harry excitedly sniffed them.

Cathy sneezed in agreement.

The two cousins sank into the Jacuzzi. Cathy slid in over her head and bobbed back up.

"It looks like the house is going up pretty quickly," remarked Andi, her eyes closed.

"I think it's possible the basics could be finished by mid-October. Al's a miracle worker. With no neighbors to be concerned with after-hours noise and a nice bonus for accelerated construction, everybody seems happy enough. I bring his crew caramel rolls every Friday morning."

"What a surprise," Andi stated without surprise. "Speaking of, have you mentioned anything to the kids?"

"I just haven't been able to come up with..." Cathy's voice trailed. "I talk with them all nearly every week, but I just..."

"Cathy, this is not bad news." Andi opened her eyes and looked at her sternly.

"No. No. But I keep thinking if only I'd found it sooner, their lives would've been so different. It's my fault, really."

"It's no one's fault. How were you supposed to know Perry had a fortune stuffed in the cover of a book you'd never read?"

"What am I supposed to say? By the way, we had millions sitting in the bookcase all through your childhood, but it was better for you to have those after school jobs so you could pay for every outing and extra bit of clothing anyway? To drop out of football because it got too expensive?"

"The stock increased exponentially this way," Andi consoled her.

Cathy sighed, squinting her eyes shut. "The Lord must have been shaking his head every time I asked for provision."

Andi persisted, "The Lord puts all sorts of things in front of people all the time, and they fail to see it. People are wealthy in ways they don't recognize. They live their whole lives and miss what's at the tip of their fingers just because it doesn't hold the picture of a president and fall apart in the washing machine."

"Amen, Sister Clemens," Cathy replied with slight annoyance.

"It *is* a commentary on how thoroughly you dust your furniture, though," Andi teased.

Cathy laughed and splashed her cousin. Andi leaned back and closed her eyes again. "Did you notice the beginnings of your patio?"

"I did. It's wonderful. And I see I'm having a swimming pool in the shape of a pond?"

"I'm actually trying something new, or rather something old that's new again. It's going to be a natural swimming pool. You won't have to treat it with chemicals because plants and gravel will act as water filters. I'll use algae-resistant materials and use plantings around it to soak up excess water."

"Are you absolutely sure I won't have green pond scum?"

"I'll have pumps and UV filters for extra water filtration. They'll run on solar energy. That way you'll have your 'quiet, peaceful piece of property' with surroundings befitting a cottage and still be able to swim every day."

"Every day?"

"Best for your arthritis. You need to talk to Al about an indoor pool."

"He's waiting for my approval to increase the square footage. He's no fan of sky lights, but he'll do them, he says."

"Will he now?"

Cathy opened one eye and looked at her cousin. "You knew I was blathering mindlessly when I mentioned it before. It's not my thing. You put him up to the indoor pool idea."

"Me?" Andi smiled.

"It's in the interest of health," murmured Cathy, wishing very hard for an excuse to skip a daily swim.

"Absolutely. You know, if you had a cell phone Al could reach you anytime with his questions."

"I get a ringing in my ears sometimes the way it is."

Harry walked in and licked the floor, coughed, then snatched up Cathy's towel laying by the side of the hot tub and trotted out.

"You'll get yours," Cathy called after him. He certainly was no longer the dying, scrawny puppy with matted fur she'd found shivering in the ditch on her drive home ten years ago. She'd spent that gray evening, bitten by the chill that comes with mist, combing through his fur and disposing of ticks in a cup of kerosene. He was never claimed by anyone, but he'd found his place with Cathy and had thoroughly claimed her. "He's going to love all that space to run. I called Hap Skalinski's former landlord," Cathy noted, changing the subject.

"And?"

"After six calls, he picked up. He said he no longer had a forwarding address for him."

"What a shocker."

Cathy squinted, thinking. "I don't know why I haven't gone through the phone book. Maybe I'll do that. Call every Skalinski listed."

"That should take all of two minutes."

"I saw Britty standing in a bus shelter down the street from the church last Sunday. It could have been my imagination, but I thought I glimpsed one of my notes sticking out of her purse pocket."

"Well. That's something."

"It is."

"I wonder what the church would think if they knew they were being spied on?" Andi laughed.

Laughter bubbled up from Cathy as she considered. "I sent a note for her with someone walking past the church building. Now that you put it that way, it was rather James Bond-ish."

Andi looked at her inquisitively.

"No verse this time. Just the scripture in a sentence: Jesus loves you."

"*That* she'll understand. I don't know if she'll believe it, but she'll understand it."

The two women looked at the ceiling, sending up a prayer, and then at each other.

"That is some huge boulder at the property entrance. What does 'Post Tenebras Lux' mean anyway?"

"After the darkness, light," Andi answered.

"Maybe you could jot it in English on a note card. I'll tape it to the rock for myself and the rest of the bourgeois."

"How did little Stevie Cartwright and his fiancée find Sunday school?" Andi took a sip from her cup at the edge of the whirlpool.

"I didn't get a chance to meet her, actually. She apparently refused to come, and he came alone."

"Brave man."

"He seemed to enjoy the brunch."

"Brunches are wonderful things."

"So did Alison."

Andi opened her eyes and looked inquisitively at Cathy.

"I cannot help what happens in people's lives," Cathy said, rather defensively, "It is not my fault that his fiancée thinks she's better than God."

"Tsk, tsk."

Cathy sighed deeply. "I didn't mean for it to take this turn, Andi. You know I'd never dream of disrupting the plans of..."

"...Never in a million years."

"It did seem to be a rather long engagement," Cathy said to herself.

Andi closed her eyes again.

"Steve and Alison hadn't seen each other since he graduated from high school and left for college. As I recollect, they did have a little something going during his senior year."

"Mm hm."

"Don't blame me. All I did was invite them to Sunday school."

"Such a harmless thing," murmured Andi.

Cathy looked around her, grateful for the warmth and comfort. She grabbed her pink cup from next to the hot tub and sipped. "Nice of you to bring me two cups. And pink!"

"The other one was on sale. I bought it against my better judgment. You're welcome."

When Cathy had drained two thirds of the second cup, she said, "This *is* decaf."

Andi didn't open her eyes.

"Andi. This *is* decaf. It's well past midnight, after all."

Andi opened one eye and shut it again.

"Andi?"

"I forgot."

"What?!"

"I'm tired, Cath. I congratulated myself for getting anything for us at all."

"Dare I ask?"

"Best not."

Cathy groaned. She leaned back and stared at the ceiling.

Andi yawned loudly and hoisted herself from the tub. "I'm going to bed. 'Night."

"'Night. Shall I wake you at 3:00 or 3:30?"

Andi chuckled. "I'll set the timer, so you don't overcook."

"And then?"

"Mmm," Andi said thoughtfully, "There's always cable."

"Ugh."

Cathy suddenly brightened. "Do you have a season DVD of that police drama? Ach! Name's on the tip of my tongue. You know which one."

"Sorry, no. I'll get one for you for Christmas."

"Which isn't tonight."

"*War and Peace* is in the library on the second shelf, fourth from the far wall."

# Chapter 23

*The expression 'Be sure your sins will find you out' is, indeed, in the Bible. It's in Numbers. Hosea says it this way: 'they do not realize that I remember all their evil deeds.' Either way, class, you might fool everyone around you, but you'll never fool God.*

"Thank you anyway, Mrs. Kipton." Cathy turned to leave. The bank's carpeting muffled her steps.

"I told you she wouldn't tell you if he had an account there," Andi said as they crossed the street to Grammie Mae's Confectionery. "Though your rendition of *Sleigh Ride* seemed of interest to the bank manager in the front office."

"You heard that?"

"Oh, sweet cousin." Andi shook her head. "I wonder what she thought of your curiosity."

"There's more than one reason to ask a question," Cathy countered. "Sometimes it's to get an answer, and sometimes it's to put the question in the other person's mind. Now that Mrs. Kipton has heard Dowling's name, she'll pay closer attention if she crosses it."

The smell of peanut butter fudge wafted over them as they entered the store. After picking up a sampler paper cup of Brazilian Bonanza coffee, Andi browsed by the bins of candy while Cathy went straight to the fudge counter.

Andi savored the coffee for a minute and asked, "Who came up with today's name, Mae? It has a nice flavor. Deep. Rich."

A small, wrinkled woman with white hair stirring an enormous vat of fudge looked up. "Me – as usual. My son suggested Brazilian Brainwash," she chortled. "Imagine. Are you through your last bag of coffee yet, Cathy?"

Cathy glanced at the coffee display. It was an end of the season closeout offering a variety of flavors. "I'm still scraping the bottom of my bag of Midnight Muse," Cathy replied. "In the meantime, I'd like some rocky road fudge to go with it, Mae."

"Karen!" Grammie Mae called. "Ka – ren!" The timbre of her voice carried through the small store with the authority of a marine sergeant. The old woman looked over at Cathy and Andi. "The younger generation always thinks they need a break."

She was about to call again when a young high school girl came from the back room and stood behind the counter. The freckles that dotted the girl's face wandered down onto her shoulders and arms and showed on the part of her bare legs that her capris didn't cover. Her dark brown hair was the same color Grammie Mae had when she was a girl.

"I'd like a half pound of your rocky road." Cathy pointed.

Grammie Mae watched as the girl cut the fudge with a cleaver. "Give her a bit more, Kare dear. She's a favorite customer."

"Everyone's a favorite customer," Karen muttered.

Cathy laughed.

The mayor's secretary walked in, made a pretense of looking at a few things, took one of the peanut butter fudge samples grouped on a small tray on the counter, popped it in her mouth, and walked back out again.

"Not everyone," Grammie Mae replied quietly, lifting the fudge in the air and letting it fall back into the pot.

Karen put another eighth of a pound in the bag and rang up the sale.

Andi bought a jar of peach salsa and a half dozen turtles, and brought a smile to the face of the salesgirl by complementing her on her service. She winked at Grammie Mae on the way out.

"You get a free turtle next time you're in the store, Mrs. Clemens!" Grammie Mae called after her.

"Even if Kipton came across his name, the bank wouldn't be concerned about his deposits." Andi continued their conversation from before they entered the candy store. "They don't care where the money comes from unless something gets their attention."

"Like what?"

"Like a deposit over, say, ten thousand dollars. That's the flag they use to look more closely into things."

"Per transaction?"

"Per transaction."

"So you're saying that if he keeps his deposits under ten thousand he avoids detection?"

"Pretty much. I mean he could make deposits in various banks in the city. Some banks are better than others at noticing things like that. Multiple accounts could undercut bank alerts, but if they're astute, they could catch it."

Cathy thought for a moment. "What if someone else made the deposits?"

"It's the account they pay attention to, not the person making the deposit."

"So he needs Masotic to have an account in his own name."

"Bingo. Or even another name." Andi handed Cathy a turtle and took a bite of one, herself.

"Accounts kept under different names wouldn't be noticed," Cathy repeated to herself, tapping the turtle on her lips.

"This does have you distracted," remarked Andi. "You aren't even eating your turtle."

Cathy took a bite.

"Happy?" Cathy replied through a mouthful of chocolate.

Andi shook her head. "This is what happens when you do something for all the wrong reasons," she teased.

"That's how half the stuff in this world gets done; you said so yourself."

"We know about Dowling and Masotic." Andi slid into the driver's side of her car. "I wonder if others are involved?"

"He strikes me as small potatoes. He probably justifies the things he does as something that anyone would do to get ahead."

Andi nodded.

Cathy continued, "If he keeps it small, there's less potential for detection; but there was a man I didn't recognize at the Farmer's Market that day I told you about."

"The guy in the tan sedan."

"Yes. Perhaps, Andi, we should drive to the DVS and look into the name listed on that license."

"My, aren't we getting astute. Do you have the correct address?"

"Not only do I have the correct address, but I also have a vague idea of how to get there!" Cathy pumped her fist.

"Let's stop at the house first and drop off the candy. I don't want melted chocolate on my leather seats."

"See? That's what happens when you drive a vehicle made in the current decade."

"Ahem. Need I say yellow Jeep just off the assembly line?"

"Oh. Right. I forgot. You know," Cathy turned to Andi, "having money takes away some of your reasons to criticize."

"Tsk, tsk. Everything has its price." Andi smiled, roaring onto the country road that led to her house.

# Chapter 24

*Jesus would get up early in the morning while it was still dark and walk to someplace where He could be by Himself to pray. If the Son of God went to all that trouble to keep communication lines with the Father open, class, you can bet we should.*

Cathy blew a puff that momentarily lifted the hair from her forehead. "Honestly. You'd think you could actually talk to someone at a phone company of all places."

"How long have you been on hold, anyway?" Andi took a bite of her sub sandwich.

"At least half a week," Cathy replied with irritation. She set the phone on the table with a thump, stood in the frame of the French doors onto the patio, and whistled for Harry. He looked at her over his shoulder and continued sniffing the ground.

Andi picked up the receiver and listened to a looped recording that told her how important her business was to them. Finally, a service rep came on the line.

Andi listened a minute, then quietly said, "My name is Andi Clemens. A-n-d-i C-l-e-m-e-n-s. I have a substantial amount of stock in your company that I am about two minutes from unloading unless my friend gets a helpful response right now. She has already spoken with at least two others by my count. Here's the deal. She will not wait while you speak to your manager or co-worker. She will not wait while you take your break. I want you to gather your wits and figure out what to do and I want you to do it now. That is your job. If you don't do your job, someone else would love to take your place. That is the way business works. If, when my friend hangs up, she is not helped, do not doubt that I will personally make a call to the CEO of this fine company and have an intense chat. Any questions?"

Cathy returned to the table with Harry at her heels. Andi held out the phone to her. Andi smiled and toasted her with her bottle of cold lemonade tea.

When Cathy hung up, Andi asked, "So who do we visit today?"

"Feel like a drive to the state pen?"

Andi rose from the table and grabbed a wide brimmed hat that rested in the window seat nearby. "A new acquaintance! Let me get my pepper spray."

The two women were accompanied into a narrow visitors' room where they sat in front of the clear partition. Andi pulled some disinfectant towelettes from her purse and wiped down two phone receivers.

"Really?" Cathy shook her head.

Andi proceeded to wipe down the counter and her chair. "You don't know who's been using these things nor where they've been. The number of possible diseases alone makes my head spin, not to mention other things the composition of which I don't even want to..."

"Okay, okay," Cathy whispered, furtively looking at the door to see if anyone had heard them.

A door opened and an inmate walked to where the guard pointed and sat down. His hair no longer brushed his shoulders as it had years ago. Now it was clipped short. Cathy thought it a good change. He was taller and broader, with firmer muscles than when Cathy had last seen him, but his walk wasn't quite the same cocky strut of times past. He looked across the counter at Cathy with deadened eyes. Then he blinked.

"No way," he said.

"Hello, James," Cathy said warmly.

"No damn way," he said a little louder.

"Ah, ah, ah. While I'm here, please refrain from cursing. You and I both know there is plenty of damning to be done, but not by you nor me, and not until judgment day."

"You always were full of it."

"Full of what?" Andi removed a hat that had previously kept her face in shadow.

James sucked in his breath, then began breathing heavily. The guard standing behind him smiled broadly and retucked his starched shirt.

"What?" he whispered.

"Full of what," Andi stated in a tone that didn't allow for compromise.

James shifted in his chair. "I just meant, ya know."

"I really don't know," Andi stated firmly, sitting back with one arm across the remainder of her chair, looking for all the world as though she was willing to wait a week for a clear answer.

"I believe James meant to say that he doesn't put much stock in what I say. Is that right, James?" Cathy said with a slight smile, raising her eyebrows.

"What're ya here for?"

Cathy looked at Andi and Andi looked back at her and shrugged. Cathy sighed. "I wanted to know how you're getting along."

"In here?" James looked at his surroundings and back at Cathy. "Great. Just great."

"Oh, James," Cathy replied softly.

He stared stonily back.

She sighed. He never had been won over by kindness. He'd always responded better to stern words. "Obviously it's not a place you prefer, but, again, it was your choice to live here for the time being..."

"Right, lady."

"...In that," Cathy pressed, "you had to know this was a possibility when you went ahead and robbed that little convenience store and then shot the clerk."

"He was disrespectful."

Andi's voice was quiet and immovable. "I don't know in whose world your stealing from someone and then calling him disrespectful makes sense, but it's not this one."

"Politicians aside," she added under her breath.

"Is there anything I can bring to you while you're here? Muffins? Oh wait." Cathy remembered what Nibsy Mehan had said. "They don't allow those, do they? Harmful things, muffins. A good book?"

James did not reply.

"Are you taking any of the courses they make available here?"

The inmate cracked his knuckles.

"Okay, James. I can see you don't care to visit. I'll get to my point and be done. I've known you since you were two."

The guard cleared his throat to avoid the laugh that stopped abruptly as Andi glanced at him without humor.

"Even as a youngster you carried a chip on your shoulder. You seemed to gain some degree of satisfaction from saying the opposite of what should be said, doing the opposite of what you were told."

James gave a short laugh.

"I see you haven't changed."

"Oh, yeah. I'm gettin' reformed in this here place."

"There are plenty of men in here who have had a tough childhood. While it's no excuse, it makes crime a bit more understandable to some."

"Speak for yourself," Andi remarked, simultaneously assessing the visitors' area.

"Anyway, you don't even have that excuse. Your parents have done everything they could for you and having been dying by degrees since you were ten. Because of you."

For just an instant, it appeared to Cathy she had hit a nerve. James' face twitched very slightly and for a split second. He squinted his eyes at her. "You don't know nothin'."

"On the contrary, James, I've done more checking on you than your lawyer, the judge, the parole board, or even this fine establishment. I have spent hours – and I mean *hours* – talking with former teachers, friends – if you can call them that..."

"I really don't think you can call them that," Andi interjected.

Cathy turned to her. "I think they had a sense of camaraderie."

Andi shrugged.

"Granted, I did not enjoy the neighborhood at all," Cathy acknowledged.

"Misplaced pride."

"Certainly confused, I grant you," Cathy replied to her cousin.

James observed the two women with inescapable interest.

206

Andi smiled. "The word 'confused' here is like an old tea bag in warm water. Is it confused when one's pride is in someone's number of conquests instead of family relationships..."

"Or tough acting snobbery rather than decent communication," Cathy finished. "You're right. Misplaced is the better adjective." Cathy turned to James. "Tough guys are the only ones who believe they're tough. To everyone else, they're just jerks. Where were we? Oh yes. And neighbors and girlfriends."

"No way."

"Does Tiffany McCraig ring a bell?"

James gasped, his eyes darting beyond Cathy, quickly surveying the visitors' area.

She had his full attention. "Tiffany has begun coming to Sunday school – at my invitation. We've had some very interesting, very cathartic chats, I think."

"No way."

"Perhaps you would like to consider – I don't know – what do they have in here, a Bible study or some sort of chapel service?"

James looked across the counter and said nothing.

"Look, James. I know you've never had time for the church; that you came only at the insistence of your parents and after a while not even then. I know you don't care for some little old Sunday school teacher taking up your time. But let me just say this, and then I'll leave and I'll not bother you ever again. During childhood, you were given, perhaps, too much. You did not suffer privations of any sort. Your parents were always there for you, even when you didn't deserve it. I believe they still are. In a way, that is the way God is."

James crossed his arms in front of this chest.

"He gives us more than we deserve. He lets us off the hook more times than we are even aware. But if someone – you, for instance – doesn't want anything to do with Him, He leaves them alone. Is that what you really want, James? Your pride has been your best friend for a long time. It's cost you the goodness of a decent job, your parents, a lovely girlfriend, and – oh yes – your freedom. Let's see what good company your pride is to you on the last day." Cathy looked around and sighed.

"You're sighing," said Andi.

Cathy dabbed the beginning of a tear from the corner of her eye. "Not anymore. Now I'm leaving."

Cathy and Andi rose in unison.

"Mrs. Covington?" James tapped on the glass to get her attention.

Cathy looked at Andi, her eyes big. She picked up the receiver again.

"Tell Tiff I might go to one o' them things."

"The road to hell is paved with good intentions, James."

"Man, that is why I never liked you. You never let up, do you?"

Cathy raised her eyebrows.

"I'll go."

Cathy nodded, then tilted her head to assess his truthfulness.

"I will," he persisted.

Cathy began to put the receiver in its place.

"I guess you can visit me again, if you want."

"I'll be here Tuesday after next." As an afterthought, she said, "In the meantime, ask around about the name 'Masotic.'"

James looked as if he was considering a math problem for which he didn't know the formula.

"Just curious," she offered with a shrug.

Cathy left then, slipping a note addressed to Britty into the outgoing prison mail on her way out: *"Correct me, Lord, but only with justice – not in your anger, lest you reduce me to nothing."*

# Chapter 25

*When most people think about Jesus washing the disciples' feet, they think about Jesus' example of humility or of Peter saying he didn't deserve it. They don't think of Judas, who didn't say anything at all.*

"So you think you can make it back?!" Cathy's heart leapt. "Label me stunned. I left the message on your service just to keep you in the old neighborhood loop. I never dreamed it would work out, but I'm thrilled it will."

Cathy scribbled on a notebook she kept by the phone. "Yes, the Serling girls are actually practicing up, can you believe it? They said something about flaming batons, but as long as you're there, I guess we won't worry about burns."

Cathy gave self-conscious laugh. "Yes, John, Christy is married. She has twin boys. She'll be playing her flute, though." She paused. "Ah. Well, she liked you, too, as did every other schoolgirl in Pine Point."

Cathy pulled last night's meatloaf from the refrigerator and set it beside the bread she had out on the counter. "I can't imagine why you're not, a handsome man like you." Cathy thought for a moment. "I suppose they keep you so busy at the hospital."

Cathy balanced the phone on her shoulder as she made a sandwich. "I can believe that. Women tend to throw themselves at men in more obvious ways than when modesty was viewed as an admirable trait."

Frowning, she returned the remaining meatloaf to the refrigerator.

"Really?" Cathy raised her eyebrows. "Pine Point would welcome you back with open arms; you know that. There are plenty of medical centers around here, as you well know.

"Imagine. Talking with the university and the Mayo Clinic in one visit. How did you manage that?

"It does seem providential that they need a department head just now.

"Yes? How interesting.

"That is terrific!

"No, I don't imagine you want to crack your wrist with a repeat performance," she laughed.

"A guitar sounds great.

"We'll see you Saturday on the south side of the high school parking lot. Great talking with you, Johnny!"

Andi shuffled into the kitchen in her robe and slippers as Cathy hung up the phone and took a bite of her sandwich.

"Who are you talking to at this hour?" Andi pulled a coffee cup out of the cupboard. "And how in the world is a meat loaf sandwich palatable at," she looked at her watch, "7:00 in the morning?"

"This, from someone who drinks caffeinated soda before bed," Cathy said, her mouth half full. "It's not that early on the East Coast. I was talking with Johnny Blakely."

"Ah. Pine Point's Carey Grant." Andi hesitated. She dropped a piece of whole wheat in the toaster. "He drove over to go out to dinner with us when I was visiting Philip at Quantico."

"You didn't say anything about that when you got back." Cathy poured Andi's coffee and gave herself a second cup.

"He had a gorgeous blonde on his arm. I hesitated to tell you, knowing that he and Christy used to have a thing for each other."

"She's married, Andi. With twins, for pete's sake."

Andi shrugged.

"Their relationship had a rather messy ending." Cathy took two long gulps of coffee. "But I always liked him; even after." Her mind drifted back to that time, and she shuddered. "You know, they were inseparable for two years and then, boom! His name was the equivalent of nails on a blackboard. We couldn't walk into a room Christy was in without getting an earful."

"What happened again?"

Cathy looked at her and shook her head. "Some misunderstanding about going to a ball game instead of a movie. Or maybe it was him saying the wrong thing to the wrong person at the wrong time. Or it could've been his taking it for granted she would be available for some dance. There was more than one argument during those years. I can't quite recall which was where. I'm sure you know as much as I, having him visit your house so often."

"All I remember is a lot of sullenness and shrugging and mumbling something about not understanding girls."

Cathy sighed loudly. "High school."

"I always thought they'd patch it up." Andi sipped her coffee.

"This *is* Christy we're talking about."

"She's quicker at forgiving now than when she was in high school," Andi defended her niece.

"I always wondered if Johnny reminded her a little too much of her dad and he got the brunt of her untapped feelings."

"I didn't realize Christy left any feelings untapped."

Cathy half-nodded. "There *is* that. I wish," Cathy sighed, "she would let go of the old grudge."

"It seemed to me the blonde was more of a convenient date than anything else anyway; though she didn't take her eyes off him the whole evening," Andi charged ahead, munching on her toast.

"John and Phil probably would've been happier watching a game on T.V. with a bowl of Doritos between them." Cathy laughed.

"Actually, they do that on occasion, I think. Philip was teasing him about his barbecue skills when we were at the restaurant. Still best friends after all these years."

Harry trotted into the kitchen and looked at Cathy pleadingly. She tossed the last bite of her sandwich in the air, and he leaped up and caught it. Cathy caught a glimpse of the microwave clock. "Oh! Look at the time!"

"Right. The final parade committee meeting. Hallelujah!" Andi laughed, nestling into her kitchen window seat with the remainder of her cinnamon toast and coffee.

"Later!" Cathy hurriedly dropped her pink coffee cup in the sink and rushed out the door.

The committee members were waiting for Cathy as she blew through the door of the Corn Hut, its bell tinkling urgently.

"I'm terribly sorry!" Cathy looked at her watch. "Ah. I guess I am on time after all, but right on time usually feels a little late."

Cathy looked at Lisa, who had approached the table with an order pad when Cathy sat down.

"Just decaf with cream for me this morning, Lisa. I had breakfast at home." Cathy turned to the others. "While you're all ordering, let me tell you about a call I got from Murtha's flowers. They're impressed and that's good news and they offered a deeper discount for parade float participants. And! And they've signed on as a sponsor."

A murmur of approval rose from committee members.

After serving them their breakfasts, Lisa pulled up a chair beside Cathy. The committee looked at her, unsure how to handle the intrusion.

"Lisa has been doing some parade work for us," began Cathy. "She and the Motocross Mamas have put in many hours, and she consented to update us this morning."

Heck had been unusually quiet during the morning's meeting. Now he looked up from his South of the Border Omelet, his fork paused mid-air. "She's not on the committee."

"Actually, Heck, she is. I've just been... running things a bit differently this year."

Heck looked over at the toddler table and shook his head. Cathy could tell he had been looking for a reason to vent some pent up feelings, and this was it. She was grateful for the fact they were in a public place and for Heck's unwavering concern over what appeared respectable.

"You got that right." He scrunched his lips and stuck them out. Then he sucked in his breath. He tilted his head and looked sideways at Cathy. "You never did follow the rules, *Chairwoman* Covington. Even in Sunday school *way* back when," he said, making a point of her age, "you weren't like a real teacher. You were like..."

Cathy leveled a gaze at him. "Like what, Heck?"

"You brought all those frogs and stuff." He took a breath. "You washed our feet! What kind of a teacher washes the students' feet?!"

Cathy looked at Heck and blinked once, slowly. He glared back. She sighed. "Lisa, you have the floor."

Lisa laid out the part of the parade that the Motocross Mamas had planned. Everyone but Heck grew excited. Even Mrs. Kipton's eyes showed a hint of sparkle. The table grew increasingly animated as the rest of the committee shared their progress.

It was fairly bubbling when it was Heck's turn. He said something that no one could hear.

"Heck?" Cathy leaned forward.

"I don't have the bands, okay?"

Conversation came to a standstill. Throughout the diner, the sizzle of bacon from the kitchen was all that could be heard after a teenager's narration dwindled to nothingness when he was shushed by the glares of those around him.

"But, Heck," Cathy murmured, "You told me you do the bands. What...?" Cathy was at a loss for words.

"We got started too late. Everybody's booked – for ball games or contests or who knows what bands do when they aren't in a parade."

Mrs. Kipton doodled on her napkin while some of the other committee members sipped their drinks. Adele came over, climbed on Ashley's lap, and stuck her thumb in her mouth. The whispering voice of someone ordering a chicken salad with chips echoed through the small space as though it was a cathedral.

"What about Pine Point High?" Ashley ventured.

Heck glared at her. "Oh sure. We've got Pine Point High School. Whoop de doo. We've got ten thousand people from all over the metro *and* outstate comin' to hear Pine Point High with its one tuba and seven trumpets."

It was as though a pin had pricked Heck's bravado and he had completely deflated.

215

"Seven trumpets isn't a bad..." Lindsey Mayberg began, her voice fading as Heck scowled at her.

Carl nodded his head in an effort to support her, but stopped mid-nod when she didn't see him.

"I suppose you'll want me to resign." Heck's shoulders slumped.

Cathy was tempted to enjoy the pathos that had entered their little corner of the Corn Hut, but she resisted. She put her hand on Heck's arm.

"Of course not, Heck. We need you more than ever, don't we?" Cathy nodded her head and looked around the table.

The committee nodded back doubtfully, but dutifully.

"It seems to me," Cathy began slowly, formulating the idea as she spoke, "that some of our small private schools don't have the opportunity to march in parades. Why don't we visit a few of them; see if maybe they'd like to put something together with the students who play an instrument and march as a school individually or to join forces with some other private or charter schools, hmm?"

Heck's breathing slowed perceptibly.

"Well, then," Cathy said bravely, "it looks as though there are a few more things to do today." Cathy went to pay her bill and the others gathered their things.

Heck stood uncertainly.

"Looks like your *old* Sunday school teacher just washed your feet. Again," Lisa chided him as she got back to work and started clearing the table.

# Chapter 26

*This section of Ecclesiastes reminds us that life is bound to have a little of everything and we must understand that it will see death as well as birth, war as well as peace. No, Barbara, it is only those willing to delude themselves who think there is not a proper time for such things.*

Whoever could not have his spirits lifted at the sight of the church on this perfect early October day probably was in serious need of a kick in the pants or, at the very least, an injection of chocolate. If the grounds gave allusion to what was within, she guessed it would be a visual feast: one from which to gorge without guilt. Every detail around her seemed to celebrate the special day. Branches on the bushes boasted tiny pale pink ribbons. The edges of the lawn were sprinkled with rose petals. Three-foot-tall clay vases brimming with sumac lined the walk and, once Cathy and Andi entered the church, exploded into mixed arrangements of dried hydrangeas, baby's breath, berry vines, pussy willows, bittersweet, and roses. Stepping over the threshold felt like crossing into a sparkling fairyland.

The wedding was between members of two multigenerational families in the congregation. To say the entire community of past and present members, as well as sister churches' members, had shown up would be only a slight exaggeration.

Andi leaned close to Cathy and whispered, "Well?"

"You weren't paid enough," Cathy replied, her eyes sparkling.

The spacious foyer was filled with people at various stages of signing the guest book, awaiting the next usher, and hugging old friends. Down the hallway, Justin was exiting the restroom. He appeared to be wearing a new pair of jeans and a dress shirt. The tie was from a thrift store, if Cathy didn't miss her guess; and she felt inexplicably proud of him for wearing one.

A sudden burst of loud laughter echoed through the room from near the sanctuary entrance. Cathy glanced over to witness a scene as familiar, though not as comfortable, as an old easy chair.

It was Francie and her mother, no doubt regaling those around them with their latest experience. She observed the grouping around them with half pity, half amusement. Francie's narrations typically ran in the direction of her in the starring role of the recitation and any missteps she might have made as harmless and amusing. She laughed the loudest at her own humor and felt those around her must be charmed. Those who knew Francie's mother knew she came by it honestly.

The guests around them, initially entertained, were growing weary as the one-sided conversation grew longer. Some were glancing at their watches, others glanced furtively at each other, but the crowd, being one of decent upbringing, showed as much attention and proper emotion as they could muster while fervently hoping the stories would soon end. Cathy knew there was no hope of that. They were trapped by the chain-linked stories of Francie and her mother, an unfortunate malady, but not fatal. Cathy chuckled under her breath, relieved to not be one of them.

There is, often neglected, an art to conversation. Naturally concerned and familiar with personal situations, it is easy for people to speak only of what they know, of what pertains to them. A minority of others are naturally guarded and find sharing about themselves a challenge. Both take up too much space, either by too many words or too much silence. Sharing and being shared with is part of speaking with one another, while including observations of ideas and events outside of personal experience makes conversation more complete, and introducing new thoughts and knowledge is more comprehensive yet. Speaking, listening, and thinking are so simple, yet not infused together nearly enough. It is rare to experience such a person, but a good conversationalist is a delight and not quickly forgotten.

Andi squeezed Cathy's arm and pointed.

"Be there in a minute," Cathy whispered. She waved to them as Andi joined her sons' and daughter's families who had run into those of Cathy's own family who had come to the wedding. They stood together talking and laughing in the short family reunion it afforded them. Their numbers alone took up a sizable part of the foyer, and a few of them branched like tributaries visiting here and there with old church friends and acquaintances they had not seen in a very long time.

Cathy signed the guest book, and turned to see Steve Cartwright.

"You're at the wedding of the season!" she greeted him.

Steve reached over and hugged her. "And I have you to thank for my date."

"I can't imagine," Cathy replied, looking around for Alison.

"She'll be back in a minute. She ran into an old friend." Steve nodded in the direction of Alison McCormick talking with a short, balding fellow and his wife.

"What happened to your fiancée?" Cathy asked innocently. She scratched her nose.

Steve shook his head. "It didn't work out. I'm just glad we figured it out before the wedding. The first time I came back here – at your express encouragement – I ran into Alison and it was like the years in between had never happened."

"You don't say."

Just then, Alison came over to join them. "Hi, Mrs. Covington!"

Cathy grabbed her hand and squeezed it. "Hello, dear. Is this guy keeping you from your MCATs?"

"He's helping me study." Alison cast an affectionate gaze at Steve.

Christy was motioning her mother over. They were ready to be escorted in.

"Bravo. Excuse me. I'm being called. You two enjoy the wedding!" She turned to leave, then stopped. "Take care of each other."

"We will." Steve nodded. Steve and Alison gave a short wave as Cathy left them holding hands.

From her pew, Cathy glanced over to see Britty walking in with her parents. Her skirt could not have been much shorter. However, it was a marvel that Britty had come at all. The path of progress was more often laid with pebbles than boulders.

Leaning over to Andi she whispered, "You'd better watch your mascara."

"I saw her. You proved once again that the pen is mightier than the sword."

"Scripture's underrated," Cathy replied as Katie shushed her mother, jabbing her lightly in the ribs as the processional began.

"I miss church basement receptions," said Cathy between bites of canapés.

She was talking with Andi in the park across from the church while their family members continued to mingle. Green grass blanketed the park that boasted a playground, three picnic shelters, two horseshoe pits, and a kiddie pool. Pines and black walnut trees dotted the acreage, and the walnut trees' leaves had turned to an iridescent yellow, bathing the air and the ground beneath them with golden light.

Three white-clothed tables were spread with buffets, another with a punch fountain and coffee, and on another stood a beautiful four-tiered wedding cake decorated with buttercream roses and fresh pansies. Uniformed servers roamed through the crowd with hors d'oeuvres on silver platters.

"The park is beautiful. As long as the weather holds..."

"And no black walnuts fall in the fruit salad. You're right. But I still miss church basement receptions. There's something, I don't know, something common, something homey, something familial about them. It's like going home for Christmas. It might not be the most beautiful or roomiest place, but it feels more right than even the most spectacular space."

Andi shrugged her shoulders. "God owns the park, too, and this way no one will care if someone spills his punch."

"Or drops his plate." Cathy stepped aside just in time as children, dressed in their Sunday best, darted in and out of the guests milling around the park.

The ceremony had been beautiful. Aside from the five-year-old ring bearer holding his hands over his ears during the soloist's rendition of *Jesu, Joy of Man's Desiring*, all had gone as rehearsed. Too bad marriage, itself, couldn't be as perfect. Cathy watched the couples around her on what she suspected was their best behavior.

Cathy had promised to call said ring bearer's mother when she started up with her piano students in the not too distant future. At least he was able to discern when a note was a hair sharp, she thought hopefully.

Someone was striding toward her and she shielded her eyes against the sun to see who it was. It was Dillon. "You look like a million bucks!"

"If only." Dillon laughed.

"Any progress with the AG pressing charges?"

Dillon shook his head. "The guy who sold me down the river is invisible. They've as much as closed the books on it." After a minute, he continued, "You know, I always thought I was the smart guy. Quiet, under the radar, observant. The guy who might not be the most noticeable, but alert and astute; maybe understanding things somebody else missed."

Cathy nodded in agreement while he shook his head.

"But this. This has me wondering if all this time I was just the guy others could see as a mark."

"Not true! Not true at all, Dillon. And you never know. Maybe Mr. Buford or whoever he is will be exposed yet." Her mind wandered to the papers stashed in her bedroom at Andi's house.

Dillon rallied. "I'm climbing back out of the hole." He gave her a valiant look, and Cathy nodded encouragingly. "And I had the strangest thing happen. Someone put several thousand cash in my mailbox one day. In an envelope. Addressed to me! I tried to track it."

"Any luck?"

"No."

"Imagine that. Did it help a little?"

"You've no idea. Do you have any idea of who could've put it there?"

Cathy threw back her head and laughed. "Do I look like I would know a philanthropist?"

Dillon laughed with her. Everyone knew the riches of his old Sunday school teacher were described best as 'intangible assets.' He laughed again. How comical it would be for the woman before him to know his Good Samaritan, much less be affluent, herself.

Something unexpectedly made Dillon stop laughing and look more closely. His eyes narrowed slightly. "Your dress looks like it's out of a magazine."

Cathy laughed. "My cousin, Andi." She motioned to Andi who was chatting with a man Cathy didn't recognize. "She's always nudging me to join the decade."

Dillon studied her.

"She gave me these earrings as a gift," Cathy continued. "She's pretty extravagant when she wants to be."

Dillon nodded, satisfied once he looked over toward Andi. He wiped a hand on the side of his pants, shot a look at the man talking to her, then shook his head as if awakening from a daydream.

Christy wandered over to them with a cup of coffee in her hand.

"Christy, why is it that I never see you without coffee?" teased Andi, who had extricated herself from her latest visitor.

"One word. Twins," answered her niece. Christy had just begun to suggest they all get together afterward at the little house on Maple Lane to see the progress when Cathy interrupted her.

"I wish we could get together, but I want to make dinner and have you all over at once to see it, remember? Besides, we have that thing after this." She looked pleadingly at Andi.

"Yes," Andi nodded, "the thing we have." She looked back at Cathy, then at Christy, then became unusually interested in the hammered gold bangle on her wrist.

Christy's mouth smiled while the rest of her face was a puzzled frown. "O-kay."

Andi snapped her fingers. "You know, I think you should all go out to my house. You can tear it apart like you did in the old days. And you won't miss your mom or your auntie with all the ruckus."

"Oh! But stay out of the small guest room." Cathy's eyebrows shot up in alarm. A bird tweeted in the silence, and Cathy looked up at it, studying it as though she had suddenly become an ornithologist. She looked back at Christy who was studying her.

Cathy cleared her throat.

Andi explained, "I'm working on a project that I..."

"Top secret," Cathy said hastily.

"And Harry," Andi said frantically, "is... is... at my house. We thought," she said, looking at Cathy.

"We thought," said Cathy returning Andi's frantic stare, "that he might want..."

"... A change of scenery," Andi said quickly.

"So... I let him stay there while we're here," Cathy concluded brightly.

The two women smiled cheerfully at Christy. Christy opened her mouth to say something and shut it again.

As she turned to rejoin the others, Cathy kicked Andi with the side of her foot. "The thing we had? Really?"

Andi shrugged her shoulders helplessly. "You didn't give me much to go on. I froze. Besides, you don't have a leg to stand on. 'Top secret'? That's sure to diminish any questions Christy had."

Christy looked over at them from a group of former schoolmates she had joined a few yards away. They waved back at her in unison.

"Look at her." Andi pressed her hand to her heart. "Even now she's forming some idea in that head of hers that's going to go viral by the end of the evening."

Cathy felt a gnawing anxiety starting near the tip of her toes.

"I'm telling you, Cath, the longer you keep this from the kids, the more stressed I get. Pretty soon I won't be able to remember my own name."

A brief smile crossed Cathy's face. How nice for Andi that she actually thought her last sentence was unbelievable. There were some things her cousin recalled like an encyclopedia, but names were her nemesis.

"It never seems to be the right time." Cathy sighed. "I just hope they don't swing by my house on their way out to yours." She emptied her glass of punch in a few gulps. "After all, I did ask them to stay away so they could see the remodel all together. They've gone along with it so far."

Andi rubbed her temple, and grabbed two canapés from the platter of a passing server and stuffed them both in her mouth.

A man they didn't recognize came over and introduced himself to Andi. After some polite conversation and an even more polite brush off, he wandered off.

"What is that? Number five?" Cathy raised her brows.

Andi gave her a look of annoyance.

The ring bearer ran past them just then, fleeing from the flower girl in hot pursuit just behind him.

"There's one member of the wedding party who will be glad to see this day end." Cathy followed their progress across the park.

"I can sympathize."

They both looked heavenward at the same instant, as they felt a water droplet hit. A few sprinkles fell, then the cloud passed and the sun shown again.

"So, Cathy, where are we going to go when we go to 'that thing we have' since, now that the kids are going to my house, we have to stay away from there?"

Cathy shook her head. "No idea. I'd feel silly browsing at the discount store dressed for a wedding and I'm not sure I want to wander around in a party dress investigating Paul Dowling either."

"Maybe we can just drive over to your property and wait out an hour in the car. We could take a walk through the property. We could cheer on your nationally renowned indoor/outdoor designer."

"Let's take some chicken salad croissants to go." Cathy started over to the buffet table.

Mrs. Kipton was in the buffet line behind her husband. Her lips were pressed together in a kind of unproductive effort to smile. She was nodding while the woman behind her chatted away. A white blob suddenly fell on Mr. Kipton's shoulder. Everyone in the vicinity looked up to see some sparrows sitting in the branches above them. A startled Mr. Kipton dropped his plate into the fruit salad. A smile crossed Mrs. Kipton's face. She picked her husband's plate out of the fruit salad and held it out to him as he crossed his arms and put his hand to his mouth looking quite perplexed. Then Mrs. Kipton laughed out loud, a lovely infectious laugh. Cathy watched in amusement and delight. No one, including Mrs. Kipton, herself, would have guessed that the most beautiful laugh in all the world belonged to her. It surprised everyone around her and pulled them all, including Mr. Kipton, into a chorus of hilarity.

And that, Cathy decided, as she picked up a plate of her own, was why marriages were better off with some imperfection thrown in after all.

# Chapter 27

*When Jesus said, 'By their fruits you will recognize them', He wasn't talking about trees. Life is not a Homecoming Royalty election, class. You can tell who is on which side of good and evil regardless of the color of their hats. Just look at the trail they leave when they walk away.*

Sheets of paper were spread over the counters and table in Andi's kitchen. Their investigation of P. F. Dowling was in full swing. They had copies of transactions with a variety of businesses, bank receipts and correspondence retrieved from their foray into the back alleys, an Internet address, and a large tag board full of lists, names, arrows, and question marks.

Cathy's mouth was full of a pastry, and Andi was just swallowing some coffee when Harry began barking and jumping maniacally.

The women gave each other curious looks as the doorbell rang.

Andi hurried to answer it. Her voice came from the foyer. "Christy? Katie? Well, this is a surprise."

"Auntie Andi," came two greetings from the doorway.

"Your mother's here – she'll be *so glad* to see you!" Andi practically shouted.

"I hear you loud and clear," thought Cathy, looking helplessly around the room.

The three made their way back to the kitchen to find Cathy standing frozen behind the table. She wiped a pastry crumb from the side of her mouth and smiled innocently.

Christy and Katie looked at each other in the same instant.

Christy said, "What's going on, Mom? I noticed your Bible on an end table in Auntie Andi's library when we were here after the wedding."

Cathy shrugged as Andi said, "So?"

"By a chair. By the fireplace."

Christy began pacing back and forth, reminding Cathy of Perry when he was carrying on about something that upset him.

"I asked myself why it was here and not at your house. You wouldn't have taken it to church for the wedding, so wouldn't it still be where you had set it down after reading it that morning? This is the conversation I had with myself, Mom."

Cathy bit her lip. That book had a way of telling the truth one way or the other.

Katie leaned against the kitchen entryway, quietly studying her mother and her aunt.

"Something wasn't quite right, so I thought I'd just swing over to Maple Lane to see how the renovation was going, despite your desire for us to stay away and what was it? Oh yes. All see it at once. I drove over there expecting, I don't know, maybe a pickup truck with a Mr. Fix It sign painted on the side and some tools in the back, maybe even the beginnings of a double garage..."

"What is it with you people and double garages?" Andi asked.

Christy turned toward her aunt with the hint of a glare. "...and instead discovered the neighborhood was decimated!"

"Mrs. Serling's house is still there," Cathy pointed out.

"What happened to the *neighborhood?*" Christy persisted.

"I... um... bought it."

After a stunned silence, Katie straightened.

"Mom, you don't have that kind of money." She looked helplessly to Andi for support.

When Andi didn't respond, Katie continued, "Christy came to the restaurant, frantic. I told her she was nuts."

"Well there's something new."

"Mother," both daughters said in unison.

"When she insisted, I left my manager in charge and went with her. We drove around the block. Twice," added Katie. "I literally felt my blood pressure increase. Do you know what that's like?"

"Mine has increased gradually over the years; so, no."

"Ah. Yes, you do. Remember when you saw the boy who took Katie to the prom?" Andi interjected.

"Oh, yes. You're right. I do know what that's like."

"Mom, this is no time for joking." Christy furrowed her brow.

"Who's joking?"

Katie continued, "My heart was beating loud enough for me to hear it. It felt like an old episode of..."

"I'm offended," interrupted Andi, "One: that you'd even dream of comparing my work to something on T.V. and two: by your obvious lack of appreciation. That property hasn't looked this good in a hundred years. Don't you like the fruit trees? There's a miniature orchard just down from where Tab used to do wheelies. Did you notice the darling little copse where the Blakely's yard used to be? Not to mention the well-placed Pines. Plus, plus, oh you'll love this. I had a rainwater capture tank installed as the outdoor water source."

"Your distractions won't work, Auntie. Sorry." Katie gestured to the papers laid out all over the kitchen. "What's this?"

Cathy glanced at Andi who was moving quickly from the cupboards to the refrigerator. All it would take to send her daughters into a panicked one-sided conversation on societal standards for senior citizens would be for them to think about their mother and aunt foraging into the topsoil of the underworld.

"Would you girls like some soda? Tea? Coffee? I've got just the thing." Andi snapped her fingers. "Hot coffee with a dollop of whipped cream, drizzle of caramel and a cinnamon stick! Come on," she coaxed, "Let's all sit down in the library. I'll get us something to eat."

The two daughters gave each other knowing looks and headed for the study.

Andi began setting a tray with what she considered to be comfort food.

"You're going to leave me alone with them?" Cathy whispered on her way out of the kitchen.

"Face it, cousin. You're busted," Andi whispered back. Under her breath she added, "I knew I should've put *Nil Desperandum Auspice Deo* on that boulder instead."

Cathy and Andi stood at the door, waving goodbye while Harry barked, chasing the car to the gate.

"Well. That went well."

Cathy let out a deep breath in response. "I should've told them sooner, but, oh well."

"Oh well? You have such a gift for words."

"Thanks for suggesting a conference call."

"It took Alden a while to get to the phone, but he can be a charmer once he washes the blood off his hands. I'm glad I had yesterday's chicken salad in the refrigerator." After a moment, Andi added, "And that you didn't eat it all at breakfast."

"Well-fed daughters are so much easier to talk to than when they're hungry."

"I didn't take those cooking classes for nothing, you know." Andi closed the door as the two women walked back to the kitchen. "Your kids' response came as no surprise to me."

"One could hardly fault them for screaming and shouting, I guess." Cathy began stacking dishes in the sink.

Andi laughed. "Besides that."

"You mean that they consider it my money to do with as I choose?"

"Their rather laissez faire attitudes *and* the humor they found in it. And I applaud you for not bursting into tears as I know you felt like doing."

"It's the regret, Andi. That regret, it's like a hornet's nest, with its little inhabitants following me around and stinging me with the thought of every dinner that could have been more complete, every experience they would have benefited from and didn't have, every denial instead of help. And me without an Epi Pen."

"Stop. It's good, remember?"

"I don't know why I was so hesitant to tell them." Cathy shook her head. "It can't make up for a childhood of shortages, but I believe I'll be writing six checks for Christmas even though I don't usually care for that kind of thing." She laughed. "Despite their attitude, there's no doubt in my mind they'll expect more than socks this year."

"Why not give it to them at Thanksgiving, instead? Keep Christmas focused."

Cathy paused, thinking it over. "What would Christmas morning be without new socks for everyone anyway?"

"Besides, you know Katie will just pour it back into the restaurant."

"She's got plenty mortgaged on that thing. It would certainly help to whittle down the debt or maybe make it disappear." Cathy began to smile. "Christy will sock it into savings for her kids."

"Cam is probably already planning Christmas bonuses for his crew," Andi thought aloud.

They sighed together.

"Just like their mother," Andi concluded.

"Are you kidding? I'm building a house for myself..."

"And a very large guest house not for yourself."

"I bought my neighbors' homes..."

"At top dollar, though you didn't need to, and gave them more opportunity than they would ever have had in this lifetime." Andi took Cathy's hand in hers and looked at her affectionately. "You're forgetting I sit on the boards of a few local charities. We find out when large sums of money are donated. "And who else would spend her own time and money investigating some miscreant just because he was making life miserable for a fellow she taught in Sunday school years ago and who, I suspect, came back once at your request, but not since?"

Cathy shook her head. "Enough of this. Half the day is gone, and we still haven't made much headway into this mess." She gestured to the scattered paper. "You'd think he'd use his shredder more, especially in his business dealings. Even a nobody like me uses one."

"Yes. Well, a shredder in the shape of a shark chewing what you feed it is rather irresistible. I still don't know how you got your hands on that thing."

"And you never will. I promised." Cathy frowned at a memory. "He probably has one of those ever creative rectangular box shaped things." Cathy slammed her Ex Caliber letter opener down on the table. "Honestly, Andi. I don't know how boring people live with themselves!"

"He might be so used to getting away with things, he's getting a bit careless," replied Andi, avoiding another side discussion.

"Help me finish sorting?"

"Are you kidding? I'm meeting a couple of very buff college guys in about twenty minutes. I don't know who's more excited."

"They are, trust me."

Andi made a face at her cousin. "I mean about the work. I promised myself I'd get over to your property and get a few more things laid out. The blizzard of '91 still haunts me."

"Those poor little kids in their Halloween costumes, buried in snow up to their necks by the time they got home," Cathy reminisced.

"I can feel the cold weather coming: little wisps at first, then steady breezes, next icy rains, and before you know it, you've got a blizzard. We don't want your little kitchen garden without a home when spring arrives."

"And a big garden."

"Already measured out. You knew when you gave me this, it would be done right. No worries." Andi smiled as she pulled on her Wellingtons. She grabbed her jacket and gloves, and waved as she walked out, closing the door tightly behind her.

Cathy walked over to the stove, brewed herself a cup of strong tea, and sat down, resting her elbows on the table. Her eyes drifted over the material; then she gazed out the windows. She hoped the weather would stay mild at least until Logjam Days was past. They'd rarely had trouble for the mid-October celebration, but Minnesota weather – well, there was a reason weathermen got paid a bundle in these parts.

That evening, the aroma of beef stew drifted through the house as Andi came into the kitchen.

Cathy finished stacking some papers, making a note on a Post-It at the top. She popped the last of the cheese balls from a snack bag into her mouth.

"Appetizers?"

"Just a little starter." Cathy washed them down with some cranberry juice.

"Looks like you've been busy."

"Couldn't let you have all the fun, now, could I? Sit. I'll tell you my discovery over dinner. Oops!" Cathy turned to the stove, "Almost forgot the biscuits."

"You always do." Andi washed her hands and set the table. "I'm finding burned biscuits are an acquired taste."

"So I'm looking at this address..."

Andi looked where Cathy pointed. "I can't believe you used the computer."

"Tab called back after everyone left. He wanted to make sure I was okay. He thought I sounded a little breathless over the phone. What do you know: he's a regular IT guy!"

"That's progress for you. It used to be the It girl."

"Slap your mouth. This is my baby we're talking about. Anyway, I got on the blame thing and found this address and, after some time of back and forth with Tab, figured out what it is." Cathy waited expectantly, incapable of holding off her revelation any longer.

"Yes?"

"A phony lottery!" Cathy clapped her hands. "And I believe that is only the beginning."

"Not everyone gets this excited when they discover a phony lottery."

"It depends why you're looking at it. I feel like a kid who just got her driver's license!"

"I will definitely remember no caffeine for you tonight. Are you ready for some more news? Good news for you, although I don't know what I'll do without burned biscuits once a week?" Andi's eyes danced.

Cathy looked at her blankly, then a hint of understanding came to her face. "No. Really?"

"Al told me I'll have more room to work on the interior design as of next week and to tell you that you can move in anytime!"

# Chapter 28

*When we are told to be salt, we are being encouraged to bring interest and excitement to the world around us, like salt flavors food; and when we are told to be light, we are being told to expose the truth like the lamp in a room shows what is actually there and like a lighthouse that signals where the danger lies. In other words, class, don't be a low sodium Christian who prefers mood lighting.*

The day dawned crisp, night's chill having left a thin layer of frost on the fading grass, the tops of mailboxes, and car windshields. Not two hours into the light, however, the sun's brightness obliterated all thought of the coming winter with intensifying warmth.

Cathy had been up since 6:00 with nothing left to do but pray for blessing. She sat back in her rocking chair by the fire, again gazing around the kitchen with the same gratefulness she had felt when she'd stepped inside her new home the day she'd moved in. The space was exactly what it should be and it suited her perfectly. Sure, she'd had to step around a stray power tool here and there, and more than once in the middle of the night tripped over two by fours stacked along the wall. She'd had to stay out of a couple of rooms until Al's boys were finished and then a while longer until Andi was satisfied with the interior design, but it was a small price to pay for living in a house of which every pore exuded 'home' to her.

Al Kastellanos had lived up to his excellent reputation and then some. He had cheerfully met Andi's every request for subtle design changes and added details. Andi, despite her modesty, was truly a wonder, and Cathy relished the skillful design her cousin had spread around like sparkles on a sun-drenched lake. The fireplace's extra stone shelf at chair height as a perfect perch for her Bible, the cupboard nook in the kitchen made especially for Harry to lounge, and the spanking new Baby Grand piano were only a few of a multitude of additions that Andi had seen to it were included in the project. Though Andi had taken care of everything down to the last piece of furniture and picture, the thing that spoke best to her cousin's skill was that Cathy's new home exactly reflected its owner, only better.

She looked at her watch. The Kiddie Parade started at 1:30. The Logjam Days parade was at 2:00. There was plenty of time now for her to relax before she needed to be downtown. She got up and grabbed a brownie from a container on the counter. She took a bite, then set it down again. It was tasteless, a casualty of nerves. She'd been able to eat a couple spanakopitas for breakfast, but nothing else besides her El Nino Special Brew coffee, a free one-ounce sample Grammie Mae was trying out on a few select customers to determine the possibility of a pre-Christmas promo.

The weeks that transpired before this day had determined most of the parade's destiny. The remainder of its fate rested in the quirkiness of life; of things going right or wrong for little reasons that had a way of popping up like weeds in a garden. The citizens of Pine Point and the visitors pouring into town would be the final judges, and this year's parade would find a place in the town's history as a success, a failure, or worse, unremarkable.

Cathy had a feeling in the pit of her stomach reminiscent of what she felt before piano recitals as a young girl. She had nailed those performances each time save one. She still remembered the song. It was a simple one: *Sonatina In C, Op. 36 No. 1* by Clementi. She had known it well, could have played it half-asleep, but upon sitting at the piano in the church basement of long ago, she had missed a few first notes, then froze and all memory of the piece had frozen with her. She had stumbled through it, missing notes that her fingers should have played even without her concentration. She had risen from the bench upon completion of the performance, nodded her head in thanks for the pitying applause, had walked home in silence despite her mother walking alongside her and her soft words of encouragement, and had cried herself to sleep. That one time colored every recital she attended ever after. She had never forgotten the embarrassed sadness, but she had never returned to it either.

With that thought, Cathy felt herself relaxing. The determination to never again relive such an experience, if it was at all within her power, had served her well in life. She had never taken an assignment, an event, or effort of any kind for granted again. She had developed the habit of not leaving one stone unturned, not resting in the assurance of things going as planned. No last minute change or challenge had ever after been met with anything but determination and focus. There had been mistakes, of course, but she did not allow them steal her focus or purpose. Cathy lifted her coffee cup toward the Lord in a toast.

"To learning from mistakes. And to hoping for a good recital from my own students in the spring."

Harry stretched his front paws out of his cushioned nook. Cathy looked over at him and could have sworn he was smiling. The nook was already a favorite spot. He seemed to sense it had been made especially for him. His paws hit the floor. Then, stretching the rest of his brown and white splotched body, he got up and trotted over to her. The now deserted nook revealed a chew toy, a sock and a wooden spoon Cathy had been missing for a few days. He licked the top of her bare foot as she patted his head.

While she had learned to keep her cool under pressure, her responses amid the minutia of daily life were another thing entirely. Cathy shuddered. If she allowed herself, she would be able to recall numerous times she had tripped up, said the wrong thing at the wrong time, misjudged, miscalculated, and miscued. While not often finding satisfaction in it, she again found a reason to be grateful that she blended into the scenery around her. Her faux pas were not much discussed by anyone beyond those whom they immediately affected. Unfortunately, today might be the exception.

The phone jolted Cathy from her thoughts. She reached for it just as she spied a red squirrel outside robbing her old bird feeder.

"Hello?" Cathy opened the broom closet made to her specifications with a vertical rack designed especially for the BB gun.

"Mrs. Covington! This is Pete Cornell from down at the *Pine Point Press*. I was hoping to get ahold of you before you left home this morning. Somebody told me you don't have a cell phone. Heh, heh. Z'at true?"

Crack! Cathy got off a shot, missing the squirrel by a tail's hair. "That's right, Mr. Cornell. How can I help you?"

There was a pause on the other end of the line. "We've got a bad connection maybe. Did you hear something like a crackle?"

"I think our line is fine."

"Maybe firecrackers?"

"It could be that someone in the neighborhood is beginning their celebration of Logjam Days early." Cathy looked out over her acreage of trees and gardens. She sipped her coffee, then picked up the gun again as another red squirrel scrambled toward the feeder.

"Anyways," Pete continued, "we'd like to get a picture of you down at the parade source."

"You mean the high school parking lot?"

"Right."

"When would you like to do that?" Cathy sighted the varmint.

"Ohhh. How's about five minutes ago? Heh, heh."

Pete had been doing a piece on the Lumberjack Days Parade time out of mind. Parade committee chairs were typically harried and eager to please. There had been one, Hank Robertson, who'd been slightly gruff, even surly, but when it was all over, Hank's wife had taken him down to Alabama for a long vacation and he'd come back a new man.

Another shot rang over the phone line, and he crossed off the word 'sweet' from under 'ideas' for his column's description of this year's parade committee chair. Come to think of it, he might be safer throwing 'cute little widow' out the window, too.

Pete's shallow breath came over the phone. "Mrs. Covington?"

Cathy threw open the screen door to prevent any further excited scratches from Harry. "I'll meet you in the school parking lot in thirty minutes."

"We'll see you there," Pete said, quickly hanging up.

Cathy thought he suddenly sounded a little winded or something. She shook her head. She'd heard that one of *Pine Point Press*'s reporters had lived in Minneapolis at one time and never gotten over it, but one could never be certain what prompted the actions of people. Maybe he'd had a turbulent childhood or, perhaps, just too much coffee. She looked at her watch and sighed. There would be no time to relax after all.

Lawn chairs and blankets lined the parade route, having been set out the night before to claim a spot for their owners. There was a line wrapped around the block outside the Corn Hut, waiting for a table where waffles were sold for a quarter each as a Logjam Days special. Caramel Cappuccinos for a buck were flying out of the Java Hut. Harriet Harper's Hair Haven had opened at six a.m. to accommodate customers. A sign in the window said 'Get a Fresh Do for the Day's Doin's.' Dick's No Nonsense Cuts was closed. Grammie Mae's Confectionery was stocked with penny candy, and cars were backed up for three miles on the highway into town.

The floats, politicians, and bands weren't due to arrive for another five hours. However, the Boy Scouts had come this morning to pick up litter from the parking lot as a troop project. Lindsey Mayberg and Carl Stein were setting up some tables for the refreshment table, a last minute addition Mrs. Kipton had suggested following the Collins wedding.

Since what everyone in the church was now referring to as 'the Collins wedding incident,' Mrs. Kipton had broken into a smile nearly every day and people had begun calling her not even by her first name, Delores, but her newly preferred derivation, Deedee.

Lindsey had loved the idea of refreshments and volunteered to set up some tables. Carl Stein had quickly volunteered to help her. Deedee Kipton had contacted Morten's Catering for a variety of sandwiches and chips, and Lindsey had tripled her bottled water purchase.

Cathy looked around. It didn't appear to her that anyone from the *Pine Point Press* was anywhere in sight. She grabbed a box of handouts listing the order in which the parade entries would line up and wandered over to Lindsey and Carl.

"Hi." Lindsey looked up from locking the legs of a long table into place.

Carl waved as he went with a Boy Scout to get another table from the back of his truck.

Cathy grabbed the opposite end of the table and the two women set it upright.

"I know we said a refreshment table thinking of mid-day snacks," Lindsey explained as they walked to Carl's truck, "but Carl and I were thinking it would be nice to have donuts and coffee for anyone who comes early."

She slid a large box of bakery donuts from the back of the truck and Cathy lifted out a 100-cup coffee maker. Another Boy Scout pulled out a cardboard box filled with a canister of ground coffee, Styrofoam cups, plates, and napkins.

Carl, having lugged over and set up a third table and a generator, went back to his truck one more time. He came back with a sign that said 'Deedee's Snack Table' in flowing script.

"I made that last night," Lindsey explained. "I just thought wouldn't it be nice to put Deedee's name on it since it was her idea. She seems so quiet. I thought it would help bring her out a little."

Cathy gave her a one-armed hug. "Perfect. And your sign is terrific!"

"She was an art major," Carl said with admiration.

Cathy set down the box holding the parade entry order for participants to take as they picked up a snack. As they were arranging the donuts and paper products on the table, Deedee Kipton pulled up in her hatchback. She lifted a large bakery box from her trunk and headed over to the table.

"I thought maybe..." Her voice drifted into thin air. "Huh." She looked at the donuts and coffee maker on the table.

"Great minds think alike," laughed Cathy.

Mrs. Kipton stood stunned when she saw the sign Lindsey had made. She blushed, and Cathy took the large box from her arms to avoid her dropping it in her distraction.

"I almost feel famous." Mrs. Kipton put her hand to her chest.

Carl toted over a thermos jug of coffee he'd made before picking up Lindsey and they all helped themselves.

"This smells like Grammie Mae's Signature Blend," noted Cathy as she inhaled.

"Is there any other kind?" Carl chuckled.

Cathy held up her cup. "To small town parades."

"To hard work," chimed in Deedee Kipton.

"To new friends," toasted Carl.

"To reasons to celebrate," added Lindsey.

They tapped their cups and the flash of a camera momentarily blinded them. Pete Cornell had gotten a great start to his parade report.

By noon, stanchions tagged with parade entry numbers had been set in place. Parade committee members trickled in, congregating by Deedee's Snack Table.

Ashley charged over with Adele in tow. Cathy had never seen her so harried in all her life. She jerked her head at Denny, who scrambled over to her as though adulthood had never come upon them and he, once again, was the younger brother doing his sister's bidding. She yanked Adele's hand his direction and he took it, stooping down to reassure Adele, who was beginning to cry.

Ashley groaned. "Kent was called in to work at the last minute. Can you believe it?" She briefly covered her eyes with a hand, then drew a breath. "Where is the Kiddie Parade line up? Our part starts in," she glanced at her watch, "twenty minutes, I've got kids runnin' all over the east end of the parking lot, dogs goin' doodoo any ol' where they please, and three skinned knees! Not to mention the Porta Potties are clear the heck on the other side of the lot. And that is no small matter where pre-schoolers are concerned, ya know what I mean?"

She took another breath.

"I told you so," Heck said helpfully.

Ashley gave him a look that would have seared the skin off anyone's bones.

"The school is unlocked, Ashley. I got permission last week for them to use the facilities inside."

"Oh, right. I forgot. I tell you, I'm a ball of nerves, Mrs. Covington, ya know what I mean?!"

"Tell your group they can use the school bathrooms. They'll be relieved to hear it," Cathy grinned at her pun. "You'll line up right at your stanchion," Cathy directed. "Sharon and Tess, why don't you go on over and start lining kids up now."

Ashley's friends grabbed a donut and coffee to go and headed across the parking lot.

"They shoulda been there from the start," Ashley whispered to Cathy, glaring at her friends.

Cathy gave Ashley's back a friendly scratching and handed her a tissue just in case things got worse. "I'm glad we have you. I don't think they meant to desert you; I think they just got a bit distracted with socializing."

"Socializing, my eye. Does this look like the time to socialize?" Ashley was clearly not in a forgiving mood at the moment.

Ashley had been persuaded to join the parade committee by a subtle guilt-inducing expression that Cathy had purposely allowed to cross her face. By now, Cathy guessed, Ashley was becoming capable of a guilt-inducing look or two of her own. Ah, motherhood. The parade committee chairwoman looked around.

"Where's Tawny Newquist? She agreed to be the first aide responder, didn't she?" Cathy searched for the high school girl who had just completed her Red Cross training.

"She's late." Ashley sounded as though everything that could go wrong was on its way to doing so.

"There she is!" Deedee Kipton nearly shouted.

Cathy swallowed. Conversation came to a halt as people jerked their heads toward the sound. Mrs. Kipton had raised her voice. In the silence, people looked around as though they expected a point six tremor in Minnesota at any minute. Between the parade committee and the Collins' wedding, there were sure to be changes in the Kipton household. Cathy didn't know whether to laugh or cry, and found herself, for the first time in her life, wishing Mr. Kipton well.

"I'll get her!" Ashley ran to Tawny's car as though children were lying maimed in the street rather than crying over skinned knees in a school parking lot.

"Denny, go see what you can do about the dog stuff." Cathy pointed.

"Ashley told the neighbor's little boy he'd get paid to be the Kiddie Parade clean-up crew."

"And?"

Denny shrugged his shoulders and, still holding Adele's hand, went to find a plastic bag.

Heads turned as Lisa and the Motocross Mamas roared into the parking lot. They assembled by stanchion number one, turned off their engines, and walked over to the Deedee's Snack Table which, by this time, had become the unofficial parade headquarters and meeting place.

Lisa looked at the gathering activity and fist bumped Cathy.

Cathy looked across the parking lot as exhaust from six buses filled the air. The results of her telephone calls, notes and patient follow-up had arrived. She nodded toward them and said, "Heck, the bands."

He stopped chewing a bite of donut and stared. Then he stared at Cathy.

"I made a few calls and called in a few favors," she explained quietly.

"Hot dang!" A donut crumb flew from his full mouth.

"Heck." Cathy put her hand on his shoulder. "A favor from you if I might. 'Dang' is 'damn' with its face washed. There will be no damning by anyone today unless it's from the Almighty, Himself."

"Yes, Ma'am." The clear memory of what it was like to be thirteen and sitting in Mrs. Covington's Sunday school class appeared to hit him full in the face.

"Secondly, there are a few very small schools that will be participating, and we will do everything, and I mean everything in our power to make them feel like they deserve to be in the Rose Bowl Parade."

"Yes, Ma'am."

"Thirdly, we have a loosely structured neighborhood group that will march to *When the Saints Go Marching In.* They have a variety of instrumentation and production and I expect they will be treated with the utmost respect and kindness regardless of what you or anyone else expects a band to look like."

"Yes, Ma'am."

"That is all."

Heck swallowed his donut and started over to the bands. He stopped, turned back, and planted a wet kiss on Cathy's cheek. Then he walked off without a word.

Lisa laughed. "It does my heart good to see him speechless."

"It won't last," said Cathy under her breath, discretely wiping her cheek with a hanky. Cathy looked at her watch and, grabbing a cordless microphone, called the parking lot to attention. She looked out over the children lined up for the Kiddie Parade with their wagons and trikes and bikes. Tenderness crossed her face as she looked at their moms and dads; some holding a little hand, some with a child perched on their knee, a few chasing their too exuberant child. Her gaze moved to a perennial favorite: the early Pine Point cabin float accompanied by members of the town historical society dressed in pioneer garb. She scanned over the Motocross Mammas sipping coffee and polishing their machines, to the clowns, to a few politicians with their teams ready to hand out pamphlets. She admired the bands; musicians from a few small schools for which this might be their first and only parade and others for whom marching was very familiar. She smiled at the troops of Boy Scouts and Girl Scouts and appreciatively viewed the other variety of colorful and delightful floats, some with motorized moving figures and others with beautiful floral designs.

"We are heart glad you are all here today and we thank you sincerely for helping the town of Pine Point celebrate its inception. It's a day, as you know, we celebrate not only our community, but remember all of the people who have lived here over the years from the first blacksmith and inhabitants of small cabins to the lovely downtown we have today and our population living in comfortable homes. No town exists by the efforts of its current members alone, but also by the work and sacrifice of those who have lived there before them. No town lasts whose members expect to receive a hand out rather than to work hard and be good neighbors. More than that, no town exists without the permission of God under whose provision we live and under whose allowances we have our freedom. Please bow your heads while I ask His blessing on our parade today."

Having prayed and having gotten somewhat composed, Ashley and the Kiddie Parade started off down the block.

Cathy walked over toward the football field to take a minute's break before the regular parade started. As she sat in the quiet, breathing in the musky autumn air, she felt someone approach behind her.

Andi sat down next to her. "Nice prayer."

"You were here then?"

"Hanging out with a band director from a charter school," Andi chuckled, "who, by the way, stuck up for you."

"Hmm?"

"The mother of a Kiddie Parade entry – the one with the preponderance of feathers – muttered something about your not being allowed to pray. The band director told her last time he checked it was still a free country and ever so politely but firmly reminded her that she wasn't the one calling the shots today."

"Brav-o."

"Hey, great pep talk. You always have loved a good speech."

Cathy nodded and shrugged.

"The vendor on the corner sent this over for you. He's crazy about the explosive business this parade is generating for his cart." Andi handed her a boxed barbecue beef sandwich and some chips.

"Nice of him." Cathy placed the boxed lunch on the ground beside her. Her appetite was still missing.

"And I brought you something." Andi handed Cathy a larger box.

Cathy hefted it onto her lap and opened it. It was a flat river rock with the words 'Pine Point Club' inscribed in childish scrawl.

Cathy recalled when she had scratched the letters on it with a pocketknife for a club she and Andi had formed down by the river. They had placed the stone on a rickety shelf at the entry of a teepee-like structure where they had held secret meetings throughout their childhood years. The meetings had evolved from secret codes and imaginary missions to secret crushes and study sessions. Each time they, or any of their friends, entered a club meeting, they would rub the rock for good luck. Each time Cathy went to the teepee, she would trace over the initial scratching with the tip of a pocket knife until the words were permanently etched in the stone.

She looked at her cousin, her eyes misting. "You kept this?"

"All these years." Andi nodded. "I thought you could use it as a door stop or put it in one of your gardens."

Cathy rested her head on Andi's shoulder and Andi rested her head on Cathy's and, before their hearts and thoughts drifted too many million miles and years away from the football field, Andi added, "Or throw it at Heck."

They both laughed.

Finally, Cathy straightened and uttered two words. "Show time."

Andi reached over and took the box. "Here. I'll take this to your house. I've got a key. You've got stuff to do."

Cathy handed her the boxed lunch, and Andi took it with a nod.

The parade broke attendance records. Those in attendance were not only fully satisfied and entertained, but would talk about its delights for weeks afterward.

At one point, Cathy thought she saw an older, chubbier version of Hap Skalinski, but as she hurried in his direction, she was accosted by two members of the visitors' bureau of a neighboring city, and she lost sight of him after that.

Ashley's neighbor boy had showed up a few minutes into the Kiddie parade and relieved a grateful Denny from his doggie doo duties.

Pete Cornell took enough pictures to fill a book and, with the notes he scribbled throughout the day, was confident that his two-page spread on the parade would be a winner.

The bands were, in Cathy's assessment, spectacular, and she noted Heck received numerous compliments from those who knew he was always in charge of the bands. She was not surprised to witness him responding with false modesty over how he had outdone himself this year. He was in his glory.

She especially got a kick out of watching the motley group of her now-grown neighborhood kids. Having acquiesced to Mrs. Serling's demands to walk along the side of the group with a fire extinguisher, the Serling girls had, indeed, used flaming batons and had obviously polished their skills to a breathtaking degree. Mrs. Serling had tired halfway through the parade route and collared a sympathetic parade watcher to take her place. The group's rendition of *When the Saints Go Marching In* was actually not half bad jazz. This, supplemented with a few other jazz tunes, had those along the parade route tapping their toes, clapping along, and some few of the uninhibited, dancing. It was apparent that the old neighborhood was having the time of their lives reconnecting and putting on a show.

By the time the gleaming red fire engine brought up the rear of the parade, people were in a high celebratory mood the likes of which would last long after the final fireworks had drifted onto the river and the Corn Hut had closed its doors for the night.

Cathy pulled up in her driveway as dusk blanketed the landscape in silhouette and the temperature began its journey toward frost. As she approached the house, she heard Katie's musical laughter and another voice. The front door opened easily, revealing Katie seated on the living room couch petting Harry. Sitting rather closely next to her was John Blakely.

"Mom!" Katie jumped up as Cathy walked in. "I didn't expect you for another couple of hours. I thought you'd be wrapping up the parade details."

"Consider them wrapped," Cathy said slowly, giving Katie an inquiring look.

"I guess the time got away from us." Katie looked back at her mother with pure innocence.

Her daughter had picked up that little mannerism perfectly. Touché.

John rose from the couch. "I had heard about your building project over here. Katie asked if I wanted to see what had become of my childhood home."

Cathy nodded her head. What in the world were these two doing here? Alone? How long had they been here and how long before that had they been, for lack of a better word, visiting? Surely she was imagining things. She could not for the life of her think of one thing to say.

"Auntie Andi was here when we came. She left the house unlocked for us." Katie smiled.

Cathy nodded again. He was as handsome as she recalled and then some.

"It's great," John offered, "I would've liked a little woods like that when I was a kid."

Katie laughed. "I loved that hand stand you did as a salute to memories."

John laughed with her. "For old time's sake." He leaned over slightly to brush a strand of hair from Katie's cheek. "The only thing that's missing is your freckles."

Cathy scratched her temple with one finger. John looked up at Cathy again.

"And your new house," he continued, gesturing. "It's gorgeous. Small, but gorgeous." He glanced at Katie.

"I'm glad you like it, John. By the way, any news from the Mayo Clinic or the university?"

The boy was getting out of hand and she had to change the direction of their private little tête-à-tête before they fell off the proverbial cliff.

"Both offer attractive possibilities." He snuck another glimpse in Katie's direction.

"Things seem to be moving breathtakingly fast." Cathy looked at Katie.

"Astoundingly breathtakingly," agreed Katie looking back at her mother.

A puzzled expression crossed John's face.

"Fast," Katie added, dusting an invisible speck from her sleeve.

Cathy wondered where Christy was just now, how soon the fireworks would start, and how impressive they would be. A few choice phrases Christy had uttered about Johnny Blakely when she broke up with him those years ago came to Cathy's mind. Seeing the sister and the ex-boyfriend in front of her was like witnessing Mentos being tossed into a Coke bottle.

"Would either of you like some tea?" Cathy raised her eyes to the ceiling. "I was just going to make myself some." Cathy headed toward the kitchen. Harry did not follow. He was staying where the action was.

"Actually, Mrs. Covington, I was just going to ask Katie if she'd like to go to a late supper. We could trek on over to St. Paul," he turned to Katie. "I've heard of a great restaurant that's anchoring a downtown development called the Riverside Rambles. If memory serves, it's called Kate's Place and has an amazing reputation."

Cathy poked her head back into the living room and raised her eyebrows at Katie.

"Its mandarin orange cheesecake was written up in the food section of an edition of the newspaper I picked up at the airport," John continued encouragingly as he detected hesitancy in Katie's demeanor.

Oh no. He even remembered her family's propensity for cheesecake.

"If we can't get in there, maybe we can go to Frost's or across the river to that Asian fusion place or even to Jack's in Northeast."

"Oh, I think they'll find you a table. Katie knows people." Cathy immediately regretted speaking.

"Really?" John was clearly interested.

Katie gave her mother a cross-eyed look John didn't see.

"I'll call ahead and ask them to keep something open." Katie's voice held all the innocence she could muster. She pulled out her cell phone as John followed her out, placing his hand on the small of her back, and Cathy crossed her arms, her hand over her mouth.

# Chapter 29

*When we're told to not let the sun go down on our wrath, it doesn't mean we're not supposed to get angry. It just means we need to iron out the wrinkle either with that person or without them, and not carry it in our hearts. Yes, Kaily, that includes the cheer leading squad.*

Cathy slept in until seven, having tossed and turned until the wee hours. This, without the benefit of a double cappuccino. She had breakfasted on the barbecue beef sandwich and chips the vendor had provided for her the day before, then leaned against the counter and stared into space, rhythmically tapping her finger on the soapstone.

She picked up the phone on its first ring. "Hello?"

"Oh, hello Mayor." Her voice was shaded with disappointment.

"No, no. I was expecting someone else, but of course I'm pleased to hear from you. Thank you. A lot of people worked hard to make it happen and they're the ones who deserve a lot of the credit. No, no. I'm just one of a team, Mayor."

Cathy shut her eyes and squeezed them tight. "While I thank you for the compliment, the answer is no. Yes, unequivocally."

"No. I mean it is an unequivocal *no*," Cathy leaned her elbow on the counter and rested her head in her hand. "There are plenty of people in Pine Point who are perfectly capable."

"Oh no, no, no. I don't think a citywide vote will be necessary." Cathy's heart beat frantically.

"Contrary to what Heck has told you, we had a ninety percent re-up rate for next year's committee. They'll find a way to elect a chair from within, I'm sure."

"Yes, thank you again." Cathy hastily hung up the phone, sat down in a chair, rested her forearms on her knees, and looked at the floor. She had heard that parade committee chairs usually took time off for recuperation after it was over, but an inner apprehension told her that there would be no such time for her.

A quick knock sounded at the door. Before she could raise her head, Andi flew in. She carried two steaming cups of coffee from the Java Hut, one of which she set down in front of Cathy. "Peace offering."

"Did it occur to you that your leaving the house open for those two might lead to something that could set off a conflagration at the Thanksgiving table?" Cathy jumped in without preamble.

"Hence," Andi motioned to the four-dollar cup of coffee, "the peace offering."

Cathy gave Andi an accusing look.

Andi shrugged. "What was I supposed to do? You weren't here. You didn't see the absolute yearning in Johnny's eyes. I couldn't leave Philip's best friend high and dry."

Cathy sighed and took a gulp of her hot coffee without flinching.

"Cathy, it was only a matter of time. That poor boy fell hard for Christy way back when, and she as much as kicked him to the curb. The minute he saw Katie, he was a lost cause; the two sisters are so much alike."

"They might have some similarities, but they have just as many differences, and this is sure to be one more. A big one."

The two women looked toward the screen door as Christy pushed it open, her twins toddling behind her. "A big what?"

"A big parade!" exclaimed Andi.

"Wasn't it great?" Christy laughed. Apparently ready for an unhurried visit, she began chatting about the parade, the old friends she had run into, and the minutiae of the day before. Christy opened a cupboard door, pulled down a box of Cheerios, and poured some into a cup, handing it to the twins. Harry trotted over and began nuzzling them for his share.

Cathy gulped her hot coffee until the cup was half empty.

Andi stretched, as though she had been sitting in Cathy's kitchen all morning. "I suppose I'd better get moving."

She sounded more carefree than she had a right to. Cathy glared at her. "Oh no you don't."

Christy's eyes narrowed. "What?"

Cathy and Andi pressed their lips together simultaneously and Harry ran to the door.

Katie walked in as though flowers were in full bloom rather than dropping their petals in preparation for the coming winter. She carefully put a lemon curd cheesecake on the counter.

"Oh good, Katie, you're here." Christy gave Katie a hug. "These two are up to something."

"And that would shock me why?" Katie cut thin slices of the cake and placed them on four plates.

Andi looked at her watch. It was 8:30 and cheesecake was being served. Christy and Katie were their mother's daughters.

"Mom? Where's the coffee maker?" Christy rummaged around in the cupboards.

"Joe and his crew bought me a new one for a house-warming present." Cathy got up from her chair to pull a pink gingham patterned coffeepot out of the cupboard. She filled it with water, measured coffee into the metal filter, and set it on the stove.

"I didn't know they..." said Andi, her voice trailing off helplessly.

"...Who knew? I have enough trouble finding pink cups." At least there was one happy thing to brighten this particular morning.

Andi massaged her temples. Pink was the last thing she needed just now.

"So where were you last night?" Christy turned to Katie. "Everyone from the old neighborhood got together at Tom and Candy's place for an after parade party. It was a blast, but we missed you!"

"Everyone?" asked Cathy.

Christy slowly turned toward her mother with a look that told Cathy she couldn't believe that her own mother had waded into those waters.

"Some people are better left uninvited." A stranger might have regarded Christy's voice as dispassionate. The undercurrent of that tone, though, reminded Cathy of the exact day and time when she had first learned that Johnny Blakely was no longer in the good graces of her teenaged daughter and reminded them all that he was one of the few she had not forgiven.

Christy had never quite managed to learn what the phrase 'even-tempered' meant, at least not with those to whom she was close. She was as effusive in her anger as she was in her love. You always knew where you stood with Christy; knew, with few exceptions, she would eventually forgive you; and knew that until then she would express with breathtaking clarity what she thought of you.

Katie got up and poured herself a cup of the coffee that was still percolating. It was the color of chicken bouillon. "So what's this about Mom and Auntie Andi being up to something?"

Cathy and Andi agreed with one look that everyone might as well get it over with.

"Hey, boys! Want to go play downstairs?!" Andi excitedly asked the twins.

"I'm right behind you." Cathy grabbed her and Andi's coffee cups and balanced two plates of cheesecake on her arms as they walked the twins downstairs.

It took about two minutes for the explosion to detonate. Cathy stared thoughtfully at the wall across from the couch on which she sat sipping her coffee. Andi politely pretended to sip out of a toy cup one of the twins offered her and flinched only every once in a while as Christy's voice rose and fell in the room above them. Harry hurried down the stairs to the safety of his master. Twenty minutes passed. The toy cups were devoured by dinosaurs. Another ten minutes ticked by. The twins fell asleep in the middle of the floor. Thirty minutes later, the back door slammed and there was silence.

Cathy ventured up the stairs and looked around.

"All clear!" Cathy called down the stairs as Andi came up, carrying a twin in each arm, Harry following behind them.

Two plates of cheesecake lay untouched on the table. Cathy looked out the window.

"Ah. There they are." She pointed. "They're walking the grounds."

"It's a good sign," offered Andi hopefully as the little boys blinked sleepily and slid off her lap.

"Yes. I believe national leaders sometimes do that at a summit," commented Cathy softly, watching her daughters, "and we all know the effectiveness of those things."

After Christy had buckled the twins in their car seats and put the remainder of the cheesecake Katie had brought on the floor of the car, the two sisters nodded politely to each other. They got into their cars and peeled out of the driveway. Cathy and Andi stood in the doorway, looking thoughtfully after them. They looked at each other, both heaving a long sigh, and quietly closed the door.

"You think it'll iron out?" asked Andi.

"A question you might've asked when you left the house unlocked last night." Cathy shook her head. "Oh, well."

"I'm beginning to understand exactly what you mean."

# Chapter 30

*The men on the road to Emmaus didn't recognize Jesus for the same reason the rest of us don't recognize Him or, for that matter, truth or opportunity when it comes our way: we're not expecting it.*

"It seems like his name should be in one of these." Cathy slurped Maple Mania coffee ground fresh at Grammie Mae's Confectionery.

Though Cathy had called every Skalinski in the phone book several weeks before, since catching a glimpse of Hap Skalinski at the parade she had decided to renew her efforts with additional resources. Neighboring cities' phone directories she had borrowed from the Java Hut and the bank were spread on the table in front of her, all turned to S.

"Are you certain it was him?" Andi bit into a Bavarian Cream-filled Long John.

"For the fourth time," Cathy looked over her reading glasses, "I *think* I saw him. He was walking down the street eating a corn dog." She licked a finger and turned the page. She moved her index finger down a few columns, then looked up and stared in front of her. "I think."

"I'm weakly reminding myself your Middle School Sunday school students are important enough for this malarkey." Andi peered across the table at the few names Cathy had copied down.

"Former. Former Middle School Sunday school students. They'd be much easier to find if they were still teenagers. It's the adults that cause most of the trouble in life. I told the Lord I'd do my best to work through the list," Cathy sipped her coffee, "and leave the rest up to the Him."

"The Lord isn't as much of a pest as you are."

"Sometimes He is and sometimes He isn't. He gets to do whatever He jolly well pleases."

"It *is* His property," Andi murmured.

Cathy grabbed the last phone book from a pile on the chair beside her and turned to the S's. "If Hap was at the parade, then he probably lives within fifty miles of here."

Andi dropped the rest of her pastry under the table, where Harry swallowed it in one gulp. She got up, refilled her coffee with the pink gingham coffee pot from the stove, flinching only slightly at the sight of it, and topped off Cathy's.

"Maybe. You can't tell for certain. Some people make it an annual affair no matter where they live. Or maybe he lives in another state and was visiting family."

"His family moved to Ohio after he graduated from high school," Cathy mumbled as she copied down the numbers of names spelled even remotely like Skalinski sounded. After a few minutes, she dropped the pen on the table and let out a long breath. Cathy held up a short list of names, addresses and phone numbers from varying cities and towns. "Feel like going for a drive?"

At her words, Harry bounded to the door, jumping up and down and barking.

"I didn't mean that kind of a drive," Cathy said under her breath. "Harry!" she ordered.

263

He continued to bark.

"I hate being the bad guy," Andi frowned. "He gets to ride along when I'm not with you. If you want to take him along, be my guest."

Cathy looked doubtful. "Don't let him fool you. He stays here as much as he comes with me. I don't take him to Minneapolis at all anymore; he doesn't do well there."

"Who does?"

"It might be a long ride." Cathy glanced at the list.

Harry began jumping up and hitting the screen door with his paws.

"All right, but you'd better…" She opened the door and Harry bounded to the Jeep. "…behave."

"One of those is a state park, isn't it?" Andi stepped into the powder room and rummaged through the medicine cabinet.

"We don't need insect repellent anymore. It's getting too cool," Cathy called to her.

"Good thing you told me. Having lived here for over half a century, I wouldn't have known." Andi finally grabbed some wet wipes and a bottle of aspirin.

Cathy went to her coat closet and grabbed a hoodie.

"Gloves!" Andi called to her.

"Got 'em." Cathy fished around and pulled four out of a large crock on the floor of the closet. She grabbed Harry's leash from beside the back door. "Just in case," she said as Andi nodded and picked up both their coffee cups to take with them.

Andi stretched as Cathy roared down the highway. They had made two stops and talked with two people whose names were somewhere in the range of Skalinski, but neither of them had heard of Hap.

"You realize, since you got this Jeep, that you've slowly begun to become a road hazard, don't you?"

A hint of a smile crossed Cathy's face. "I feel like nothing can hurt me; not like when I was driving my little car. It just feels so... I don't know."

"Powerful?"

"A Jeep powerful? Really? Maybe."

"Fast?"

Cathy gunned it and they flew past a full-size sedan.

"Fun?"

"Yep."

Andi nodded her head in understanding. "How goes the Blakely boyfriend ex-boyfriend situation? That was one quick move he made back to town."

"And you're the one who accuses me of not being subtle?"

"Subtlety has its place, but that place is not between us."

Cathy ran her fingers through her hair and heaved a sigh.

"Both hands on the wheel!"

"Huh. Didn't see that." Cathy recovered from a swerve to avoid a raccoon whose demise had apparently been sure and swift the day before.

"They said they'd take him as soon as he could get here. He had a good relationship with the department head out east and was able to do things on his time table."

"They held out an open-ended offer for him there, I hope?"

"Oh, yes. No hospital, including highly-regarded ones, likes to lose a good surgeon."

"And?"

"I believe Katie and John have been spending copious amounts of time together." Andi started to say something, but Cathy continued. "Christy has begun speaking in one word sentences."

"Yikes," Andi whispered, biting her lip.

"And instead of running to the door and jumping up on either one of my daughters when they visit, Harry has been running out of the house the minute one of them opens the door."

"Oh well."

"Exactly."

"By the way," Andi picked up the map, "you realize you missed our exit back there, don't you?"

"I thought the number looked vaguely familiar. You shouldn't give me directions so far ahead of time. I'm not a savant."

After a moment, Andi replied, "You should be proud of me for resisting the comment that's even now resting on the tip of my tongue."

"Congratulations."

They drove another ten miles.

"Ha! How about that? There's a state park ahead. Wasn't one of the Skalinskis a park ranger?"

Andi picked up the list on the seat between them. "Mm hm. This is the park all right. We might as well go exploring."

They pulled into the visitor's center and were told that Ranger Skalinski was out assessing some damage from an earlier storm.

"Do you mind if I get his first name?" Cathy raised her brows.

The worker shook her head. "Honestly, Ma'am. It says H. N. Skalinski on his tag, but we all just call him Ski."

"Thank you anyway, Ms.?"

"Everyone calls me Digger." Upon the sight of both women looking at the floor, she added, "Or Jamie, if you prefer".

After getting a general direction and a park map from Jamie, they drove several miles further into the forest and parked in a small lot off the side of the road.

Andi unzipped the top of her cap, shook several aspirin into it, zipped it up again and put it on her head. Cathy snapped her key ring onto her belt loop, shoved the map into the pocket of her hoodie and attached two water bottles to Harry's collar.

"Good ol' boy," she scratched his neck. "I'm glad I brought you after all."

Andi handed Cathy some thin gloves as she pulled some on over her own hands. "I love how the blue and black almost match."

Cathy glanced her direction with a crooked smile. "Perhaps I was a bit distracted when I grabbed them out of the *very dark* closet, Miss Runway."

Cathy looked down at the pair she had pulled on. One was teal with a black fur cuff. The other was pink and white striped.

"Ready?"

"If we walk two miles, I'll be ready to turn around and come back to the car," Cathy cautioned.

"Right. A five mile limit."

"The absence of persuasion in your voice is not reassuring," called Cathy as she followed Andi's quick pace into the woods.

Harry was in his glory. He ran ahead of them, sniffed to his heart's delight, swept over the area, and ran back again in a kind of Springer Spaniel dance.

It was around two hours later that the women came to a log by the edge of a lake.

Andi walked along the edge of the water and studied the map Cathy had handed to her a mile or so back. Cathy plopped onto the log, then, finding it not restful enough, sprawled into the wooded beach.

Andi turned to look at her. "What in the world are you doing?"

"Resting," mumbled Cathy, getting some dirt in her mouth for the effort.

"That can't be comfortable."

"And hiking six miles is?"

"You know, I think the gal at the desk was off somehow. If Skalinski went to Black Bear Lake this would be it and I've seen no fresh boot tracks of any kind. Perhaps he gave one set of directions and then changed his mind and ended up on another trail."

"Black Bear Lake?" Cathy raised her head. "Named for the shape of the lake I hope?"

Andi looked at the lake on the map and shook her head.

Harry, who had been sniffing up and down the water's edge began barking maniacally.

Cathy laid her head back down. "I'm too tired to fight. Tell the bear to take me first. It will give you time to run."

"Oh, for pete's sake, Cath, it's just some people. It looks like a group of, hmm, early thirties is my guess. Ah. I believe we'll have visitors. You might want to comb the twigs out of your hair."

Cathy grunted as she pushed herself to her feet and began to pull a few loose twigs and leaves from her hair.

Six adults in three canoes paddled over to them.

"Hello," Cathy greeted them as a few of the group pulled their canoes onto the shore. There were three men, one of them a bit chubby, two others health club fit, and an equal number of women. The chubby man knelt on the beach, working to repair a strap from his backpack. One of the members stayed in her canoe.

"Hel..." one of them began, his voice dropping away when he caught sight of Andi.

They all stared at Andi, wordless, until one of the women stepped toward the cousins. A brown baseball cap covered her short blond hair, her nails were caked with dirt, and it appeared that her enjoyment of the trip had been left behind somewhere back two lakes or so.

"We've been portaging around the area. Sidney sprained her ankle this morning." She gestured to the gal in the canoe. "So we thought it was time to head on back."

"Are these canoes yours?" Andi tugged a lock of hair behind her ear.

The man who had begun to greet them earlier shook his head. "They're park rentals."

"And how do you portage with an injury?" Cathy furrowed her brows.

"Not well," a few of them answered at once.

The chubby man looked up suddenly, then shook his head as if to clear it and went back to his task.

"We could take a canoe off your hands," Andi offered.

Cathy gaped at her cousin.

"If we find Hap, he can carry it back for us," Andi reasoned quietly.

"And if we don't? And if he's not Hap?" Cathy whispered urgently.

However, four of the group were already gladly hefting only two remaining canoes on their shoulders while the other member let the woman with the sprained ankle lean on her as she hobbled down the trail. It was apparent that they were anxious to seize Andi's offer before she could retract it.

Cathy looked down.

"You left one of your bags!" she called after them.

"Keep it!" someone called back.

Andi picked it up and emptied its contents onto the beach.

"Ha! A granola bar!" Cathy delightedly ripped off the wrapper. "Mm. I didn't realize how hungry I was. Wanna bite?" She offered the bar to Andi with her mouth full.

Harry was diving into the pile where he grabbed a package of beef jerky and, looking guiltily over his shoulder, trotted a few yards away.

"I was thinking we could paddle around faster than we can walk. Maybe find Skalinski along the perimeter of the lake."

Cathy sat on the log and started in on a second granola bar.

"We can make faster headway in the water," Andi persisted.

Cathy swatted a rogue mosquito and rummaged through the contents scattered before her.

"Or we could take a lunch break." Andi sighed, sat beside her cousin, and picked up a baggie of trail mix.

"Are those dried apricots?" Cathy pointed. Andi held the baggie out and Cathy picked two out of the mix. "Mmm. It's been too long."

Andi rolled her eyes.

Harry trotted over to them, his tongue hanging out and his breath smelling strongly of teriyaki beef jerky. Cathy untied the water bottles from Harry's collar and handed one to Andi. They both drained them within a minute. Harry lapped water at the shore's edge.

"Okay then. Let's take a personal moment in the woods and we'll be off." Cathy went one way while Andi went the other.

The women dropped their shoes in the bottom of the canoe, rolled up their pant legs, and pushed it into the water, where they climbed in. Harry jumped in after them and shook the water from his fur, spattering them in the process. They soon paddled into deeper water.

"Reminds me of the old days and our adventures on Pine River." Cathy sighed.

"We jumped into a boat a bit more spryly then," Andi remarked.

"We did everything more spryly then."

"We're smarter now."

"No contest, although I think we didn't wade in water quite this cold when we were younger." Cathy shivered.

"Sure we did. Remember the Halloween when we were fourteen?"

"Oh, my. You're right. I wore my father's wool socks to bed and slept with a hot water bottle on my feet that night."

"We're less impulsive. Well, at least *I* am."

"And your not being impulsive is why we're in a canoe in the middle of Black Bear Lake? In November?"

Andi grabbed Harry's collar before he leaned too far out of the canoe, rocking it precariously while he looked at the fish. Andi laughed. "Oh, that's right. We celebrated All Saints Day at church Sunday. Let's remember who started this mission, shall we? I wouldn't have volunteered to take a canoe had we been at, say, a knitting class."

"Let's keep this conversation grounded in reality, shall we?"

"Okay, okay. My not being impulsive is why we're in a canoe in the middle of Black Bear Lake with a spastic dog playing chicken with the fish."

Cathy cleared her throat.

"In November," Andi added.

"I don't see this ending well." Cathy heaved a heavy sigh. "But a person can talk themselves out of everything if they spend too much time thinking about it."

"I absolutely agree. Which is why we'd better not discuss that dark cloud behind the trees over there."

"What?" Cathy looked in the direction of Andi's gaze.

"It's still a bit distant," Andi noted.

"Mm hm." How in the world would she be able to lift the canoe onto her shoulders and how long it would take them to carry it back in the rain? Then a worse scenario occurred to her. "What was the temperature going to end up at today?"

Andi splashed her paddle on the water, kicking a few droplets up at Cathy. "No worries. It's been a balmy fall. I think only down to the 40's today."

Harry began barking furiously and both women looked over just in time to see a bear wading into the water at the shore they had just left.

Cathy whispered, "How 'bout we paddle a little faster?"

There was no hope of keeping the canoe upright unless Harry calmed down, no hope of quieting Harry until the bear was out of his sight, and no hope of calming herself until she was out of sight of the bear.

"He's fishing." Andi shrugged. "He's not interested in us."

"Were her famous last words," Cathy held the paddle more tightly.

They were out of sight in a matter of semi-stressful minutes, and Harry calmed down enough to peer over the edge of the canoe at the fish again.

They made their way around a bend and caught sight of some movement in the woods.

"Hey there!" Cathy waved.

A man poked his head out of a profusion of resplendently red sumac lining the water's edge, made his way to the shore and waved. Then he turned and walked away.

The cousins looked at each other, then up at the sky as the first raindrop fell.

"The thing is, even if he wasn't Hap Skalinski he should've waited for us to get to shore and offered to carry our canoe." Andi warmed her hands on her cup.

"He's probably been slapped upside the head one too many times for being chivalrous."

Andi was sipping hot cocoa, wrapped in a velvet robe of deep purple. Cathy sat across from her, wrapped in a peach-colored chenille robe, sipping from her pink cup. Harry lay snoring in front of the fire. They had come straight to Andi's house from the state park in a driving November rain, jumped in hot showers and carted a late supper to the library/music room. Andi had insisted Cathy stay the night rather than driving back to her house, and Cathy hadn't argued.

"My shoulders are going to ache for weeks to come." Cathy bit into a roll stuffed high with roast beef and green peppers.

"At least the strain of hauling the canoe back kept us warmer than if we'd hiked back without it. I'm rather proud of you. It's obvious you're in no need of a knee replacement. Strong legs, girl!"

"Desperation gives a person strength they didn't know they had." Cathy looked gratefully at Andi. "Thanks for taking periodic breaks, though I'm not sure it helped all that much. I really have got to lose twenty pounds."

"If only I hadn't dropped the map in the water when I tried to keep Harry from jumping in," Andi mused, ignoring the fact that her cousin needed to lose more than the twenty she always claimed.

"He was a lost cause when he saw the rabbit on shore. Sorry about swamping."

"Mm."

"I don't think the rain bothered me as much, having already been soaked in the lake." Cathy sneezed.

"Bless you."

"If we hadn't gotten lost, we wouldn't have found that little homemade grotto."

"There's got to be an interesting story behind that."

"Or found that itty bitty lake," continued Cathy, "though I could've done without the snake."

"Agreed. I wonder where Hap Skalinski is." Andi brushed crumbs from her hands.

Cathy yawned. "The Lord only knows and it appears it's going to stay that way."

# Chapter 31

*When the Bible says the church is one body, it's saying we all have different things we're good at, and things work best when the one who's good at something does it. Your mother wants to lead worship singing, Emma? Perhaps she might learn to read music first. Ahem. Let's turn to Romans, class.*

A ndi pulled up behind the banana yellow Jeep outside of the county courthouse. She patted the hood of her car with a gloved hand as she stepped onto the curb. Cathy materialized beside her and looked at her watch.

"Okay, I know and I apologize with an excuse. I had a seven o'clock exercise class this morning, then needed to review some board minutes and that had to be done before I came here. The minutes didn't come in the mail until yesterday and, as we both know, there was that situation with the thing in that place yesterday which precluded any reading, leisurely or otherwise."

Cathy nodded, waiting for more.

"There's a meeting tonight at seven and who can tell if I'll even get home before then? We might just get buried in papers and unable to extricate ourselves before six."

"You must be thinking of working with someone else. I love working with papers and forms as much as I love a daily swim." Cathy eyed her cousin meaningfully.

The two women stared each other down until Andi said, "You win. For now."

They found their way to an office near the back of the building and asked about viewing some property records.

"Aughh!" echoed through the office to where the two women stood.

Cathy and Andi looked toward the back of the office area where a red-faced clerk was extricating his crushed fingers from a filing cabinet.

"Which ones?" The clerk behind the desk sounded bored.

Cathy pulled out a list.

The cousins found a table in a corner of the building, plunked down the records they'd been allowed to look at and settled in. After ten minutes, Cathy sighed loudly. Andi kicked her under the table as Cathy looked up in time to see Andi rub her neck and pick up another file.

Cathy was reading the same sentence over for the fourth time when a soft noise made her look up.

Andi was squinting at some papers.

"I wonder if he's restructured enough of these things to avoid the tax liabilities that would come with them," Andi whispered.

"And if I had an idea of what you just said, I'd have to slap myself silly."

Andi shook her head. "Never mind. I'll explain it to you later."

Two hours later, as Cathy yawned for the sixth time in a row, Andi whispered, "Do you want to call it a day?"

Giving her a grateful look, Cathy nodded. "A day, a year, an eternity." Cathy looked down at the file folders and papers spread out in front of her on the table. "We're nowhere near to getting a clear grasp of what property belongs to whom or who bought what with which account; not to mention anything else this guy is involved in."

Cathy's face was growing red. "I feel as though I'm looking at what Van Gough would have done had he worked in an office like this."

"Just let me ask them to make a few more copies, and I'll meet you outside."

Cathy gave her cousin a limp wave and started toward the door.

"Mrs. Covington?"

Cathy turned as a young woman walked quickly down the hall to catch up with her.

"You don't recognize me, do you?"

Cathy held up a finger.

"Give me a minute." She studied the girl's face. She finally shook her head.

"I'm Emma Knightley's cousin. I thought I recognized you when you walked in, and then when I heard your voice, I was sure it was you. I used to... "

"You visited Sunday school with Emma on a couple of occasions," Cathy interrupted, remembering, "Krista, isn't it?"

Krista seemed pleased. Cathy stuck out her hand and Krista shook it.

"So you're working here? Have you been here long?"

"My mom worked here. I started helping her out after school when I was in high school; filing, things like that. Eventually, they hired me."

"That's nice. You can take lunch breaks with your mom. She must like that."

Krista shook her head. "When she hit fifty, she retired. She's living in the Bahamas."

Cathy choked from an involuntary intake of breath, but managed to regain her composure. "The Bahamas. How nice."

"When I was younger, she always talked about moving someplace warmer. She finally took off."

"How nice." Cathy couldn't think of anything else to say even if it had meant winning a round trip to the Bahamas herself.

"Fifty's young, I know. But I'm happy for her."

"Indeed." They were about to part, when Cathy suddenly thought of something. "Krista?"

Krista turned back. "Yes?"

"You must like this, hmm? Forms, papers, records, that type of thing."

"Oh, I'd get lost in the stacks if I could." Krista smiled.

Cathy smiled back.

As they stood outside in the brisk fall sunshine, Cathy did a little victory dance.

"Okay, already." Andi surreptitiously looked around them. "When I left you, you were half asleep."

"I love Sunday school." Cathy looked at Andi. "I ran into a gal who visited my class several times. Krista Knightley. She, my dear, loves records. She loves old entries. She loves the smell of ink."

A smile slowly spread across Andi's face. "You found an investigative Sunday school student!"

"A Nancy Drew of records!" Cathy nodded.

"A spy of names and numbers!"

"You better watch yourself, or you'll start dancing with me and then we'll be in the newspaper. Technically, she was only a guest. Her mother who, by the way, is living in the Bahamas..."

"The Bahamas?"

"Retired at fifty."

"Fifty?"

The two women momentarily stared into space, imagining.

Cathy waved it off. "As I was saying, technically she wasn't my student. She was a guest. Her mother didn't care much for churchy things, as I recall; though Krista did seem to have more of a spiritual sensibility. Ah ha. Just a minute."

Cathy hurried back into the building. She returned to Andi five minutes later. "I had to invite her back to Sunday school."

"Of course you did."

"Anyway, she agreed to look up anything I throw her way. And she looked interested. She actually smiled." Cathy held up Krista's card.

"I love Sunday school," Andi said to no one in particular, as she slid into her Porsche and Cathy climbed into her Jeep.

As Andi pulled out, Cathy motioned her over. She idled her car next to Cathy's and rolled down the window.

"Do lunch at my house? I'll pick up Chinese." Cathy grinned and sighed. "I've always wanted to say that."

"Sure. I'll let Harry out when I get there."

"It won't take me long." Cathy revved her engine. You could take the energy out of the cousin, but the girl would always remain.

Andi rolled her eyes as she rolled up her window and drove off.

The two women sat in Cathy's spacious kitchen and dined out of little white cartons.

"I love these little handles." Cathy stifled a yawn.

"How are you holding up? This list of yours got out of hand the day we started." Andi broke open a fortune cookie. She folded the fortune into a crinkle snake and flicked it across the table at Cathy.

Cathy grabbed it and stuffed it into the bag with their used paper napkins. She got up to open the door for Harry, who was waiting to be let inside. Suddenly, she took a few quick steps to the broom closet and threw open the screen door. Three consecutive shots echoed through the fall air.

"Get it?"

"I got two leaves, one black walnut, and who knows what; probably a limp rhubarb stalk. But," Cathy peered through the window as she replaced the BB gun, "it appears he's run somewhere else for now." She plopped down on her chair. "I'll admit, I'm worn out, Andi. I think the effects of that parade will last long after the new year." She yawned loudly this time.

"You didn't set out to research a barbarous idiot of a second-rate property manager."

"Oh, my. Now look who's getting grumpy."

"Admittedly, I'm a little tired, myself." Andi wrapped her arms to grip either shoulder and crack her back. She stretched her legs under the table. "I warned you about this. Things just seem to pile up when you start a project."

Cathy held up her hand. "I went in with full knowledge," she agreed, "and, as it is, I haven't been able to pick up full speed with my piano students. I still have three who haven't started at all. Although, it's more their problem than mine."

"Fall sports," the two women said at the same time.

"How're the Coleman twins doing?"

"Same as last year. One week, one has practiced and one is dreadful. The next week, the other has practiced and his twin is the one seemingly unable to discriminate between bass and treble clef." Cathy sighed.

"You don't have to give lessons, you know."

Cathy looked up at her and wrinkled her eyebrows.

"You have money, remember?"

"Well so do you, and you're still a designing maniac."

"With a style sensibility unequaled on either side of the Mississippi." Andi smiled.

"Besides, who wants to live in the Bahamas?" Cathy shrugged.

Andi hesitated. Looking up and seeing Cathy's arched eyebrows, she replied, "Not me."

# Chapter 32

*God doesn't love you because you're good, but because He is. He extends His hand to pull us out of trouble and hell's reach, too; but it's up to us to grab it.*

Andi opened the door and poked her head into the kitchen. Cathy was sitting at the table, swirling her coffee in its cup from which it occasionally sloshed onto the table into a coffee-colored puddle. She wore a red speckled sweater thrown over a pink turtleneck, gray sweatpants, and her fuzzy pink slippers. Her supper dishes were still in the sink, unwashed. There had been no breakfast dishes. Harry was nowhere to be seen.

Andi slid into the chair opposite her cousin and shrugged out of her coat. "When did he disappear again?"

"Two nights ago." Cathy shook her head. Worry lined her face as she glanced up at Andi. "The temperature has been dipping pretty low lately. He usually does his business and comes right back in. Of course, he roams around farther with the larger property."

"And he's been loving it," Andi interjected.

"Loving it," Cathy nodded. "But that last night he didn't come when I called."

"Not that unusual."

Cathy gave a short laugh. "No. But he didn't come back at all. I was out half the night looking for him, calling his name."

"It could've been the lightning. That was quite a show we had."

"Snow mixed with thunder and lightning has always seemed a bit bizarre to me. He doesn't like storms, but he's not wacky about them like some dogs."

"Still. Maybe a thunder rumble spooked him for some reason."

The two women sat silently, thinking of the dog that had been Cathy's friend for so many years.

"I wish I could tell him how much he..." Cathy's voice drifted off.

Andi got up and poured herself a cup of coffee. On her way back to the table, she squatted down and peered into Harry's kitchen nook. A chewed up new tube of hand cream lay inside along with his bone and an empty cheese ball package from the wastebasket. "Remember the time he pulled the ham platter off the counter at Easter?"

The effort of a smile touched Cathy's face, but didn't succeed.

"At least it was after dinner, not before" Andi continued. "There went the leftovers for a week of ham sandwiches."

"He drank the equivalent of a small pond and had a small bout of intestinal issues the next day. Nothing that would've taught him a lesson, though." Cathy sighed.

The two women looked up as Christy and Katie entered the kitchen. They looked at the growing puddle of coffee on the table in front of Cathy, then glanced at each other.

"At least the snow didn't stick." Christy hugged her mother.

"Where're the twins?" asked Cathy quietly.

"Dan took the day off. He had just one court appearance anyway, and they agreed to move it."

Katie poured two cups of coffee and brought one over to Christy, who was already sitting at the table.

"He can't have gone far," Christy said.

Katie nodded.

"If he didn't go far, he would be back," Cathy countered. "He always comes back."

A single snowflake drifted in the air. Cathy studied the window for a minute, then pretended to take a sip of coffee.

"Remember when he buried Tab's baseball cap by the peony bush?" Katie asked.

"It was Tab's favorite," Christy added.

"Tab kept his things picked up a bit better after that," Cathy noted.

"Or the time he caught that bunny and snuck it into the house?" Christy wrinkled her nose.

"It hadn't grown completely stiff by the time I found it under the bed," Cathy muttered.

"There's always something for which to be grateful," Andi chuckled softly, shaking her head.

"But he could always be counted on for a listening ear," Cathy defended him. "For knowing when a person needed encouragement. For playfulness. For love of life."

They all nodded.

Andi leaned back. "Remember when he scared away that fellow, oh what's his name, the one with the big SUV..."

"Mel Platt," Cathy said. "The girls don't know about that."

"Oops." Andi grimaced.

"What?" Christy furrowed her brows.

"Oh, this fellow kept dropping by your mother's house. I think he thought if he expressed enough interest in her, she would reciprocate. Finally Harry did what your mother was too polite to do and growled at him..."

"Ooo. I'll bet he bared his teeth, didn't he?" Katie interjected.

Cathy nodded.

"And he quit coming around after that," finished Andi.

"Thank heavens," added Cathy.

Katie got up and looked out the window. "Tom's out looking for him now. Alden and Tab said they'd drive out later."

"Maybe we should drive around town," Andi suggested.

"Did. In the middle of the night as well as the next day. No luck." Cathy crossed her arms and leaned back in her chair, her chin quivering. "He's a good dog."

"He's good company for you," Andi agreed. "Hey. How 'bout I drive around again? You write down all the places you think he might like and I'll check them out and everything in between."

Cathy stared without seeing, blinking back worried tears.

Andi laid her hand on Cathy's arm. "It won't hurt to look again."

Cathy nodded. Finally, she said, "You'd better look for a body on the side of the road. He's badly hurt or dead or he'd be under the table right now."

"I can put up missing dog posters while I'm out," Andi offered.

Cathy shook her head. "I've never liked those things. They get ripped in the wind and wilted in the rain and end up just looking pitiful rather than helpful."

"I'll spread the word then." Andi rose from her chair. "We'll find him."

"He doesn't wander off. At least, not far. Ever."

Andi nodded her head and pressed her lips together as she headed out the door. After a moment, Katie stood, leaned down to give Cathy a hug, and followed her out. Christy patted her mother's hand and got up to wash the dishes and make a lunch that they could pretend to eat.

The morning's snowflake had come and gone without note. One by one, the searchers had returned without success. Andi had cooked up some scrambled egg and bacon burritos for them all and, after an 8:00 supper, everyone had gone home.

Cathy remained at the door after seeing the last person out, and when she could no longer see their car exhaust, she stepped out into the dark. Little puffs of her breath appeared and evaporated in the air as she walked around the yard. Her heart was heavy and aching in her chest. The evening held the kind of quiet that lies heavily in the air.

Suddenly a howl punctuated the darkness from far away. It was a howl, wasn't it? She wasn't in such a state that she was imagining things, was she? She turned toward it, then turned around quickly as a howl seemed to come from the opposite direction. Cathy listened intently, but heard nothing else.

"Harry! Harry!" The sound of her voice fell dead in the intense quiet that muffled sound and hope.

Soon the cold penetrated her sweater and her slippers became damp, forcing her back to the warmth of her kitchen.

Cathy wandered into the library/music room and switched on the electric fireplace. She stood where Harry usually lay snoring as she remembered the exuberant, mischievous, loving, loyal dog that was both a bother and a help and wondered what in the world she would do without him. Her thoughts ran through episodes of head shaking mischief and tongue lolling laziness that comprised the mundane hours of living with Harry. He was a dog whose presence had not been planned but had been gradually welcomed and then become a customary part of daily life.

Restless, she turned away and walked through the house, looking out every window as she did so. Finally returning to her rocking chair in front of the fire, she picked up the prayer that she had been praying off and on for two days straight. It wasn't that Harry was indispensable, she explained to the Lord. It wasn't that he was heroic or noble. It was just that she loved him; and as a small favor in this big, wide, world with so many other, more pressing and important matters, she would boldly ask this favor. God knew about love. He would understand.

She left the yard light on and his food dish and blanket on the step.

As a dim sun crossed its well-worn path and hoisted its ancient, persistent presence again to mark another day among the millions of days it had begun, a sleepless Cathy opened the kitchen door and whistled. A light, cold wind caught the sound and silenced her effort.

She turned as the sound of an engine in her driveway caught her attention. Going to the front of the house, she opened the door to John Blakely who was pressing a bloodied cloth to his hand.

# Chapter 33

*The parable of the unmerciful servant shows us that we're to forgive everything; or why should Jesus forgive us? It doesn't even require someone saying they're sorry. Their bad behavior might send them to hell, but we needn't let it send us. No, Kevin, forgiveness has nothing to do with being easy or fair; that's only for second grade math tests.*

"John! What in the world?" Cathy opened the door wide to let him in.

He took his shoes off at the door. His clothes were muddy and his ears were slightly pink from the cold.

"I found Harry. Mind if I use your sink? I think I need to tend to this pretty quick."

"By all means. You know where to find it." She peered out the window, then hovered near the hallway.

Words of thanks tripped over themselves as she sent silent shouts heavenward. Cathy listened to the sound of running water and rummaging in her medicine cabinet.

"The antiseptic is..."

"I found it," John called back.

Cathy stepped back into the living room and sat on the edge of the couch.

In a minute more, John walked into the living room, his hand expertly bandaged.

Cathy stood. "Let me get you something, John. You're a little pale. Would you like a cup of tea or toast?"

John shook his head. "We really need to get to Harry. He looks pretty wasted. Katie told me about his disappearance so I thought I'd take an hour or two this morning to look for him. He managed to get himself into a culvert about a mile from here."

"A mile. I can imagine the naughty thing wandering that far, but can't imagine how they missed it."

John shook his head in defense of those who had searched for Harry. "It wasn't obvious. It was in the ditch with earth covering all but the opening. I can see how someone wouldn't have noticed it. Added to that, a few bars cover the trough leading up to it. Harry probably got in easily enough, especially if he was chasing some little animal..."

"No doubt."

"But getting out of it would have posed a problem for him. Not only that, his collar appears to have caught on something down there, and after a couple of nights in the damp some of his fur could be frozen to it as well. I reached in to try to free him, but he was pretty defensive. I don't think I'm the one to get him out."

"I'm terribly sorry about that bite." Cathy grabbed a towel, some leather work gloves and her coat. "You're not going to be selling used cars anytime soon?"

John laughed. "He got me pretty good, but no. It won't slow me down at work. I still have all my moving parts."

Harry was right where John had said he would be: wedged into a culvert near a road on the way out of town. Cathy stooped down and peered inside.

"There you are," she whispered. Harry barred his teeth and growled. "C'mon now."

She continued to talk soothingly while she reached in quickly, grabbed his collar, yanked hard, and pulled him out. His growl turned to a gurgle as he chomped down on her hand and arm. In a minute he was out and staring warily at John.

"I see why you brought your leather gloves." John swallowed.

"You'd better be sorry, Harry. Look what we've done. For *you.*" The dog's growl changed to a whine. He jumped up and down around them both, finally stretching up and placing his muddy paws on Cathy's torso. She gave his ears a vigorous scratching, then gave him an all-round good pet and kissed him on the mouth.

"In with you." Cathy ordered Harry as she pointed to the towel spread across the back seat of John's car.

She slid into the passenger seat as John started the engine while eyeing a spot of blood beginning to appear beneath the coat at Cathy's wrist and spreading steadily.

Cathy looked over at him. "I trust there's some antiseptic left?"

A small smile crossed John's face as he nodded and pulled onto the road.

"You might want some stitches," he said diplomatically.

"Not unless some Superglue won't hold it."

Cathy stood at the door and waved.

"Thanks again and again," she called as John drove off. She turned to go inside just as Andi pulled up.

"I'll make some coffee," Cathy said cheerfully, "just as soon as I patch myself up." She held up her arm and Andi winced.

"Want me to throw that coat in a cold tub of water?" Andi squatted down momentarily to pet the top of Harry's head.

"I've got it," Cathy called down the hallway.

Andi pulled a white bakery bag from her purse and tossed a glazed donut in the air for Harry to catch. It fell to the floor. He was too tired to catch it as usual, but not so tired that he didn't snatch it up and carry it with him under the table.

The phone rang just as Cathy had returned from the bathroom and turned on the stove.

"Christy! That's right. John Blakely found him. How'd you hear so fast? Ah. Well cell phones are good for something, I guess. He didn't waste any time calling her. Katie's always at the restaurant at the crack of dawn. No doubt she'll have an omelet with the works ready for him by the time he goes home to change and swings by on the way to the hospital. Fine. Fine that you told Katie and fine that you told me. But the one you need to tell is John, himself. Don't ask me what you should say. You said plenty to him those years ago. You'll figure out what to say to him now. Yes, I do think there might be room for him at the Thanksgiving table. I love you too, dear."

Cathy hung up the phone as the coffee finished percolating. She filled two cups, then sat with Andi in a relieved silence as they sipped their coffee. A spot of blood stained the bandage on her wrist as Harry licked her ankle.

# Chapter 34

*Since Barak was a coward and wouldn't go to war without Deborah, credit for the victory went to a woman. Jael drove that tent peg into Sisera's temple clear through to the ground, class. God hates a coward, and finds a variety of ways to drive that point home. Sorry, couldn't resist.*

A ndi breezed through the back door while Harry barked a greeting. Flames were blazing, as they had every morning for decades. However, now they danced from a full sized kitchen fireplace.

Cathy closed her worn Bible, laying it on its special shelf. She crossed the room, patted the soapstone center island counter as she passed, and pulled open what appeared to be large cherry wood cupboard doors, revealing a refrigerator. She peered inside for a minute.

"I've got toast or last night's pizza," she announced.

Andi put a hand on her hip, then pulled a white bag out of her purse. "Here. Glazed donuts, and one for you, too, Harry. I'm thirsty."

Cathy pulled her coffee pot from the cupboard and began making coffee the old-fashioned way.

"And I can't get water from the indoor pool since you nixed it."

Cathy tilted her head to one side. "You know I wouldn't use it enough to justify the expense."

Andi looked toward the ceiling. "Will you ever understand that you don't have to pinch pennies anymore?"

"I have a new house, don't I?" Cathy sat down long enough for the coffee to percolate. "Oh, by the way, have I told you how much I love, love, love my pink toile bedroom?"

"Only every day since you moved in. I thought if I kept it to an isolated area..."

"Oh, you're just complaining now. I love the fuchsia leather chair in my library/music room."

"I did make a concession there, didn't I?"

"And the pink lacquered dresser there to go with it?"

"Don't remind me. It's a testimony to how much I love you."

"I saw a sparkly pink toilet lid cover at the discount store I thought we could..."

"You can't be serious," Andi interrupted with alarm around the edges of her voice. "We have enough to keep us busy the way it is. What day are we on with this? Harry's little episode threw me off count. Once he was back safe and sound, you seemed to gain the energy of a puppy, yourself."

Cathy rubbed Harry's back under the table with her foot. "Who keeps track? It seems to never end. First the phony lottery," Cathy sighed happily. "I so loved finding that."

Andi looked at her cousin.

"Don't look at me as though I'm a three-year-old in need of a nap."

"Who said anything about a toddler?"

Cathy loaded her arms with the temporary stack of papers on the kitchen counter, and carried them to the table. She pulled the tag board from inside the new dishwasher that she had yet to use.

"Thank heavens for Krista Knightly. That girl found things I wouldn't have dreamed existed, much less looked for."

"It was nice of you to pay for her to take a vacation down to visit her mother."

Cathy sighed. "Families are important." Gingerly spreading some papers out like a deck of cards, she continued, "Then the – oh what did you call it again?"

"Bank restructuring."

"It's not that hard to find if you have a cousin as sharp as well-aged blue cheese," Cathy elatedly announced to the walls. "Only it was rather boring – all that..."

"You gonna talk or deal?" Andi interrupted, tossing the last bite of her donut to Harry under the table.

After the two women had poured themselves some coffee, they began making notations about the papers Cathy had spread over her kitchen table.

Around lunchtime, Andi looked up suddenly, screwed her eyebrows together, and picked up some papers she had passed by an hour before to re-examine. "Bingo," Andi said under her breath, "There's the lynch pin for his non-existent rental contracts."

She slid some papers over for Cathy to see.

"Mm hm." Cathy rose half-way out of her chair to make more notations on their tag board. "No, no. Put it in this stack here."

"Oh, yes. Mortgage fraud and kickbacks are two completely different entities. What was I thinking?" Andi snapped her fingers.

"Referral fees," corrected Cathy.

"Also known here as kickbacks. Don't buy into seductive excuses."

"Righto. Leave seduction to the devil and strip clubs."

For a time, the only sound was Harry's claws clicking across the kitchen floor and the thump of him finally laying down in front of the fireplace. The quiet crackle of the dying flames was interrupted now and then by the voices of the women with another new discovery.

As the sun began to touch the tree line, Andi walked over to the fireplace. She knelt, laid kindling and two logs on the long-cold grate, and struck a match, bringing it to life. Cathy poured two cups of Harvest Spice coffee. Andi slid into a rocking chair on one side while Cathy brought her a cup of soup and coffee and sat down in a chair on the other side of the fire to slurp her own.

"I feel as though we should be knitting." Andi rocked slightly.

"I hate hand work. It makes me want to scream." Cathy hummed as she rocked back and forth.

"Besides, this is far more interesting. Whatever did we do with our afternoons before this?"

"I would like to check out that last phony address. Maybe find a contact who can shed some light on that area of the city."

"You mean the one next to the grocery on 7th? I can do that."

"You look overly pleased." Cathy narrowed her eyes.

Andi smiled mischievously. "I've an idea, that's all. My own little amusement."

"So Masotic is only one of several intermediaries."

"Looks that way."

"And Primary Properties is a shell corporation," Cathy continued.

"It couldn't be more of a shell if it was polished and sitting in a beach house."

"Dowling avoided detection with some pretty solid bank restructuring."

"He probably doesn't file his nails either."

"And with good old-fashioned money laundering, he..."

"...kept everything as fresh smelling as a spring day," Andi concluded. "Sufficiently nailed?"

"Clear through."

# Chapter 35

*"I am sending you out like sheep among wolves. Therefore be as shrewd as snakes and as innocent as doves." Class, what do you get when you cross a snake and a dove? Ha, ha, Jack. Actually, 'Christian' is the answer I was going for, but from someone as cheeky as you I'll accept 'Sunday school teacher.'*

A s Cathy passed him, the doorman gave her a courteously disinterested nod, as if she wasn't there. The maître d' hurried to her and deferentially asked where she wanted to be seated.

Cathy smiled, placing her hands in his as she would an old friend, and replied in a voice that could've been mistaken for a teenager if she had not been standing right in front of him, "I'm joining Mr. Dowling for lunch. He'll pay. He may need to leave a little early."

The maître d' noted her harmless smile, nodded and smiled back, and motioned for her to follow him as he slid the fifty she'd slipped him into his pocket.

"And so you see, Mr. Dowling, it's only a matter of time before that house of cards you have so deftly built – and beautifully, I might add – will come crumbling down; not unlike some little cheesecake tarts I made just last week. Poor things. They just couldn't hold it together." Her eyebrows screwed together as she thought about it. "Though I think if they'd just had a little more butter..."

She picked up her knife, using as a pointer. "You know, the problem these days is that everyone tries to make desserts less fattening." She shook her head and gave Mr. Dowling a slight smile. "Some things just aren't meant to be, are they?"

"So you're the one who bought the buildings on 24th? You're Jericho Juncture Ventures? And sold them back to me at that ghastly price while promising the tenants places in more favorable locations?"

"Caveat Emptor." Cathy tilted her head. "I guess I did learn some Latin after all."

Mr. Dowling talked very fast, she thought, for a man pushing 50. She nodded courteously and didn't say a word.

Finally spent, he slouched in his chair and said, "So what're you going to do? Report me to the police? Call the papers?"

"Oh no, no, no, no, no. No, Mr. Dowling, I'm not a policeman nor am I a policeman's mother. And, although I read the newspaper every morning, I don't put much stock in half of it. How in the world can they live with themselves publishing subjective reporting, a self-contradictory term if ever there was? A child can see it. No, I simply thought it would be helpful for someone to point out to you that what you're doing is wrong."

He started to say something, but she held up her hand to silence him. "And to suggest that you make things right – to your tenants, to your investors, to your creditors, and – I might add ever so discretely – to your wife; though I left that out of our earlier discussion."

"And if I don't?"

She motioned to her mouth, chewing on a piece of steak. Swallowing, she said, "I like this restaurant because they are so very thorough. Attention to detail makes all the difference. When it comes to detail, I'm a bit compulsive, myself. They have some of the best steak in the city here, don't you think?"

Dowling's breath became shallow. "I'll pay you whatever you ask."

Mrs. Covington's mouth dropped open and her eyebrows shot up. "Mr. Dowling, I may show wrinkles in unattractive places, I may burp after a Diet Coke, I may even forget the speed limit now and then, but I can assure you I do *not* blackmail!"

She motioned to the waiter. "I believe we're ready for that dessert now."

Clearing the table quickly, the waiter brought Mrs. Covington a hot fudge cake and Mr. Dowling a sherbet.

"Really, Mr. Dowling. Life is short. You should live a little." Cathy gestured to his tiny dish.

The businessman rose from his chair. "I need to get busy if I'm to do all those things you suggested. Please excuse me."

Mrs. Covington smiled charmingly. "Any efforts you make to cover things up will be useless. As I mentioned before, I'm very thorough. I'll have someone check with you next week to see if you need any help."

"Anything else?" He nervously scanned the room.

"Well, now that you mention it, there is the matter of Sunday school."

"What?"

"You should go. I should think to one of those churches that actually takes the Bible seriously. And, Mr. Dowling?"

He looked down at her.

"Never underestimate a Sunday school teacher."

She'd just finished dessert and was lingering over her coffee, when the maître d' approached.

"Mrs. Covington, the man who just left asked me to hand you this."

She peeked inside.

"A guilty conscience is a funny thing, Fred." she shook her head pityingly.

She removed one of the hundreds and handed it to him. "Share this with our waiter, won't you?"

Scanning the room, she added, "Isn't that the president of a news station over there? The one that has a coat drive every year?"

"Yes, Ma'am."

Cathy handed the envelope to Fred. "Would you please give this to him? Tell him it's a donation."

"My pleasure." Fred paused. "Mrs. Covington?"

"Yes, Fred?"

"You're the most beautiful woman I know."

Cathy laughed. "You must be seeing things."

Across town, the lithe, shapely woman slipped the hundred-dollar bill into a tray of cupcakes and handed it to the grocery manager. Smiling, she said, "I don't believe I'll be needing these after all."

He bowed his head slightly, slipped the bill out of the tray and into his pocket and tossed the tray back onto the bakery display. It landed on its side, crushing the frosting against its container.

"I'm always glad to serve our customers, Mrs. Clemens. Do come again."

She tilted her head and replied in a well-modulated voice, "Until next time, then."

As she turned to leave, a display of oranges from the opposite side of the produce area rolled to the floor as a red-faced couple tried to stop them. An intern on his break from the accounting firm two doors down ran his cart into the lettuce bin, and a voice over the intercom said, 'Clean up in Aisle One.'

She walked out the sliding doors and into the bright November sunshine. Sliding behind the wheel of her Porsche Spyder, Andi checked her lipstick and pulled into traffic. She deftly punched a button and waited.

"Cathy? Got it. Name's Rand. He's very observant, and talked as fast as a kid on Christmas morning. He seems glad to be contacted anytime," she paused, "You just never know what you'll turn up at the corner grocery." A series of beeps sounded. "You don't have to push any buttons, Cathy. It isn't a walkie talkie."

"I was trying to increase the volume. Why in the world did I let you convince me to get a cell phone?" Cathy said with exasperation.

"When does the wall fall down, cuz?"

"I took care of it over a very gratifying lunch. The little piece of information you got is just an insurance policy. Mr. Dowling was, shall we say, stunned and very apologetic. He's expecting to be contacted next week, though I believe there could be an expression of surprise on his face when you're the one who walks through the door. By the way, it's probably time to call that friend of yours. Oh, you know who I'm talking about. Police Chief something or other."

"Now who's having trouble with names?" Andi's laughter echoed down the highway as she hung up and accelerated.

Cathy tapped the Thanksgiving week snow from her boots as she unlocked the door of her house. She slipped out of her boots and into her pink fuzzy slippers as Harry jumped up on her and barked. She scratched his head and went into the kitchen to make Java Christmas Jubilee coffee.

With her pink cup full of steaming coffee, Cathy wandered into the library/music room and switched on the gas fireplace. Pulling a small notebook out of her desk drawer, Cathy tilted her head to one side and checked down a list with the stub of a pencil. She lay the list on the desk, picked up her coffee and moved to her favorite rocker.

The list was only partially finished, and even after she was able to check off every name, she felt an unfortunate conviction there would be more to take their place. Cathy momentarily stared into space, thinking of her classroom and of the students who sat in it this year, those who had populated it all the years before and those who would learn there in the years after this one.

For now. Be still for now.

After the quiet of unhurried thought, she decided to take a break from tracking down her former Sunday school students during the weeks of thanksgiving and celebration. The end of the year was a time to fill with family and music, other kinds of good works, and the delicious scents and tastes of special recipes. Who knew? Maybe a few of those errant students would show up at the church for the Christmas Eve service.

In two days' time her house would be filled with laughter and reminiscence and heaping platters of good food. There was a lot for which to be thankful, and the blessings from the trying years were every bit as wonderful as blessings from a year of abundance. Blessings had a way of hiding themselves, anyway, until you were miles down the road, looking in the rear view mirror.

Cathy put her feet up on the ottoman as she sat back, closed her eyes, and began humming a Christmas tune. Outside the long windows of her favorite room, sun glinted off a pure, white layer of snow that had fallen the night before, nearly blinding in its brilliance. One bright beam ran down the library/music room wall, onto the wool carpet, touched Harry's ear as he lay in front of the fire, and landed squarely in Cathy's lap.

CPSIA information can be obtained
at www.ICGtesting.com
Printed in the USA
BVHW082219100821
614096BV00010B/522

9 781735 123141